Copyright © 2019 by Joshua Dalzele

All rights reserved.

No part of this book may be reproduced in any form or by any electronic or mechanical means, including information storage and retrieval systems, without written permission from the author, except for the use of brief quotations in a book review.

Battleground
The Unification War Trilogy
-Book One-

Joshua Dalzelle
©2019

First Edition

1

This war was inevitable.

Centuries of peace had been shattered when a single alien ship came into Terran space and began destroying worlds. After that threat had been defeated, we turned on each other just as quickly as we came together. But what is peace? Is it simply the absence of conflict? I sometimes wonder if we—humans—really even know what the word means.

For hundreds of years, we colonized worlds and expanded our territory unchecked. The glut of resources and worlds we found far outpaced our population growth, so there was little to fight about. But even then, we divided ourselves along the old borders of our home world, creating enclaves and regional governments within the old Confederation, where we could remain in our ethnopolitical comfort zones.

Once something appeared that punctured our illusion of supremacy, our alliances crumbled, and we slid back into old habits, dividing along nationalities that don't even exist on Earth anymore. After the Phage War showed us just how vulnerable we were, the regional governments stoked the embers of distrust within their respective enclaves and, before we knew it, the Asianic Union and Warsaw Alliance split away from the Confederation to form the Eastern Star Alliance. They sealed their borders and refused contact with outsiders. These populations were primarily descendants of Russia, Eastern Europe, and China. The new Terran Federation, built from the remaining three enclaves, had peoples who hailed from the former United States, Western Europe, Japan, and parts of Central and South America.

The old hatreds, it seemed, were alive and well.

The history of our species is awash in blood...our *own* blood. I think that the lull in conflict we saw in the centuries before the Phage found us was an anomaly. Now that the alien threats are gone and our love of fighting has been rekindled, we'll show the universe our true nature as we turn our terrible machines of war upon each other.

I have a unique perspective on this, being from Earth. During most of my career, I was discriminated against by nearly everyone I encountered, denied opportunities that were given to less qualified officers from New America or Britannia. What I learned during this time is that, for the most part, people don't truly hate each other. It's the governments that sow discord, encourage people to distrust and fear those who come from someplace else. Large groups are easier to control if you give them two things: something to fear, and a solution to protect them from it. With those two things, people are willing to turn over control of much of their lives to a government. Perhaps my perspective is skewed being from a planet that unified under a single government long ago, or maybe my wife is right and I'm just a cynic at heart.

Either way, here we are. The Phage are gone, the Darshik all but extinct, but there's still one more fight left. I would have much preferred a diplomatic solution, but neither side is willing to give ground, and so, for the first time since the Third World War on Earth, humanity will go to war with itself.

So, as a species, have we ever really known peace? Or, as I think, were we always destined to fight ourselves?

—An excerpt from the personal log of Rear Admiral Jackson Wolfe, Chief of Combat Operations, Seventh Fleet.

2

"Computer, report."

"There is no indication that the target has detected our approach. The two patrol ships in this system are still out of effective range, one near the boundary opposite our position and the other in orbit over the second planet."

"Looks like we're still a go, Agent," Specialist Halsey said. The NOVA operator had been on the flightdeck of the Broadhead III with Senior Agent Pike since the ship had popped into real-space just inside the system's heliopause.

"Looks like," Pike agreed. "Better get your people suited up and ready."

"Right," Halsey said and slipped out of the seat. He floated across the flightdeck to the hatch in the .125G that Pike had set the artificial gravity to. While it was uncomfortable, it also allowed him to reduce the power signature of the small, stealthy ship by fifteen percent. A full 1G was far more comfortable, but it took a lot of power to generate.

The latest Broadhead, version three, was a marked

departure from the semi-luxurious fast-transport its predecessors had been. Rather than being a repurposed executive courier from the Tsuyo Corporation, the United Terran Federation had designed and built the latest iteration of the near-mythological ship in its own shipyards. What they produced was a much more utilitarian, purpose-built craft than the luxurious personal toy of the ultra-rich and powerful that the previous versions had been. It was still fast and stealthy, but now it had room for an entire NOVA team and a bit more armament in case they found themselves in a situation they had to shoot their way out of. All things considered, Pike missed the plush interior of his old ship.

"Target is now sixty thousand kilometers away," the computer said. "Still no indication we've been detected." The AI that ran the Broadhead III was much more advanced than what Pike was used to from his previous ships. There had been a quantum leap in artificial intelligence research and practical application within the last five years, and the new generation of AI computer was just making its way into the Fleet. He had to admit that having a voice that was a bit more...personable...made the long missions a little less lonely. It was still nowhere near being sentient, but it gave a damn good impression of it.

The target loomed in front of the tiny ship as they approached one of the maintenance docking arms. The ubiquitous com drone platforms had existed for hundreds of years, most heavily populated systems having two or three of them to handle the traffic, and yet Pike was always shocked at the size of them whenever he had need to be aboard one.

Faster than light communications still didn't exist in any practical form—at least not for commercial or civilian applications—and using starships to ferry messages back and forth between systems was grossly inefficient. Instead, a network of tiny, warp-capable drones were used. The enormous, autonomous platforms they operated from would recover, refuel, and launch drones as needed to create an interconnected web that allowed humanity to maintain a sense of community in a growing federation that spanned thousands of lightyears.

Since the drone platforms were autonomous, they were also a weakness that could be exploited. The ESA—Eastern Star Alliance—had never upgraded their system after breaking off from the old Terran Confederation. They'd simply updated and replaced their encryption protocols, but the hardware they were using was all vintage tech from well before the Phage War. What it meant for an enterprising Federation intelligence service was that even though they couldn't easily break the encryption schemes to access the ESA's network, they could board the platforms themselves and get in behind the encryption.

"Stand by for final approach," Pike called over the intercom to where the NOVAs were prepping in the cramped cargo bay. "Are we still clear to dock?"

"Transmitted codes have been accepted," the computer said. "The platform thinks we're a maintenance crew. Unless there is an emergency com drone launch, you will have three hours until the next scheduled departure to upload the package and erase the log entry of our docking."

"Copy that," Pike said, watching as the ship guided itself in smoothly to the spindly docking arm. He was skeptical of their mission, but he was still just an Agent, so when orders came down, he went.

"We're ready back here, Agent Pike!" Halsey's voice came over the intercom.

"Standby. We'll be making hard dock in...fifteen

minutes," Pike said as he climbed out of the captain's seat. The new Broadhead was so advanced that there was no longer a traditional helm, all piloting duties were turned over to the computer. Pike was a mediocre pilot at best, but he still didn't like the fact that the ship designers had taken the option of manually flying completely out of his hands.

Pike slipped on his tactical harness, checked his weapons and the mission payload, and then pulled on the sleek helmet. One of the NOVAs came up behind him and fastened the umbilical from the back of the helmet to the device on the back of his harness that housed his rebreather and com gear. The helmet HUD booted up, and he immediately began receiving a telemetry feed from his ship's AI. The Broadhead had aligned itself with the docking arm and was now stopped in space relative to the massive platform. It would now use a low-power RF link to hack into the platform's command and control systems so that they could dock and enter without tripping any alarms.

"Now we'll see if the ESA was smart enough to change all the access codes to every platform," Halsey murmured.

"Relax," Pike said. "This is the easy part." The mission planners had picked six targets within ESA space with sparse interstellar traffic because they were still the old second generation com drone platforms that had dozens of security vulnerabilities, some of which even the maintainers weren't aware of.

The old GenII platforms were no longer authorized for sensitive information by either government, but Pike's team wasn't there to try and tap into the ESA's military communication channels. It was the relatively unsecure civilian broadcasting system he was there to exploit. Pike agreed with psyops in theory and had seen it used effectively, but he had grave misgivings about this mission. He felt it sent up a flag that told the ESA that the Federation was becoming desperate and was buying for time...which they were.

In the last two years, ESA raids into Federation space had gone largely unanswered as the Fleet still struggled to recover from its war with the Darshik. The border systems that were being targeted weren't fooled by the platitudes coming from New Sierra, and the message from them was clear: if you can't protect us, maybe we'll have better luck with them. So far, three systems had officially declared secession from the Federation and had opened diplomatic talks with the ESA. With that in mind, Pike was adamant in his opinion that the stunt they were about to pull with the public broadcast system made the Federation look weaker and gave the ESA yet another tool to use against them in a propaganda war they were already losing.

"Docking control and internal security override successful," the computer's voice said in his helmet. "Standby." They all swayed in the low gravity as the ship fired its thrusters and pushed gently across the remaining gap to bump up firmly against the platform's docking collar. Pike watched as the lights over the airlock hatch flashed red, then amber, and then went to a solid green as the pressure on the other side was normalized and the mechanical locks were fully engaged.

"The ship is docked, Agent Pike. You may board at will."

"Copy," Pike said. "Open the hatch. Let's get this over with."

The lower levels of the ancient installation had obviously not been used in some time, likely decades since a human had actually been down there. The newer maintenance docks that were well above them had been added nearly fifty years ago when the newer launch cradles had been installed. There would be no reason for someone to come down to the lower decks unless there was a problem reported by the onboard diagnostic system. Most of what they were looking at now was either disused support equipment that the government didn't want to pay to have removed or empty space converted into storage.

"It's like a damn museum down here," someone said. Pike's HUD identified him as Specialist First Class Marco Costa. He was the NOVA team's techie and was peering into a cage full of old terminals that had to be a hundred years old.

"Let's hold up here a moment, Commander," Pike said to Halsey. "I want to be sure that the AI was able to circumvent *all* of the station security and not just the sensors on an unused old maintenance hatch."

"It's your mission, Agent," Halsey shrugged and began deploying his team into a loose defensive formation around the airlock. The NOVAs held their position while Pike waited for the AI aboard his ship to let him know that it had successfully infiltrated and bypassed the platform's security measures, meager as they were.

"*I have successfully deactivated the personnel trackers on all decks*," the computer's voice came over the com. "*Cameras in the main crew area and drone launch complex are still active.*"

"Copy," Pike said. The cameras were able to be remotely accessed by the ground control station on the planet so they'd decided to not risk tampering with those, even just to tap into the feeds, since they didn't need to access those areas to accomplish their goals. The only downside was that there could feasibly be a maintenance or security crew aboard the platform and they wouldn't know about it. "Halsey, we're a go."

"Cooper, Barnes...you're on point," Halsey said. "Let's move."

Two of the NOVAs peeled away from the cluster and ranged ahead down the dark corridor. There was something decidedly spooky about the lower levels of the old platforms. They almost looked abandoned, and one was quite aware that the hull was hundreds of years old. Explosive decompression was a spacer's greatest fear regardless whether they were wearing a protective suit or not.

"Agent! Take a look at this," Specialist Cooper called out from the front of the group.

"What is it?" Pike asked, elbowing past the other operators. Cooper gestured to the three ladder wells he was standing in front of. There was only supposed to be one. "Shit."

"We in the right spot?" Halsey asked.

"The technical specs on this platform are ancient." Pike gave an exaggerated shrug in his tactical gear. "We found it in the Tsuyo archives but those were the original prints this floating pile of garbage was built from. The Asianic Union has been operating and maintaining this station for nearly three centuries."

"Meaning?"

"Meaning I have no idea which ladder will take us to where we need to go," Pike said. "We don't have the time or personnel to go exploring right now either." He went over and looked up each ladder well. The one on the left had been sealed off at some point only a few meters up, the one in the center was also sealed, but with a hatch instead of a solid plate. The ladder on the right went up at least two more decks and that was as far as his low-light optics could make out on their own.

"Easy choice...we're taking the right one."

"You sure?"

"It's the only one that goes anywhere," Pike said. "We need to go up five more decks."

"You heard him, let's go," Halsey said, waving his team into action.

Climbing vertical ladders in full tactical gear was painstakingly slow and it took far longer than Pike would have liked to get the team—minus two that were staying below as a rearguard and com relay—to make the fifty-meter climb. The engineering teams at New Sierra had indicated that gravity would likely be lowered or turned off entirely to save power. The fact that they were sweating and grunting in a full 1G indicated to him that there could be a crew on the upper decks. Or worse, a crew was inbound from the planet and might notice their ship hanging off one of the disused docking arms.

"Any of this look familiar?" Halsey said, looking around.

"No, it doesn't," Pike said. The team had run through a dozen simulations before they launched from New Sierra and, so far, it looks like the re-creation Fleet Research and Science division had provided was far from accurate. They should have been looking at banks of servers that, while having been upgraded years ago, were still active and used as backups. Instead, they were looking at more cages full of old junk.

"This looks like another storage area."

"We're already at docking plus ninety minutes, Agent Pike," Halsey said. "Do we chance staying past the one hundred and twenty minute mission allotment?"

"We stay until we're finished," Pike said, studying the engineering prints he'd been given on a holographic projection from his wrist-mounted mission computer. "I think the sims we ran on New Sierra may have been mirror imaged.

According to this schematic, these storage cages exist, but they're way the hell over there—" Pike pointed down a dark corridor— "and the server farm we're trying to access should be here."

"Logically, the servers should be over on that side then, right?" Halsey asked.

"That's my assumption, Commander. Let's get moving."

The team moved quickly to traverse the deck, nearly ninety meters wide, to find that the server farm was indeed in the opposite location they thought it would be in. Pike idly wondered if the engineers at Fleet R&S were actually wrong or if Tsuyo hadn't built it to the engineering drawings centuries ago.

"Status lights show this connection is active and tied into the main array above," Pike said. He examined the lock on the cage door for a moment before pulling out a device from a thigh pocket and placed it over the lock.

"CIS toy?" Halsey asked.

"Inductive link that should be able to crack the code on a simple lock like this," Pike said. "It's not meant to keep anyone determined out, just protect the servers from any overly-curious workers who might happen by." A second later, the device beeped twice, and there was a *clank* as the lock released. Pike winked at Halsey and pulled the cage door open. "I'll need at least twenty minutes to deliver the payload, maybe more."

He quickly located the main console for the array and slipped another device out of a pocket on his harness. This was a black box with rounded edges that appeared completely seamless save for the single connector at one end. Pike picked the appropriate cable out of the five he was carrying and connected the box to one of the maintenance ports. When the light on the console port began to flash amber, indicating it was talking to the box, Pike pulled a glove off and pressed his bare hand to the black box. There was a muted *beep* as it read his bio-signature and almost immediately the screen on the console changed as the device began forcibly hacking into the secure system.

The device he'd hooked up had some of the latest AI intrusion software CIS could provide. It came from the same labs that made the Broadhead's incredible AI interface. Pike had a suspicion where all this new and wondrous tech originated from, but he kept his speculation to himself. Even a full Agent wasn't privy to some secrets.

"Tricky little machine," Halsey said as he watched the box slice through the ESA security firewall with ease.

"It is impressive considering over half the space inside the box is taken up by explosives," Pike said.

"What?! And you were carrying that in your pocket?"

"If I'm captured or killed, and someone tries to take a peek inside this thing, it will make sure it's the last thing they ever see. It's no more dangerous than the concussion grenades your team carries."

"We don't carry them within a sealed hull," Halsey grumbled. "There are better ways to—" He was interrupted by chaotic chatter breaking in over the open channel. "Quiet!" he barked. "What's going on?"

"Just heard from Memphis," Conner said. "Our ship contacted him and said we have another ship inbound that came from the planet."

"Shit," Pike said. "I was afraid of this when the gravity was turned all the way up. It's likely a scheduled crew, but we still need to hurry. Tell Specialist Memphis to ask the ship for a projected timeline. We need to know how long until we'll be spotted trying to leave."

"Yes, sir." Conner sprinted down the corridor the way

he'd come. To minimize the chance of being detected by the more robust security measures on the upper decks the team was using a low-power com mode that limited their range considerably. It was why they'd left two behind so that the ship could keep them informed about local space without switching to a high-power mode.

"Where are you at?" Halsey asked.

"The package is uploading now," Pike said, looking at the status bar the device was transmitting to his HUD. "Once it's in the buffer, it'll have to be flagged by the system to be moved to the main server array and embedded in the payload for all outbound drones."

"I should have specified how much longer. I don't care about the technical details. I was just told to get you here safely."

"Around forty minutes," Pike said.

"The ship estimates that we have less than an hour before the inbound ship is within detection range," a breathless Conner spit out. "It says that it was flying cold and that's why it was able to get so close before being spotted."

"Well," Pike sighed. "This could end up being an exciting mission after all. Commander, begin moving your team back down to the docking arm so we're not all jammed up in the ladder well once I'm ready to move."

"I'll stay with the spook, the rest of you get your asses back to the ship," Halsey told his team. "I want two posted at the bottom of the ladder, one up top, and the rest of you by the airlock ready to board the ship as soon as you get the word." There were some grumbled affirmatives, and the NOVA team cleared out quickly, running back for the ladder.

"They almost seemed regretful that we're not going to have a shootout here in the maintenance hold," Pike said.

"NOVA teams have been sidelined for the last two wars." Halsey shrugged. "Now that it looks like war with the ESA is almost inevitable, a lot of them are ready to prove themselves."

"I don't think a bunch of engineers and techs coming out to inspect the hardware would be much of a fight," Pike laughed. "If there were any soldiers on that inbound ship, they'd either be trying a lot harder to hide from us or they'd be coming in hot, engines blazing."

"I just said they were eager, I didn't say they were geniuses," Halsey said.

The pair stood silently as the software completed its task and began to erase its footsteps on the way back out. The whole point of this mission was that the ESA would have no idea how the Federation had compromised their public broadcast system, at least not right away. Once they figured it out, if they ever did, it would then require them to overhaul their entire com drone network to make sure there weren't any more embedded surprises waiting for them. The time and cost alone would deal a heavy blow to the ESA government.

At least that was the theory CIS brass was operating on when they sold the mission to Fleet Command. Pike's own opinion was that the ESA would look at the games the Federation was playing, laugh, and then ignore it. The populations in the Asianic Union and Warsaw Alliance enclaves that made up the bulk of the ESA weren't like New America or Britannia; they weren't predisposed to distrusting their own governments and would be ready for any clumsy psyops efforts the Federation might throw at them.

. . .

—*Beep. Beep*—

"That's it," Pike pulled the connector from the console and gently replaced the dust cover. "Let's get the fuck out of here."

They carefully put all the covers back as they'd found them and re-locked the security cage before racing down the corridor to where one of the NOVAs was waving them on by the ladder well. Pike noticed they were leaving footprints in the fine layer of dust on the steel decking, but there was nothing they could do about that now.

"The rest have already boarded, and the ship is reporting its ready to fly as soon as the hatch closes," the NOVA said as Halsey grabbed the outsides of the ladder with his gloved hands and braced the insteps of his boots against the metal poles, sliding down with a raspy hiss. Not to be outdone, Pike copied the move and hoped there weren't any cross supports on the ladder that he was about to hit and go bouncing the rest of the way down the well.

The remaining five members of the boarding party were sprinting down the passage to the docking arm when all hell broke loose. Red lights began flashing and audible alarms blared as the airlock hatch slammed shut, trapping the remaining NOVAs and CIS Agent on the platform.

"*Unable to override the airlock hatch,*" the computer told Pike on a private channel. "*Your presence was detected and automatic security protocols were enacted that have completely locked out all maintenance hatches.*"

"Has the platform sent out a distress signal yet?" Pike asked.

"*No transmissions have been detected. Initial intrusion to lockout the security system seems to have interrupted the automated response somewhat."*

"And that inbound ship is still approaching at the same speed?"

"*Affirmative*," the computer said.

"Disengage and withdraw," Pike said. "Move out beyond the orbit of the sixth planet and go dark. Observe everything, and if it looks like they're mobilizing a military response, send an emergency point-to-point com drone back to New Sierra and report mission failure. We'll find another way off the platform and send a signal for pickup when we can."

"*Acknowledged.*"

"We're on our own," Pike said, quickly relaying his conversation to Halsey and his NOVAs.

"You still have operational command of the mission," Halsey said. "What's the play?"

"The service boat coming out won't be able to open the airlock either, at least not at first. They'll have the tools to force their way aboard, but that will take time," Pike said, thinking aloud. "We can either meet them at the dock and take their ride—"

"Which will ultimately give away the fact we've been here and tank the mission," Halsey pointed out.

"—or we can find an alternative way off the platform and hope for a pickup by the Broadhead," Pike finished.

"Killing a bunch of techs and taking their ship would be easier, but it would mean a mission failure for not only us but for the five other teams," Halsey said. "That's six months of prep and planning down the shitter. You think there's another way off this thing?"

"There's something else," Pike said. "If we let that tech team board and investigate the alarm, they're going to quickly find that *something* tampered with the security systems since the alarms went off before our AI intrusion software could erase its tracks."

"You sound like you have a plan that mitigates that risk," Halsey said.

"It's extreme, but it'll work."

"How extreme?"

"We'll have to destroy this entire com drone platform."

"You CIS spooks don't fuck around, do you?" Halsey breathed. Destroying an entire com drone platform was an almost unthinkable act of sabotage given that it was the lifeline for the entire planet's population to the rest of humanity.

"There are still a few starships in this system that will be able to get word out about what happened, and it will cover our tracks," Pike argued. "Look...this whole mission was a dumb idea, but it's all that CENTCOM was able to come up with to hold the ESA off while Starfleet gets its feet back under it."

"You're probably far more privy to overall strategic doctrine concerning the ESA than we are," Halsey said. "I'm assuming you don't want to just blow the platform with us still on it?"

"No...I'll explain on our way up," Pike said. "We have to be at that airlock by the time the tech crew makes entry. If they're able to report back we're screwed."

"This should be interesting," Halsey muttered before taking off after Pike, his own men fanning out behind him.

3

"Stop fidgeting at it."

Admiral Jackson Wolfe glared at his wife but pulled his hand away from the area where his prosthetic leg mated up to the socket Fleet Medical had installed permanently just above where his knee used to be. The leg had been making an odd whining noise when they'd been walking into the auditorium, and he'd been probing around the joint through his dress blacks to see if he could figure out the issue.

Jillian Wolfe, dressed in a fashionable business suit, was seated next to him on the stage as the Starfleet Chief of Operations was finishing up his remarks. The event was a combination promotion ceremony for Jackson being given a second star and an announcement that he was being given command of Seventh Fleet's newest task force, as well as responsibility for Starfleet's overall strategic outlook. Jackson had at first balked at the idea of being put in that position given the fact that the cold war between the ESA and the Federation was about to go hot, but in the end, he had conceded there was currently nobody else for the job who wasn't already being used elsewhere.

His wife and friends had mistakenly thought that his quick acceptance meant that he was finally coming to terms with the fact that he was a crucial component if the Federation was going to win. The truth was, he took the job out of fear. The ESA knew where all of the Federation's planets, major installations, and production facilities were, including the planet of Arcadia where his children were currently living with Jillian's parents. The image of ESA cruisers appearing in orbit over that planet and landing troops on the surface while his children slept at night was a recurring nightmare he'd been having since they'd begun minor incursions into Federation space.

Along with that fear was something else. Something...darker.

As he shifted Starfleet's strategic outlook from the defensive posture it had adopted during the short, vicious war with the Darshik to one that was designed to take the fight to the enemy first, he realized there was no line he wouldn't cross to keep the ESA from harming the only thing he loved. It frightened him that the people entrusting him to do the right thing didn't see this lack of empathy within him, but he'd be damned if he stood aside again as his home was attacked.

"...so, with that in mind, I'd like to introduce the new commanding officer of Task Force Vega, Seventh Fleet, Rear Admiral Jackson Wolfe."

Jackson cut his ruminations short and stood, the prosthetic whining again as he did. The thunderous applause the now-standing crowd was giving startled him as he walked to the podium, nodding to Admiral Victor Lazonic as he passed the new Starfleet Chief of Operations.

"Thank you, Admiral," Jackson said, clearing his throat. "I'll make this brief since we all have a lot of work to do and not a lot of time to do it in.

"When the threat of the Phage appeared in our space, Starfleet was woefully ill-equipped to deal with such an implacable enemy. For centuries, we'd done little more than ferry messages and fly in demonstrations before something determined to end our existence attacked the planet Xi'an. But we—*you*—rose to the occasion. Even after losing the planet Haven, and things looked their bleakest, the enemy was defeated.

"From the ashes of that dead enemy we were attacked again, this time by a species convinced they were the instrument of the Phage's will, and that the alien core mind spoke through them. Our decimated fleet once again, rallied, and pushed back, defeating the Darshik and eliminating the threat once and for all. We did this without the help of two entire enclaves that decided to break off and leave us at the mercy of an alien power bent on our eradication. Not enough to take away major resources and production capability when we could least afford it, the ESA then cut deals with an alien power, helping them kill Federation citizens by the thousands.

"I know we're all war-weary. Believe me, there's nothing I want more than to return Starfleet to peacetime footing and pass the torch to the next generation of officers coming up. You've all given too much already, but I'm afraid our job isn't yet done. The ESA has begun pushing into Federation space with raids designed to test our resolve and further destabilize the area along the border zones. We've stepped up patrols and had some success intercepting these incursions, but it's clear at this point that the ESA will not be satisfied with this stalemate."

Jackson paused to take a sip of water, looking out at the crowd. Their eyes were fixated on him, and they were looking at him with what could only be described as hero worship, bordering on adoration. The crowd was made up of politicians, top military brass, invited members of Starfleet—many of whom had served with Jackson—and a lot of representatives from the Federation's military industrial complex. He'd been asked to make some remarks during the re-christening ceremony for the newly expanded Eternis Pax Shipyards to allay the fears of the last group, but he felt he wasn't doing a very good job. Was a pep rally full of meaningless platitudes really helpful in this situation?

He set his glass down and pressed a control on the podium to kill the holographic teleprompter that had been scrolling his prepared remarks and looked out at the crowd. The prolonged pause seemed to be generating a bit of anxiousness, most notably among the political class who had flown in from New Sierra.

"Let me just speak plainly," he said, stepping from around the podium, the microphone hidden in his lapel broadcasting his words over the PA. "Despite our best efforts to avoid it and to find a diplomatic solution, the ESA is pushing us into an armed conflict. We still have critical resources they want, and they're willing to use their substantial military might to get it. They've been able to keep most of their fleets intact, even during the Phage War, and we were not. They're banking on that fact to intimidate us into backing down or, failing that, taking it from us by force.

"This is why we're here today, officially spinning up the

fifth major shipyard since the Federation was forced to dissolve Tsuyo Corporation and take over production of ships and weapons for Starfleet itself. This facility—and those of you who work here—will be the ones who win this fight. The new classes of starships coming from Eternis Pax are unlike anything humans have ever built, and as you go about your work don't forget that every man, woman, and child in Federation space is relying on you. I have no doubt you'll continue to rise to the challenge. Thank you."

As he walked back to his seat, the cheering was noticeably strained, nothing like when he'd first been introduced. He'd told them that giving inspirational pep talks wasn't something he'd ever been good at. Maybe now they'd believe him.

"Not exactly the rousing speech to the troops you had written down," Jillian murmured as he sat. He just grunted in reply.

The next hour was exceedingly awkward as the next two speakers tried to recapture the festive, upbeat spirt of the event after Jackson had dumped a bucket of ice water on it. When, mercifully, the assembly was dismissed, Jackson slipped out a back entrance with his wife and met up with his aide and Marine guard. The latter wasn't typical for flag officers when not aboard a ship, but there had been enough credible threats against Jackson's life that CENTCOM wasn't taking any chances.

"A rousing and inspirational speech, sir," the Marine in fatigues said.

"Shut up, Barton," Jackson growled.

"Of course, sir," Gunnery Sergeant Willard "Willy" Barton said, nodding to Jillian. "Mrs. Wolfe."

"Willy," she said, hiding a smile. "How's the family?"

"They never see me and Fleet keeps paying me on time," Barton said. "My wife says it's the ideal marriage."

Gunny Barton was wearing camouflage fatigues instead of the normal black that most shipboard Marines wore. It was unusual but technically authorized, and something Marines that had served in a ground infantry unit did to separate themselves from the detachment Marines who had only ever served aboard starships. Barton was one of the very few still in the service that had actually seen combat on a planet called Juwel when he'd been inserted to try and repel a Darshik incursion.

Barton's entire battalion had been close to being overrun and wiped out when a starship captain with more balls than brains had run the Darshik blockade with an underpowered assault carrier. Then-Captain Jackson Wolfe had managed to deploy his drop shuttles full of reinforcements in time to save the day. Barton had requested to serve aboard whichever starship Wolfe was commanding, and the two had been together since.

"Where's our VIP?" Jackson asked.

"The party in question is waiting through that secure hatch, sir," Barton said, pointing to secure hatchway. The hatch was open, but there was a civilian contractor standing guard and checking IDs.

"Ah, Admiral Wolfe," a raspy voice said once Jackson's party had made it through the security checkpoint.

"Dr. Ito," Jackson said, bowing slightly to the elderly man of Japanese descent sitting in a chair that hovered nearly half a meter off the deck. "A new toy, sir?"

"A simple trick," Ito smiled. "This only works on ships and installations with the newest artificial grav generators. All the older platforms or on a planet's surface and I'm back in a traditional wheelchair. Thank you for coming to see me."

"I was already here." Jackson shrugged, ignoring the elbow from his wife.

"I wanted to personally thank you for your public support for the new generation of starship we're building here. Maybe that's not correct. Maybe this is the *first* in a whole new philosophy of shipbuilding." Ito had been propelling his chair down the curved walkway, and he stopped in front of a large, panoramic window that overlooked the illuminated docking complex. Jackson didn't bother looking since he knew what was down there.

"Do you think we're making a mistake, Admiral?" Ito asked, gesturing to the graceful ship moored below them. "Beautiful, isn't she? The *Nemesis* is likely to be the last of the great starships. The new MCMSDS vessels will be effective but lack the beauty and soul of ships like this." Ito pronounced the acronym like *mick-mids*. The new ship design architecture that Jackson had helped push through committee was called the Modular Constructed, Mission Scalable Deployment System. In a very military move, the clunky description that had been the title of the original whitepaper study had stuck as the official nomenclature. Most of the spacers had already shortened that and had taken to calling the new ships *Mickeys*.

Jackson took a moment to look at the *Nemesis*, the ship he used to command, feeling a pang of regret and the weight of the stars on his shoulders pressing down on him. Ito had been one of Tsuyo's lead ship designers before the Federation moved to disband the megacorporation. He'd survived the witch hunt that had seen a lot of Tsuyo's top people imprisoned for helping the enemy. Ito was politically oblivious; he just wanted to build starships. He was so emotionally connected to his work that he sometimes lost objectivity, so Jackson considered his next words carefully before continuing. Ito was nearly ninety-seven years old and was known to have an erratic, prickly personality.

"This is a temporary situation," he said. "You were right when you brought this proposal to CENTCOM...the Fleet needs ships, and it needs them fast. We can't spend years developing and building works of art like we did back in the old days. This new solution will allow us to replenish our losses from the Darshik and get back on even footing with the ESA quicker than they'll ever expect."

"I hope you're right, Admiral," Ito said. "Now, if you'll excuse me...I have things to attend to as I'm sure you do as well."

"Interesting," Jillian said. She was a civilian now but still carried a security clearance thanks to her work developing crew training programs for Starfleet. As such, she'd been intimately familiar with the proposal Ito had come up with as well as her husband's decision to back the unorthodox plan.

"I can never figure out what he really means half the time," Jackson said as his comlink began beeping. "Wolfe."

"*Emergency transmission incoming over Bluebird for you, Admiral.*"

"I'll be right there," Jackson said and pocketed his comlink. He looked around the deserted corridor and then gave his wife a quick kiss on the lips. Barton pretended not to notice as Jillian's eyes widened in surprise. Jackson *never* engaged in public displays like that while in uniform and on duty.

"In case I don't see you before your ship leaves," he explained. "If it's a Bluebird communique it's likely something serious."

"Be careful," Jillian said. "Remember you're an Admiral now and that the *Nemesis* isn't your ship anymore. Don't step on any toes."

"I remember," Jackson said through clenched teeth. "Let's go, Barton. You too." The last remark was directed at the nervous ensign who had just been assigned to him as an aide.

Jackson didn't like having someone trail after him like a puppy, so he mostly just ignored the young officer. Barton had noticed this and took it upon himself to tell the aide that Jackson despised the new breed of officers coming up through the ranks and that the last two aides had disappeared under mysterious circumstances. The net result of Barton's bullshit and Jackson's brusque demeanor was a confused and terrified ensign who seemed to try and blend into the walls whenever he was around his boss.

"At ease!" Jackson said sharply as he walked in through the airlock.

"The *Nemesis* has been cleared for departure, Admiral. At your command, I'll call for a push back from the dock, and we can begin steaming up the well to rendezvous with the rest of the task force."

"Very well, Captain Barrett," Jackson said to the *Nemesis's* new CO. "Get your ship underway. Once we've rejoined the formation, I'm sure that we'll know whether we're heading to the border or back to New Sierra."

"Yes, sir," Barrett said. "Bluebird communique is waiting for you in CIC."

Jackson just nodded and waved Michael Barrett back to his duties. He'd been hesitant to fly his flag aboard his old ship with a newly assigned captain who had been a direct subordinate for so long. Barrett had been with Jackson since the days aboard the TCS *Blue Jacket*, where he'd been a tactical officer when the first Phage attack happened. He'd gone on to prove himself as a smart, courageous commander and had earned his spot aboard the Fleet's most decorated and advanced warship, but Jackson still noticed Barrett tended to defer to him at times he shouldn't.

The *Nemesis* had been at Eternis Pax for three months getting her last round of system and armament upgrades before being cleared to return to active service. Jackson had come out with Jillian aboard a VIP courier ship with the rest of Task Force Vega, Black Fleet's newly commissioned rapid deployment battlefleet, to hold his promotion ceremony aboard the destroyer that he'd commanded to end the Expansion War when he destroyed a Darshik ship they'd called *Specter*. Once he'd arrived, however, he felt having the ceremony aboard a ship that was no longer his sent the wrong message to the crew, so he'd opted to do it in the shipyard's auditorium instead.

"You're cleared for number three, Admiral," an ensign manning the desk in CIC said as he walked up and cleared himself through the biometric scanners. She pointed to one of the *coffins* that lined the rear bulkhead that provided a secure place for information so sensitive it couldn't be allowed to leave CIC, not even to an admiral's office or quarters.

"Thank you, Ensign," Jackson said and walked back to the third coffin, sealing the hatch behind him. It took a few minutes to authenticate himself to gain access to Bluebird communications. Access to the system while the ship wasn't underway was strictly guarded. It was a hassle, but one he completely agreed with. The system was likely *the* most classified system in the Federation. When it was implemented, it was called a "war winner" by one of the few people in CENTCOM who fully understood what it was.

Bluebird was the codename given to the Federation's new superluminal communication system. It operated by exploiting the quantum Zeno effect and allowed for information to be instantaneously passed between two entangled particles. The system had severely limited bandwidth, and each Bluebird transceiver could only talk to its own matched pair so there were some logistical challenges, but the end result was that CENTCOM would now get real-time intel from its fleet and could send orders back just as fast.

The text-only message was brief and to the point:

EYES ONLY: VICE ADMIRAL WOLFE

TWO FULL ESA SQUADRONS CONVERGING ON ODMENA SYSTEM. ODMENA HAS WARP LANES INTO FOUR FEDERATION SYSTEMS, TWO OF WHICH ARE INFRASTRUCTURE CRITICAL. SUGGEST TASK FORCE VEGA REPOSITION FOR POSSIBLE INTERCEPT. CIS PROWLERS INBOUND.
AUTHORIZED FULL AUTONOMY. KEEP ADVISED.

Jackson reread the message as he tried to remember what he knew about the Xiwang System. It was part of the former Asianic Union and, other than being a convenient refueling point for ships traveling between Britannia and the AU, it had nothing of note other than all the mapped warp lanes that converged to it. He frowned, wishing he had access to a computer within the secure coffin. It was possible the ESA was going to use Xiwang as a staging or jump-off point for a push into Federation space, but it seemed too obvious and too easily countered. The ESA fleet masters were smart, tough, and had a good idea about how the Fed fleet would respond to provocations like this.

After thinking it through, Jackson saw no reason not to take Pitt's suggestion and relocate his task force. The intel analysts were all convinced the ESA would strike soon, so it made sense to be closer to the border. Task Force Vega was also an integral part of the newly minted Wolfe Doctrine, as it was being called—and the ESA likely knew where it was at all times thanks to a distressing number of sympathizers within CENTCOM. It also posed a risk to Eternis Pax since the ESA would undoubtedly want to neutralize Task Force Vega for both practical and morale reasons.

He saw that he was still tied into Bluebird at the secure terminal, so he typed a quick response to Pitt. The Bluebird access list was told to keep messages under five hundred characters if possible so he simply told Pitt he would be taking Vega to Xiwang to await further moves by the ESA fleet. The message was then bounced to the paired transceiver sitting aboard a Fleet communications frigate, where it would be sorted and forwarded to the proper address for the recipient.

So far, Bluebird had six dedicated communications ships that would continuously fly to ensure their safety. It also meant that even though messages were theoretically instantaneous, the reality was that it could take as long as thirty minutes to get messages where they needed to go. It was still a damn sight better than days and weeks when using standard com drones.

"Please inform the captain that I'm on the way to the

bridge and that I have movement orders," Jackson told the ensign as he left CIC. Barton was waiting outside as expected and his aide, knowing when to make himself scarce, was likely sitting in his office on the command deck.

"Aye, sir."

4

"The Mickeys sure are ugly ships," Barrett commented as the *Nemesis* slid over the staging areas that trailed along behind the shipyard as it traveled along its heliocentric orbit. He stood next to Jackson as the admiral gazed at the components that would become the new generation of Terran starship through the *Nemesis's* hemispherical main display. The computer created the false-color image they were looking at and enhanced the details by stitching together data from the hundreds of multi-spectral imagers dotting the hull.

"They'll do their job," Jackson said, trying not to sound defensive. After the heavy losses they'd taken during what was now being called the Expansion War against the Darshik, Dr. Ito and Admiral Wolfe had been forced to think outside of accepted Fleet dogma when it came to replacing ships. Starfleet was a multi-generational organization steeped in the traditions of spacers going back hundreds of years. One of the things that had been sacrosanct among the top brass was how starships were built.

For centuries, the ships had been laid out and constructed much as their ocean-going ancestors had been before humans had left Earth. First, the hull would be laid, then individual systems installed, then interior spaces would go in last. This process, along with the initial design phase, could sometimes take years, and that was before the engines were ever fired for the first time for the lengthy shakedown process. Ship classes were small, made up of a handful of numbered hulls, because they took so long to build and each class had its own quirks and unique logistical considerations when it was finally put into operation.

This traditional method of building was slow, costly, and an inefficient use of labor and materials. Back when Starfleet used to keep ships for nearly a century and didn't have much to do it wasn't that big of a concern. In fact, the inefficiency kept a lot of people gainfully employed for a lot of years. But when they were trying to quickly put together a capable fighting force, it was a nightmare. What Jackson hadn't counted on was the considerable pushback when he and Ito took their proposal to CENTCOM. Humans love tradition and doing things the way they've always been done...even when that way no longer made any sense.

"I've no doubt of that, Admiral," Barrett said. "You really think this modular construction idea will be able to produce ten starships a month?"

"Once the plants building the major components are up and running, sure," Jackson said. "I think that will be a conservative estimate, actually."

Soon, the *Nemesis* was past the staging area where all the major *modules* for the new starships were stretched out with their protective covers still on. It seemed common sense to make ships from interchangeable, pre-made component assemblies to Jackson. Hell, they'd been making entire cities out of pre-built components for decades. Now, ships were simply bolted together in a configuration determined by mission. While it may have been common sense, it had been an uphill battle to get CENTCOM to go along with it.

If all the old dogs at CENTCOM bucked him that hard just to streamline starship construction to the point that build times were practical, they were *really* going to hate his Phase II proposals. After two brutal wars that could have been lost just as easily as they were won, it disheartened Jackson to see that so many people were still slaves to a system that'd been proven not to work time and time again.

"Coms, please announce us to the taskforce," Barrett called over his shoulder once the icons of the twelve ships in tight formation appeared on the display.

"Aye, sir," the com officer said.

"Helm, put us in the lead of the formation," Barret said.

"Taking the lead, aye," the helmswoman said.

In another break with Fleet tradition, the helm was now given a lot more leeway when it came to positioning the ship. Thanks in no small part to Jackson practically dogfighting with a two hundred and forty-thousand-ton destroyer during the hunt for the *Specter*, the tactical analysis teams determined that the old way of calling out ship movements to the helm was clunky and may have cost more than a few ships during the Phage War. Now the pilot and nav specialist were seated next to each other at both helm stations and shared the duty of flying and navigating, almost becoming a pilot/copilot team.

The Nemesis's first watch helmswoman was Petty Officer Kyra Healy. She was regarded as one of the most talented starship drivers in the fleet and had been crucial in Wolfe's victory over the Darshik *Specter* at the end of the Expansion War. The good news was that Barrett had kept her on the *Nemesis* when he took command. The bad news was that her skill and natural abilities as a leader had caught the eye of

CENTCOM, and she now had a slot for Officer Training School where she'd earn her commission and begin her path to get a command of her own. Barrett hated to lose that kind of talent, but he had to concede that she was too good to remain at the helm forever. She'd be the new generation of Starfleet once he was finally put out to pasture.

Jackson stepped back to let Barrett assume the middle of the bridge alone, not wanting to give any mixed signals about who was commanding the *Nemesis*. It was a lot more difficult than he had imagined it would be. Commanding a starship had been his job for so long that when he walked onto a bridge, there was a certain level of muscle memory that made him start barking orders immediately. It was a challenge to curb those impulses and trust Captain Barrett to handle the destroyer while he focused on the overall picture of the task force.

"Admiral," the *Nemesis's* breathless executive officer said as he walked onto the bridge. "I hope everything went well on Eternis Pax?"

"Commander Accari," Jackson nodded. "As well as any other change of command ceremony I've been to, I suppose. Where have you been keeping yourself?"

"Captain Barrett asked me to make sure the CIC was configured so you'd be able to more easily command the task force from there," Accari said. Jackson appreciated that he did it with a perfectly straight face. The decision to have the task force commander sit in CIC was made long before CENTCOM approved the changes to Fleet deployments, but it looked like Accari was giving his former CO a not-so-gentle reminder that the bridge was the domain of the captain.

"I'm sure it's just as good as the first time I checked it over at New Sierra," Jackson said.

"Yes, sir."

"While we're on the topic, have you picked the watch assignments yet?" Jackson asked. "I'd prefer to have a com officer that's cleared for Bluebird messages if possible."

"We only have two on the ship currently, and one is first watch com officer up here on the bridge, Admiral," Accari said. "Can you get by with the one?"

"I suppose I'll have to," Jackson said. "You and Captain Barrett come to my office after—"

"Sensor anomaly!" the tactical officer called out. "Computer is giving a thirty percent probability that it's a stealth ship hiding in the shadow of the sixth planet." Jackson bit his tongue and pretended to look interested in his comlink while Barrett walked back from the display to the command chair.

"Did the information come from our own sensors or over the Link," Barrett asked, referring to the open data link Federation ships utilized to share sensor data and telemetry.

"It was the aggregate sensor picture from Link data confirmed by our own radar, sir. It was just a brief snapshot, but the high-res array caught a return the computer says is consistent with an atmospheric engine nozzle."

"One of ours?" Barrett asked.

"Unknown, sir," the tactical officer said. "There wasn't enough data to build a full profile and match it to any known class of vessel."

"Do you think CIS has a ship out here keeping an eye on Eternis Pax, Admiral?" Barrett asked.

"I can't rule it out, but standard procedure for Prowler Fleet when doing overwatch on a friendly system is to station keep along the outer boundary and above the ecliptic," Jackson said. He would be well within his bounds to assume operational authority of the task force, but it was a little soon to jump in and override one of his captains based on something that could be nothing more than an oddly shaped bit of debris.

"Nav, adjust our exit vector so that we're getting a gravity assist from the sixth planet," Barrett said. "Update the task force over the Link and come onto new course...ahead three quarters. Tactical, maintain our posture but make sure CIC is watching that area closely."

"Coming about to new course, engines ahead three quarter, aye," the helmswoman said.

"Task force has confirmed new course, all ships falling into formation, Captain," the OPS officer said. "CIC says they're staring a hole into that part of space."

Jackson smiled slightly as he knew the officer in charge of CIC, a Lieutenant Commander Jake Hawkins, had almost certainly sent up the message. He was young and talented, but also had a quick temper that had cost him promotions. Thinking of Hawkins made him look around at the rest of the bridge crew, and he felt another momentary pang of regret, like he was not in the place he was supposed to be.

All of these officers had been picked by him, had cut their teeth under him, and had all shown themselves to be the very best Starfleet had to offer. Not commanding a destroyer as they flew towards a possible armed conflict with the ESA seemed...wrong. It was true that he was a bit young to be a two-star, but that could be said of most officers in the post-Phage War fleet. They'd all had to move up fast to cover the horrific losses they'd suffered at massacres like the Battle of Nuovo Patria and the loss of entire planets like Haven.

The problem with his selfish impulse of wanting to be a captain on a bridge was that it left nobody to do the job he was currently doing. It all came back to who he trusted to do the right thing. Fleet Admiral Pitt had been politically damaged when he'd been removed from duty for allowing Jackson to go off alone in pursuit of the Darshik *Specter*. He'd been reinstated afterward, but the sharks at CENTCOM tasted blood in the water, and the venerable old warhorse didn't carry the influence he once did. The rest of the recently promoted admirals—and a few generals in the Marine Corps—didn't see the ESA as the threat Jackson knew them to be. They felt that if they could wipe out the Phage and defeat the Darshik that the ESA's antiquated ships would pose little threat, and they were able to sell that fantasy to the civilian oversight.

It was a potentially fatal misconception that Jackson did his best to dispel. The name "Wolfe" still carried weight when he appeared before CENTCOM and Fleet Oversight Committee hearings, but he'd burned a lot of political capital trying to convince the Fleet to buy off on the Mickeys. He didn't think he had the juice left to convince them that the Federation needed to be on full wartime footing and that the ESA movements along the border weren't just games or bluffs.

"CIC reports two more hits on the same anomaly," Lieutenant Ayko Hori said from the OPS station. "No new analysis, but Commander Hawkins is confident there's definitely an artificial construct out there."

"Understood," Barrett said. "Tactical, prep four Hornets, forward tubes only. Keep laser batteries and mag-cannons powered down. Tell the other task force ships to keep their weapons powered down."

"Aye, sir," Lieutenant Falcone said. He was the *Nemesis's* new first watch tactical officer after Accari was step promoted and moved to XO. Jackson had watched his former protégé with great interest to see how he'd handle the adversity of being bumped ahead of people in rank and staying on the same ship with them. He'd pushed Barrett to transfer Accari to another ship, but the new captain politely ignored the suggestion.

"What's the plan, Captain?" Jackson asked, walking back over to stand by Barrett.

"I still think it could be one of ours, but that doesn't explain why they're so far down in the system," Barrett said. "There's the possibility that someone in CENTCOM has a ship out here spying on Eternis Pax...one of the project's detractors."

"Possibly," Jackson said.

"When the task force flies close to the planet, we should get some kind of reaction," Barrett continued. "I'm hoping it begins to move off once it detects us bearing down on it so we can identify it through its RDS signature. It'd be an awkward debrief if I fired a missile at one of Admiral Wright's new spy ships."

"It wouldn't make you any friends at CIS or CENTCOM," Jackson agreed. "A suggestion?"

"Of course, sir."

"Start stringing out the task force, move the ships out of the phalanx and into a column that makes it look like we're getting ready to push for a warp transition vector," Jackson said. "It'll put the *Nemesis* out front with room to maneuver should the need arise."

"Nav, did you hear the admiral's suggestion?"

"Yes, sir."

"Then make it happen," Barrett said. "Move the *Nemesis* out front and have the task force redeploy into a transition formation."

"Aye-aye, sir."

Task Force Vega had already been sitting in a parking

orbit near the planet, which meant they still had one and a quarter billion kilometers to cover before they were within range of the anomaly they'd detected. Given the speed the *Nemesis* was flying, it would be thirty-two hours before they covered the distance.

"Captain Barrett, I'll be down in CIC getting acclimated to my new workspace if I'm needed," Jackson said.

"Of course, Admiral," Barrett said. He looked like he wanted to say something more but turned his attention back to the display.

The task force concept was completely new to the Fleet, and there seemed to be some growing pains as people struggled to redefine their roles and responsibilities. Before the Phage War the numbered fleets all just patrolled their own space while Seventh Fleet, a repository for unwanted spacers and ships, would fly the warp lanes between systems. Deployments were always single ships or pairs, never more than two ships in a formation while on-mission. Once the Phage came, all the different numbered commands were tossed in together and ships were deployed as fleets, but even then, it was an unorganized cluster fuck with many territorial pissing matches.

After the wars had ended, and Jackson thought about how starships could be most effective when deployed against an enemy, he started combining different classes and types into task forces that could be rapidly deployed and able to respond to a wide range of threats. Task Force Vega was anchored by the *Nemesis*, arguably the most powerful ship in the fleet despite her destroyer-class designation, and contained frigates, assault carriers, heavy cruisers, and support ships. Vega could respond to a system in distress and fight off a significant enemy fleet, gain orbital superiority, and deploy Marines to the surface to repel an enemy landing if necessary.

Jackson's changes had ruffled feathers and raised eyebrows, making no sense to some, and simply pissing off others. What they didn't see was that Admiral Wolfe was quietly reconfiguring the Fleet and changing its tactics in a way that would let him quickly counter a *human* enemy that understood how he thought and what he would want to protect.

"To the CIC, Admiral?" Barton asked as he fell into step behind Jackson.

"I think I've changed my mind, Gunny," Jackson said. "Let's clock off for the rest of the shift. I could use some sleep, and I know you can."

"Don't expect me to talk you out of that, sir," Barton said. "Pulling security on an orbital platform with so many civilian contractors is exhausting. They don't screen their people as carefully or secure areas as tightly as a purely military installation does."

"But we need them as much as they need us," Jackson said, even annoying himself with the paternal tone he adopted as if he was lecturing the Marine. *When did I actually become the* Old Man?

"No doubt, Admiral," Barton said. "I've seen how hard they're all working putting those ships together."

Gunny Barton escorted Jackson all the way to his quarters, a suite that had been added by combining three officer's quarters on the *Nemesis's* command deck. It was sinfully luxurious inside, far more so than the captain quarters on the ship, and Jackson absolutely hated it. A warship should feel like a warship, even in Officer Country. His suite was more opulently appointed than his home on Arcadia, and while he knew it was put in as a sign of respect by the

Black Fleet planners, it seemed like a horrific waste of resources.

"Nice digs, Admiral," Barton whistled. "I should have gone into Starfleet instead of the Marines. I'll be sending Corporal Schmidt to stand watch the rest of the evening."

"Who?"

"Emil Schmidt. You remember the kid from Juwel, sir? The civvy we enlisted as a survivor on the initial landing to push back the Darshik? Anyway, he's in the Corps now, and Castillo pulled some strings to have him assigned to the *Nemesis's* detachment. He's a good kid."

"Tell Corporal Schmidt that I'll be in here the rest of the evening so not to worry about me sneaking off on him."

"Will do, Admiral. Enjoy the evening."

"Admiral Wolfe, please report to the bridge!"

Jackson had been sitting in the officer's mess going through the latest dispatches that had come up from Eternis Pax when the call came over intercom, the computer knowing where he was and broadcasting the announcement only in the mess. He cocked an eyebrow at the urgency in the voice and pushed the remains of his breakfast away, nodding to the steward who came to collect it as he walked to the hatch where Corporal Schmidt was standing at parade rest.

"Emil, right?" Jackson asked. When he'd come out of his quarters earlier, he'd only waved for the Marine to follow him and hadn't spoken.

"Yes, Admiral," the young man said smartly.

"You fought with the militia on Juwel?"

"I...helped, sir," Emil said. "We were all just a little overwhelmed and unprepared when the Marines showed up and saved us and, then again when you were able to run the blockade and make the relief drop."

"Detachment duty isn't likely to be as exciting as all of that," Jackson said as they walked up the ramp to the bridge hatchway. "At least I hope not."

"Yes, sir."

"Report," Jackson said as he strode onto the bridge.

"Captain Barrett is on his way up, Admiral," Accari said. "He asked me to notify you if something changed with the object. Fifteen minutes ago, it moved, and we were able to get a better profile of it on the passive sensors. It's lit up right now from the reflection coming off the planet. OPS, on the monitor if you please."

Jackson looked at the computer-generated model that appeared on the display, rotating slowly. The dimensions and recorded thermal output were listed next to it. It was smaller than a Federation Prowler, but much bigger than a Broadhead-class infiltration ship. The engine exhaust was heavily baffled, and the nozzles were recessed back into the hull to minimize the radar return of the ultra-dense alloy. It was unlike anything he'd ever seen, but it was unmistakably human in design.

"So, this is our bogey," Barrett said, walking up beside Jackson and breathing heavy. When Jackson gave him a questioning look, he explained. "I just ran up from Engineering. Your thoughts, sir?"

"It's human, but I don't think it's Federation," Jackson said. "It's got some clever stealth features, but the fact it has thrust nozzles at all rules out a CIS ship. Even the single-crew ships are all using RDS drives only...no thrust engines."

"That narrows it down to an ESA recon ship, or we have

another faction playing around," Barrett sighed. "The New European Commonwealth has been more and more vocal about their displeasure with New Sierra."

"They don't have the infrastructure in place to develop and deploy stealth ships like this in secret," Jackson disagreed. "Their star systems are almost all dedicated to raw ore mining and processing. Another thing is that I don't think this ship has its own warp drive. It was dropped out near the boundary and then flew the rest of the way in to its vantage point. The Commonwealth doesn't have any starships capable of that in their merchant fleets."

"How would you like it handled, Admiral?" Barrett asked.

"Ideally, I'd like to take it intact with the crew alive, but I have a feeling that a non-warp spy ship inserted deep in Federation space is likely equipped with a failsafe to prevent us from taking it," Jackson said, studying the image. "What do you have in mind, Captain?"

"The element of surprise, sir," Barrett said. "The task force is swinging around the planet at a distance that will make it look like we're committed to overflying it so the captain of that ship will likely choose to sit tight and pray they're not spotted. The *Nemesis* is capable of altering our course much closer to the point of no return than the rest of the task force. She can turn in harder than we've let on to ESA's spies. We might be able to take it by surprise."

"Interesting." Jackson rubbed his chin as he played the different scenarios through his head. "Your plan for capture?"

"Rush in close enough for point-defense laser batteries to disable its engines," Barrett said. "Given its profile and mission, I don't think it's packing anything that can hurt the *Nemesis*."

"I'm inclined to agree with you there," Jackson said. "Very

well, Captain. You're free to run your operation. Just know that I'd really appreciate it if you left me something to take back to Fleet Intel after you're done."

"Understood, Admiral," Barrett said and went about directing his people to put his plan in motion.

Jackson watched and felt like Barrett was onto a solid plan. The full capabilities of the *Nemesis* were closely guarded secrets to the point that disinformation had been fed to known ESA agents about her. The destroyer had been designed and built specifically to hunt and kill the Darshik *Specter*, a single enemy ship that had wreaked havoc within Federation space before it had been stopped. As such, the *Nemesis* was in many ways the most powerful ship in service. The big *Juggernaut*-class boomers could out-gun her, but they were true battleships and couldn't match the destroyer in speed or maneuverability. They were designed to come on-station and throw haymakers, relying on the heavy armor for survivability while they hammered a target with their big guns.

Though he had great confidence in the ship and crew, he thought it was unlikely they'd be able to get close enough to put pinpoint fire on the target to just disable it. The best-case scenario was that they wouldn't completely vaporize the tiny ship and the geeks at Fleet Intel and CIS could get something useful out of it to study.

"Coms, inform the task force that the *Nemesis* will be breaking formation and that they're not to deviate off course," Barrett said. "Tactical, standby for full active sensors and begin plotting firing solutions as soon as you have a fix. Helm, on my order, you're clear to free-fly the ship. I want our bow on the target and try to pass so our starboard batteries are within range."

"Understood, sir," Healy said.

"This is going to be a soft target, so don't get carried away," Barrett told his crew. "It will see us coming and likely try to flee, but it won't be able to outrun us. Keep her steady and pick your shots. Let's get this right on the first try. Execute!"

The *Nemesis* angled over, and there was a low-frequency hum from deep in the ship as Healy slammed the RDS to full power. Jackson leaned into the turn as the artificial gravity failed to fully null out their inertia in the tight turn and watched the main display as the computer plotted out the likely course the enemy would use to escape. The bridge was buzzing with tension as the destroyer roared up the well towards the target.

To their credit, the enemy didn't hesitate when they saw the lead ship break formation and come directly at them. There was a thermal bloom from the small craft's engines as it turned and flew out along the same course the computer predicted. It had been in a heliocentric trailing orbit behind the gas giant, well beyond the orbits of the planet's moons, so it was able to break free and fly an escape course directly away from the closing destroyer, but something still seemed...*wrong*...to Jackson. The captain of the small ship had to know there was no chance for escape. The ship was even turning in on a course that would allow the *Nemesis* to more easily pursue.

"Target isn't even trying to evade, Captain," Falcone said from Tactical. "Computer is analyzing the engine layout and programing the firing solution now."

"Fifteen minutes until we're within range, sir!" Healy called out. The *Nemesis* was shaking slightly, still under full power as they ran down the helpless stealth ship. Jackson, the tickle at the back of his mind now a full-blown itch, moved to one of the rear auxiliary terminals and began his own analysis. He started by requesting the data from the initial sensor anomaly that they'd picked up, and then also asked the computer to grab some frames from the high-res tactical array and begin a point-by-point comparison. It didn't take long for him to find the discrepancies he suspected were there. He pulled up one more screen, looking over his shoulder and seeing they were almost on top of the tiny ship.

"Target is losing engine power!" Falcone said. "Acceleration is dropping. She appears to have sustained critical engine, large thermal build up where the powerplant likely is."

"Helm, all reverse full!" Barrett said. "Come along beside it."

"All engines reverse, aye! Angling to port to move alongside the—"

"Belay that! Hard to port, all ahead emergency!" Jackson barked. "*NOW!!*"

"Coming about!" Healy said, yanking on the controls and pulling the destroyer off her intercept course. It was then that Jackson's fears were proven true.

The displays all washed out as the target exploded. The deck heaved, sending crewmembers not in their restraints to the deck. Jackson caught himself and rolled up into a sitting position as alarms blared and crew members began shouting conflicting reports.

"Quiet!" Barrett shouted. "OPS, I want a casualty and damage report ASAP. Tactical?"

"Forward array and imagers are offline, sir," Falcone said. "Secondary targeting array is showing nothing left of the enemy ship. CIC is telling me that the explosion is off the charts. Not even a Shrike detonates with that kind of force."

"Admiral?" Barrett asked. "Are you hurt?"

"I'm fine, Captain," Jackson waved him off. "See to your crew."

"CIC is saying we have nineteen injured, no dead, Captain," Hori said from the OPS station. Barrett's shoulders sagged with relief.

"Damage?"

"Substantial structural damage to the prow," Hori said. "All exposed sensors and antennas appear to be gone. RDS was knocked offline."

"Helm is nonresponsive with engines down, sir," Healy said. "We're adrift."

"Coms, get on a working radio and inform Eternis Pax that we need assistance. Tell them they may as well send out tugs to drag us back to dock for an initial damage assessment," Barrett said. "OPS, tell Engineering to do what they can."

"And tell Captain Carmichael that he's to assume operational command of the task force," Jackson said. "I want the ships moved back away from the *Nemesis* and in a holding orbit over the planet. Have them scanning the outer system with active sensors for any additional enemy ships."

"Aye, sir."

"How did you know?" Barrett asked.

"That it was a trap?" Jackson asked. "I didn't, at least not completely. I suspected something was off when the ship took the course that would make it easiest for us to intercept it. I looked over the sensor data and saw that the radar anomaly we thought was an engine thrust nozzle didn't match with what we saw once we were closer and using the high-power radar."

"So, we were baited in...but a suicide mission?"

"I suspect that the ship wasn't crewed," Jackson said. "There may be a tender still sitting in the system watching to see if they were successful, or this could have been dropped off and flying autonomous the entire time."

"Waiting for some dipshit captain to come in close where it could detonate the nuke aboard," Barrett sighed.

"Don't beat yourself up on this, Barrett," Jackson warned. "You made a snap-decision and it went badly, but nobody was killed, and it doesn't seem that the ship was irreparably damaged. Look at the bright side, it happened in a system with one of the largest Federation shipyards in it."

"I'll keep that in mind, sir," Barrett said, in tone indicating he didn't appreciate the attempt at levity.

"We won't get a return message from Eternis Pax for another two hours, fifty-seven minutes, sir," the com officer said. "Captain Carmichael has confirmed the admiral's orders and is redeploying the task force into an overwatch position."

"Understood, coms," Barrett said before turning back to Jackson. "So...this had to be the ESA, right?"

"I would say that it's a safe assumption this was their ship...or drone," Jackson said. "The real question becomes, what was the mission? Did we really just trigger some failsafe when it was discovered or was this thing here waiting to take out a Federation ship?"

5

"How many do they have?"

"The ident from the ship didn't include crew complement or cargo," Pike said. "From what I've found in the logs, the typical maintenance crew will be between eight and twelve individuals, and the shuttle itself has a flight crew of six."

"That's a manageable number," Halsey said. "You want them disabled or killed?"

"We're blowing up the platform with them aboard. What do you think?"

"Got it," Halsey said and began passing orders down to his men.

The team had negotiated the multiple ladders to get to the active part of the com drone platform so they could take the cargo lift the rest of the way to the main hab deck where the maintenance ship would dock and let its crew off. Pike had ordered the Broadhead to tuck in close to the platform on the opposite side of the other ship's approach rather than risk it being spotted as it tried to leave the area. So far, it seemed his plan was working as there was no unusual com traffic in the system indicating a heightened level of alert.

"I'll handle this, Commander," Pike said.

"Alone?" Halsey frowned. "That's not wise. If there are—"

"I'm aware of the risks. Believe it or not, I've done this sort of thing a few times before," Pike said. "No offense intended here, Commander, but NOVAs tend to be—how can I put this delicately?—a blunt instrument. Wait...I have a better one. You're like a sledgehammer when—"

"I get the idea, Agent," Halsey deadpanned. "And thank you for being delicate about it. So, you want us to just kick back in the galley while you kill a dozen ESA techs?"

"Ideally, I'd like for you to be doing something more useful than that, but I don't plan on simply ambushing and slaughtering the technical staff," Pike said. "We have a unique opportunity here as we're already aboard an enemy com platform. If one of the techs coming up has the proper clearance codes, we can grab a lot of intel off the buffers here before lighting the fuse."

"So, let's just incapacitate the entire crew as they enter," Halsey argued.

"You're not equipped for that. All you have are lethal rounds," Pike said. "I'd like for your team to be out of sight so, if I need you, you can storm in and save the day."

"Tell me the plan," Halsey said, resigned to playing a contingency role.

Over the next four hours, Pike worked to put his plan into action while the NOVAs went about prepping the platform for a demolition that would look like a catastrophic failure...hopefully. While most of the special forces operators rigged the fusion reactor so that they could send it super-critical when triggered, Halsey and two others used tools they'd found on the crew deck to force their way into the secure server compartments so that Pike's tricky intrusion AI could begin preparing a data dump that wouldn't set off any alarms. Halsey had impressed Pike by having a decent grasp of technical issues, so the Agent handed off the task to the NOVA team leader and let him handle it completely.

By the time the platform's proximity sensors let Pike know that the automated systems were bringing the ship in to dock, the team had finished their tasks, were in position, and ready for the unsuspecting maintainers to board. The adrenaline pumping through his system when he heard the loud *clangs* of the docking clamps erased the fatigue he'd been feeling from the long mission.

—*Beep. Beep*—

The console Pike was beside let him know that the data umbilical had been attached and the authentication handshake was complete. Standard procedure for the Tsuyo-era com drone platforms was to automatically dump all the system logs into the maintenance boat's computer as soon as hard dock was made. Pike was piggybacking onto this signal to put the first part of his plan into action. While he couldn't even be considered a novice programmer, what he was trying to do was low-level enough that he was confident it'd work.

"What the hell? The inner airlock door is jammed shut!"

"Use the manual override, idiot!"

Pike risked moving to view the monitor and quickly counted that there were thirteen bodies jammed onto the airlock bridge, one of them wearing a flight crew uniform, and none of them wearing environmental suits. He quickly activated his first script and waited. It was a few seconds later before he heard shouts of surprise coming from the airlock hatch, which soon led to banging and screaming for help. He'd successfully negotiated with the docked ship and closed its outer airlock hatch, trapping the team on the gangway. He now had to work quickly before the rest of the flight crew came to investigate the hatch malfunction.

He ran to the airlock and slapped the large red button that controlled the fire suppression system. Halon began to pump into the chamber immediately, displacing the breathable air. Pike watched the display on the bulkhead that showed the oxygen levels within the airlock while the panicked crew on the other side began to succumb to the halon. He wanted them unconscious, not dead, so once the last one sank to her knees and toppled over, Pike deactivated the fire suppressant system by pulling the switch back out, and then opened the airlock hatch, waiting a moment while the atmosphere from the platform displaced all the halon he'd pumped into the gangway tunnel.

"Halsey! Get your ass in here and secure the prisoners," Pike shouted as he checked his weapon and walked across the bridge to the hatch of the ship. As he'd intended, when the three-minute timer ran out on his program control of the airlock hatch reverted back to normal and it swung open noisily. Two crewmen looked out onto the gangway at the maintenance team strewn about, and then up to Pike, the shock clearly written on their faces. The Agent shot both center mass, dropping them before they could raise an alarm. He looked back one more time to make sure the NOVAs were cleaning up the mess before entering the ship and moving forward, dispatching crew as he went. By the time he'd finished, there were five dead spacers lying on the deck.

"Any resistance?" Halsey asked as he walked onto the bridge. Pike was in the process of going through the com log to make sure there weren't any messages sent regarding a possible breech of security on the platform. From what he could see, they never suspected a thing.

"None," he said flatly. In the course of his career as a full Agent he'd been called upon many times to kill in the name of the greater good. Over time, he learned not to dwell too much on the fact that the people he terminated in the process of accomplishing a mission were individuals with their own hopes, dreams, and maybe families who would miss them. "Did you identify a supervisor on the crew yet?"

"Yes," Halsey said. "He was wearing a badge that identified him as the crew lead and even his security clearance level, so that was helpful."

"Let's get started then," Pike said. "We have to get the data dump going, launch out the com drones with the mission package on them, and then scuttle this bastard before anybody comes looking for a reason the service barge isn't answering calls anymore."

"We have engines back online, sir," Accari said when Jackson walked onto the hectic bridge of the *Nemesis*. "Engineering warns that we're limited to forty percent power until the rest of the inspections are completed."

"Tell Captain Barrett that I would prefer to have the ship towed back to dock rather than take an unnecessary risk with the RDS for now," Jackson said.

"Aye, sir."

"Have Flight OPS prepare a shuttle to take me over to the *Blake*," Jackson said, referring to one of the escorting heavy cruisers. "I want to depart as soon as possible. I've been talking to CENTCOM over Bluebird, and they're not happy that Task Force Vega is stalled. They've dispatched the TFS *Jericho* to take the lead spot, and they want Vega repositioned to cut down on the delay. We'll warp out of this system and rendezvous with the *Jericho*."

"Captain Barrett will be...disappointed...sir," Accari said.

"I'll talk to him before I leave," Jackson said. "I hate to lose the *Nemesis* if the ESA actually escalates things, but we can't wait for her to be repaired."

"The *Jericho* is one of the new *Juggernaut*-class battleships, isn't she?"

"She is. I'm hoping her presence will keep the ESA from doing anything stupid. They may have numbers right now, but I'm sure their spies have told them about the new weaponry our battleships are sporting. That alone should keep everyone honest."

"What are our orders once we're out of repair dock, if you don't mind my asking, sir?"

"Since you're a Bluebird-equipped ship, I plan on having you rejoin the task force as soon as you're able," Jackson said. "We'll be able to send you real-time updates with our position and status so there's no point in holding you back."

"Glad to hear it, sir." Accari smiled.

Jackson made the necessary arrangements with the captain of the TFS *Robert Blake* and then had his staff gather his things and get them loaded into the shuttle while he went to talk with Captain Barrett personally. He hoped the embarrassment of being knocked out of action before the fighting even started wasn't going to cause Barrett to question his own decisions or, worse, overcompensate and do something rash.

It was more than concern for his protégé that weighed on his mind, however, as he walked the corridors with Gunny Barton trailing along behind him. The drone attack —and he assumed it was a drone—was an inexplicable move by the ESA. It would have limited success even if they managed to take out a mainline ship, and it would give the Federation every justification it needed to respond in-kind with its own series of covert strikes into ESA space. The problem he had with it was that the ESA wasn't led by idiots, and it had so far not made these sorts of strategic blunders, so Jackson could only assume it *wasn't* a mistake and that he just wasn't grasping the significance of the attack.

"You've seen the latest reports from the border systems?"

"Do come in, Admiral," Celesta Wright said to Fleet Admiral Pitt, the current CENTCOM Chief of Staff. Before the end of the Expansion War, he'd been stripped of his rank and had his court martial date set for helping Captain Jackson Wolfe take the Fleet's most advanced warship to hunt down the elusive Darshik *Specter*. After the news of Pitt's actions, and subsequent disciplining, had been leaked to the media, the politicians stepped in and squashed the court martial and put Pitt's name on a short list to replace outgoing Chief of Staff Dax Longworth.

"I knocked," Pitt grunted. "You just didn't hear me. So... have you?"

"Given that the fleet movement reports came from my Prowler Fleet, yes, I'm aware of the ESA buildup in two systems with strategic jump-off points into Federation space," Celesta said. "All of the *StarWraith*-class Prowlers are carrying Bluebird gear, so I'm getting intel updates in near-real time. You heard about the attack near the Eternis Pax Shipyards?"

"The brief just came across my desk," Pitt said, easing himself down into a chair. The admiral wasn't a young man and the rigors of his new assignment seemed to be wearing him down. "I didn't get a chance to go through the details other than Wolfe thinks it was likely a drone attack and not some spy ship's failsafe measure. How bad was it?"

"The *Nemesis* is out of commission," Celesta said. "She was the only ship pursuing, thankfully, but the blast did significant damage to the prow and the list of system damage to the ship is growing."

"So..." Pitt blew air out through his lips forcefully, "one of the most advanced starships in service, and definitely the fastest, has been taken out already because Barrett drove the motherfucker right at what seemed to be an obvious trap?" Celesta squirmed uncomfortably, well aware that Pitt knew she and Barrett were members of what the rest of Starfleet called the Blue Jacket Mafia: officers who had all served aboard the TCS *Blue Jacket* with Wolfe and were now promoted up into command positions.

"I can't speculate as to what Captain Barrett saw in the field, but his own report indicates that had Admiral Wolfe not ordered the *Nemesis* to pull off the pursuit, the damage would have been significantly worse," Celesta said. "We probably would have lost the ship altogether."

"What the hell kind of nuke was that bastard carrying?" Pitt shook his head. "It's unlikely I'll be able to keep Barrett in command of the *Nemesis* once she's back in action, and that kid Wolfe likes—Accari?—he's not qualified to take command. I'll have to move someone else from Black Fleet into that chair which, of course, will disrupt the hell out of everything. Spacers who served under Wolfe are so damn loyal to him that it even extends to *other* officers who served under him. What a mess."

"And well outside my area of responsibility," Celesta said, not bothering to offer any defense for her friend. The fact was that no matter if a board of inquiry found that Barrett had followed procedure to the letter, a vitally important Federation asset had been badly damaged and someone was going to have to take the fall. She just hoped Admiral Wolfe would understand this when CENTCOM came crashing in and began making personnel decisions for Black Fleet ships. "What did you need from me, Admiral?"

"Since you're outside of CENTCOM's chain of command, I was hoping for a favor," Pitt said. "Your boss has already showed me how many leaks there are in Starfleet so I can't pass this down through normal channels without someone catching wind of it."

"This should be good," Celesta murmured.

"We need to see if Bluebird has been compromised before we trust the system in a real-world contingency," Pitt said. "This is a shared asset between CIS, Fleet Intelligence, and Starfleet, so the likelihood that someone may have slipped the knowledge to the ESA is greater than I want to admit. Out of all the players, your Prowler crews go through a much more rigorous background screening than Fleet crews."

"You want to start passing false information and see if the ESA reacts to it?" Celesta guessed. "A counterintelligence operation that big could be problematic for my office, Admiral. Bluebird isn't *that* small to think someone won't get suspicious when my Prowlers start flooding the system with bogus ship movements. I'm assuming you think the leak is aboard one of the com ships?"

"Actually, no," Pitt said. "The com ships are tightly controlled so there's no way information is getting on or off of them. The system is also compartmentalized so that the operators have no idea what's in the message, just who it's from and where it's going...and that's only if it needs to be manually routed. Most of the time, the computers will shuffle the traffic.

"We've narrowed the possible leaks down to a handful of Bluebird access points. We'll begin with those, and if we don't get a reaction, we'll widen the net a bit."

"And you coming here directly means that—" Celesta let the question hang in the air.

"Correct. I haven't cleared this with your boss, and I've not discussed it with the director of Fleet Intelligence either," Pitt said. "Bluebird represents the single greatest strategic advantage in space combat since...well, ever. I'm playing this close to the chest in case the rat we're after turns out to be someone politically connected. I don't want to give them enough warning to shield themselves." Celesta just stared at him for a long, uncomfortable moment.

"This isn't some fishing expedition, is it? You suspect someone of actually leaking Bluebird intelligence to the ESA," she said. "You don't think it's already been compromised, do you?"

"I don't know," Pitt admitted. "I'm hoping that whoever is feeding information to the enemy is doing it through a third party on our side and that the existence of the system may still be a secret. Eventually, they're going to figure out we have superluminal communications, but that won't do them any good without knowing exactly how it works."

"But that knowledge will nullify the tactical advantage of

the system and allow the ESA fleet to develop tactics to counter it," Celesta said. "You can count on my help in this, Admiral. I think it would be best if we continue to meet in person regarding it for now."

"Agreed." Pitt stood and smoothed out his uniform. "How's that shit weasel CIS Agent you've been rumored to be involved with?"

"Pike is currently on an assignment classified above my paygrade." Celesta smiled. Pitt had made a mistake early on and told the smart mouthed Agent that he got under his skin, since then, Pike made a special effort to annoy the admiral.

"Tell him I said hello and that I hope he dies from explosive decompression," Pitt said casually as he walked to the door.

"I'll tell him, sir."

6

"The *Jericho* is making good time, Admiral." Captain Carmichael read the latest Bluebird dispatch regarding the inbound battleship after Jackson handed him the tile. "We'll only be in the system for eleven days before she joins the formation."

"And likely just in time to meet the ESA fleet that Intel says is moving into the system," Jackson said, taking the tile back and passing it to the specialist in CIC that would erase the device.

The Robert *Blake* had been in warp for the last nine days and the crew was just starting to get used to an admiral patrolling their decks. The heavy cruiser was actually larger than a destroyer, but her interior was much more cramped thanks to most of the room in the hull being taken up by ordnance. Rather than close with an enemy ship like a destroyer and scrap with it at relatively close range, the heavy cruisers would standoff and fire missiles down into the system. The strategy was accuracy through volume of fire, but since the Federation was still scrambling to prop up new sources of weapons-grade fissile material, the Fleet was much more sparing with ship buster missiles like the Shrikes sitting in the *Blake*'s magazine.

"The Odmena System isn't exactly a vital system to either the ESA or the Federation. There are half a dozen systems with multiple jump points into Fed space along this stretch of the border region. Why are they massing ships at this one?"

"Our best guess is they want to secure this system because of the *five* jump points from Odmena into ESA controlled space," Jackson said. "That's including two former Commonwealth systems that just left the Federation and signed on with the ESA. Those two systems hold critical manufacturing, and they'll want to make sure we don't send a task force to try and convince them to rethink the alliance."

"This is strange, isn't it, sir?" Carmichael said. "Fighting humans, I mean."

"It may not come to that," Jackson said, nodding with his head to leave CIC. "I'm hoping for a diplomatic solution in which we can at least coexist without the threat of violence, maybe even become trading partners as time goes on."

"Do you think that's likely?"

"They shot down the last two ships we've sent into their space with diplomatic envoys without warning so...no, I don't." Jackson said. "The problem is that they don't believe we'll allow them to keep the territory they've taken from us, so there will always be tension and distrust. One side or the other is going to make a critical first misstep and fire on the wrong ship, and then we'll find ourselves in an all-out war."

"Now, I see why CENTCOM is sending us to Odmena," Carmichael said. "With you in command of Task Force Vega, it might keep anyone from getting anxious and firing off a shot." Jackson looked at the captain but said nothing. He'd served with Carmichael briefly when he'd first been given command of the *Aludra Star*. The man was a lot of things, but a kiss ass wasn't one of them, so he let it slide without comment. As Jackson remembered it, the two didn't exactly hit it off when they'd first met, but Carmichael had been the consummate professional since the *Robert Blake* had been added to Task Force Vega.

"Admiral! Admiral, wait up!"

Jackson turned and saw the CIC watch officer running down the corridor towards them.

"Yes?"

"Another Bluebird came through just now...for you, eyes only."

"I'll see you this evening at Captain's Mess, Admiral," Carmichael nodded and strode off towards the lifts. Jackson followed the lieutenant back to CIC and went through the process all over again to authenticate himself as an authorized user. He had to assume the message he was getting was important given how adamant CENTCOM was that the system be used as little as possible for operational security reasons.

"Thank you, Lieutenant," he said when the officer handed him a secure tile clearly marked for Bluebird. Once he authenticated himself and the security measures were all active, he wasted no time diving into the message.

ADM. WOLFE...BE ADVISED CIS/FLEET ASSETS CURRENTLY IN PLAY IN ODMENA SYSTEM. BROADHEAD 3 CLASS SHIP WITH COMPOSITE CREW STILL ON-MISSION. DO NOT ATTEMPT TO MAKE CONTACT UNLESS THEY INITIATE. NO WAY TO WARN THEM YOU'RE COMING. YOUR ORDERS STAND: ENSURE

THE INTEGRITY OF ALL FED JUMP POINTS. ADM RUBACK, OUT.

"Shit," Jackson grumbled. So, the CIS was playing in the same system they were sending him to, but they weren't part of the overall mission to project Federation strength and deny the ESA Federation jump points.

Admiral Ruback was a holdover from the Phage War, a former operations officer from Fourth Fleet that had been picked to head Starfleet's overall strategic policy while Jackson had been given the job of developing tactics within that framework. While he'd never say it publicly, Jackson had a fairly low opinion of Ruback's strategic prowess and looked at him as an anachronism from the days when Starfleet admiralty was simply an extension of the old Terran Confederation's political apparatus, picked because of their family connections or wealth.

Specifically, Jackson had issues with Ruback's premise that Starfleet could be put in position to *block* the ESA fleet. Space was unfathomably big, and starships, even with the newest RDS and warp drives, were too slow. The only reason warships ever clashed with each other was either to take or defend a specific asset like a planet or orbital platform that wasn't mobile. If the ESA wanted to skirt around the Fleet's picket lines and move their ships into Federation space, there was no way to stop them.

It looked like Ruback's strategy might actually work if the intelligence was accurate, though it pained Jackson to admit. The ESA was funneling the bulk of their ships into three choke points; systems that had multiple jump points into Federation and ESA space. With their deployments, CENTCOM had no choice but to match them and marshal its diminished fleet to meet them. Jackson wasn't sure who might be playing who in this scenario.

He shook off the idle thoughts and typed in an outgoing message, this one to a friend who might be able to shed some light on what was happening in the Odmena System.

ADM WRIGHT...ANY NEW INTEL TO SHARE RE: ODMENA SYSTEM? TF VEGA IS EN ROUTE MINUS ONE DESTROYER. HEARD THERE WAS A CIS MISSION IN PROGRESS. ADM WOLFE, OUT.

He checked the clock on the wall and saw that it was the middle of the evening on New Sierra. Wright might still be in her office, so he'd give it a few minutes. As the head of the CIS Prowler program, she had access to her own Bluebird transceiver. He spent the time running through different deployment scenarios in his mind that would maximize his effective coverage now that he could no longer rely on the speed and power of the *Nemesis* to cover any gaps or unexpected moves from the enemy. So engrossed was he in the mental exercise that he jumped when the tile chimed.

ADM WOLFE...HEARD ABOUT *NEMESIS*, BAD LUCK. SHIP SHOULD BE BACK UNDERWAY IN A MATTER OF WEEKS. NO SPECIFIC KNOWLEDGE OF THE ODMENA OP OTHER THAN IT'S A JOINT CIS/SPECIAL FORCES MISSION. NO PROWLERS IN THE SYSTEM YET, AM DEPLOYING TWO STAR-WRAITH'S ON ADM PITT'S SUGGESTION. BE ADVISED THAT CURRENT INTEL SHOWS TWO LARGE FORMATIONS OF ESA SHIPS

CONVERGING ON THE SYSTEM. WILL ADVISE WHEN I KNOW MORE. ADM WRIGHT, OUT.

"Nothing like not being told the whole story," Jackson snorted in disgust and blanked the tile, tossing it onto the shelf. A second group of ships steaming for the Odmena System was something he definitely should have been made aware of. Perhaps Celesta was giving him the raw intel before the analysts had time to disseminate it to CENT-COM, and then on to the Fleet, but they were less than a day from popping into a system where they could be severely outgunned.

He left CIC and decided to skip Captain's Mess, sending his aide ahead to tell Captain Carmichael that he'd be absent. Instead of sitting around sipping expensive wine and swapping war stories, he grabbed a carafe of coffee from the officer's mess and locked himself in his office, adjusting his contingency plans based on the new information Celesta had given him. The outlook was bleak. He didn't have enough ships, and the ones he did have were vulnerable. He began to look at the other deployments to the border region, seeing if he could figure out what was different about Odmena that justified so many ships to the area. Were the other two buildups just feints to force them to divide the fleet up while they used Odmena's jump points for a first strike?

By the time the coffee ran out, and he'd pored through every intelligence dispatch on the region, he was no closer to an answer than he was when he started. What was he missing?

"That's two more drones that have docked and downloaded!" Halsey shouted over the noise. "Adding the raw data to the dump."

"One more and that's it," Pike said. "We need to get out of here. The ship just made contact through the relay team. Half a dozen transition flashes so far from around the New Kazan jump point."

"That many flashes that close together means military," Halsey said. "You think it has something to do with us?"

"Doubtful," Pike said. "This looks like a major fleet movement. They're either passing through or they're setting up here for something big. Has the package gone out yet?"

"Six outbound drones have been loaded with it," Halsey said. "It should start propagating through the ESA communication system within a few days."

"Unhook when you can and let's get moving back down to the lower dock. I'd like to be shoving off before any of the new arrivals begin taking a closer look at the platform."

The team had liberated a spare com drone data core from a parts locker to begin pulling data off the buffers. All the good stuff was heavily encrypted, so Pike was taking it as-is rather than risk corrupting it by letting his ship's computer take a crack at it. Since he was blowing up the entire platform anyway, it seemed like a low risk move that could pay off big.

Pike went about the cleanup methodically, unworried about an armada that would take over a week to reach him if they came about on a direct course. For all the advances that had come fast and furious during the last two wars, human starships were still, for the most part, at the mercy of Newtonian physics once they were back in real space. The fleet that was popping in on the other side of the system would have to fly an indirect course around the primary star to get to the platform. By the time they were at the outer edge of their effective optical detection range, his team would be long gone.

"We're ready, Pike," Halsey said. "The data core has been disconnected, and we put ESD caps on the connectors like you asked." The NOVA commander pointed at the black caps on the data connections that would protect the core against any stray electrostatic discharge.

"Start pulling them back," Pike waved him towards the lift, taking one last look around. He felt a bit of guilt at what he was about to do. A com drone platform wasn't something easily replaced, and it would effectively cut this planet off from the larger community until they could bring a replacement in. Despite his reputation as a ruthless Agent, willing to kill or maim to accomplish his mission, he was never happy when his actions inadvertently harmed innocent civilians. But their mission might have some chance at holding off any rash actions by the ESA and give the diplomats time to cool the conflict off before starships began lobbing missiles at each other and spacers started dying in droves.

He followed the last NOVA to the lift car, pushing his doubts and recriminations as far to the back of his mind as he could. As the safety cage closed, and the lift began to drop them to the lower decks, Pike tried to figure out the best way to get his Broadhead out of the system. The ship was small and stealthy, but Fleet R&D hadn't figured out a way to completely eliminate the telltale transition flash. With a whole fleet of ESA ships arriving in the system, there were now a lot of optical sensors scanning the boundary, not just one patrol boat with a bored, complacent crew.

"We're all set, Commander," a young specialist reported to Halsey as they climbed off the lift. "We can begin the process either by timer or remote signal...your choice."

"Timer," Pike interjected. "We can't risk broadcasting any sort of trigger signal now that there are so many ships in the area listening. The odds of it being missed by their passive sensors decreases exponentially with each new transition flash we detect. This has to look like an accident or we've just blown up a critical bit of infrastructure for nothing."

"The tile we're using to control the process is near the airlock, *Agent*," the specialist said. He wasn't *quite* disrespectful in the way he said "Agent." Either way, Pike had no interest in petty back and forth between CIS and Starfleet Special Operations.

The older Tsuyo platforms had no protections against intentional sabotage. Its designers assumed that the only people that would ever be aboard one would be qualified technicians, and the platforms were designed and deployed when the entirety of human space had been at peace for a century. As such, it had been ridiculously easy to rig the fusion reactor for a meltdown. When the tile they'd rigged near the airlock sent the command, charges would blow and cut the actuator arms that controlled the emergency reactor vents, preventing the system from simply dumping the plasma into space when the pressures exceeded maximum.

Once the primary safety system was damaged, it was a simple matter of increasing the fuel flow rate by fooling the computer into thinking there was a higher demand, and then blowing a second set of charges on the pipes supplying chilled water to the reactor cooling jacket. After that, it would only be a matter of minutes before the reactor case failed and the resulting explosion took out the platform along with all the evidence of the covert team's meddling.

"I hope the other teams aren't also blowing up their platforms," Halsey griped as Pike set the timer for thirty-six hours and executed the script.

"Yeah me too," Pike said. "Just so you know, this is technically illegal and a violation of the Xi'an Nonaggression Pact."

"What?! Are you fucking serious?"

"Why do you think I said it had to look like an accident?" Pike asked. "Don't worry, we won't get caught."

"It's still illegal!" Halsey spluttered.

"You've been a NOVA commander for how many years and you're still hung up on legalities?" Pike laughed. "So, you've *never* been deployed to hit a target against an enemy that we're not in a declared state of war with? Never been deployed for a surgical strike against one of the regional governments in one of the enclaves?"

"I'm sure you're well aware of our operational history, Agent," Halsey ground out. "I just don't like being a party to a major treaty violation without at least getting a vote. Got it?"

"Sure," Pike said. "Now, get in the ship so we can get out of here."

Once the computer on the Broadhead confirmed that everyone was aboard, he closed the outer hatch and made his way to the flightdeck. He could feel Halsey burning a hole in his back with a glare and resisted the urge to turn and wink at the uptight commander. They would be stuck on a small ship with a single head for a few more days, so being intentionally antagonistic wouldn't be helpful.

He slipped into the pilot's seat and told the ship to go ahead and close up the platform's airlock and detach from the docking collar. While the ship slowly drifted away from the enormous artificial satellite, he reflected on how jaded he'd become during his career in the CIS. As a full Agent, he'd routinely done things that, if caught, would have caused an uproar in the old Confederate Senate. He'd assassinated politicians, blackmailed regional heads of state, even held a high-level corporate executive's parents for ransom to ensure her company behaved the way his superiors wanted. He'd done it all in the name of peace and security back then. Now, he was doing it to try and prevent a war, but he held no illusions about himself. He was a weapon and, at times, had been wielded by people with nefarious intent. It was something he would have to learn to come to terms with as he was coming up on the end of a long and violent career.

7

"System is clear, Admiral."

"Thank you, Captain," Jackson said. "Once the rest of the task force has formed up, move us down into a trailing orbit behind the sixth planet. Maintain strict EMSEC protocols and watch the transition flashes. The only one we should see will be our inbound battleship, but let's not be careless."

"Aye-aye, Admiral," Carmichael said smartly, turning to bark orders at his bridge crew. Jackson hated to admit it, but commanding the task force with Carmichael as captain of his flagship had been less stressful than when he'd been aboard the *Nemesis*. Jillian had been right when she'd suggested it would be better to not be on his old ship that still had most of its original crew.

After a likely ESA ship had exploded so close to what was supposed to be a highly classified shipyard, Jackson was no longer taking security for granted. Once Task Force Vega had transitioned out of the system, he had used Bluebird to directly contact the *Jericho* and change the rendezvous point to a system that had been mapped, but was uninhabited save for a single automated mining platform. What the system *did* have was a jump point directly to the Odmena System, their ultimate destination.

He'd also called in a mission support request to Logistics Command for a supply convoy so that his ships were topped off with fuel and consumables before arriving. If he'd timed it right, his supply convoy should already be sitting in the system and, within the next two days, they'd be taking on fuel and consumables before pushing on to the Odmena System.

Since the latest reports from Fleet Intelligence were that the ESA was committing a large number of ships to the system, he preferred to have his battleship with him when they arrived, not waiting for a week afterward. The sleight of hand trick changing his arrival time and point of origin via the Bluebird system meant that even if his mission specifics had been leaked, the ESA fleet would be expecting him on the wrong side of the system.

Jackson moved to the back of the bridge and continued working at one of the terminals, mapping out different deployment strategies he might use depending on what they found when they arrived. Intelligence had gotten better with the advent of super-luminal communications, but it could still be wrong at the source, and he'd learned to trust nothing completely that he hadn't seen with his own eyes. He also took the time to read up on the Odmena System's orbital manufacturing facilities, the main reason the ESA was trying to coax them away from the Federation in the first place.

"Admiral, the resupply convoy has signaled," Carmichael said after a few hours. Jackson checked the time and figured they must have transmitted a greeting as soon as they saw the task force's transition flashes.

"Fire up the ident beacons, Captain," Jackson said. "Confirm the identity of the convoy ships and have them come to us to begin resupply operations. I'll be in my quarters. Alert me the moment the *Jericho* arrives."

"Aye, sir."

Jackson and Barton went back to his sparse quarters. He'd sent his aide to work with Carmichael's admin staff the moment they'd come aboard and saw no reason to call for him now. The ensign was assigned to him by Seventh Fleet HQ, and while he was a nice kid, he was an unredeemable bootlicker. Jackson didn't need his ass kissed, and he didn't need someone underfoot who seemed more interested in being seen with a *legend* than with doing his assigned duties.

"There's two racks in this room, Gunny. Call down to the detachment and get someone else to watch the door, and then I want you in one of them, getting at least six hours of actual sleep," Jackson said. "Don't even open that trap unless you're about to say 'aye-aye, sir' or 'thank you, sir, I could use some sleep.'"

"Aye-aye, sir," Barton said with a smile. "I am a little dead on my feet now that you mention it."

Jackson just grunted. Barton was the only person from his personal security detail that he'd brought with him from the *Nemesis*, and the Gunnery Sergeant had been pulling long hours, seeming to be distrustful of the Marines aboard the cruiser given how many credible threats there had been on the admiral's life already. Jackson figured if he was armed and in the suite with Jackson, the poor bastard might relax enough to actually sleep.

"I'll have someone bring some chow up, and then you can rack out," Jackson said. "I'm just going to be working at my terminal for a few more hours, and then I'm doing the same. This fucking leg is killing me."

"They make a lot better prosthetics now, sir," Barton said. "Even the grunts that have lost some limbs are getting those tricky new replacements with the pseudo-organic muscles instead of electric servos."

"I haven't had the time to get fitted, and they'll have to replace the neural transmitter in my leg for the new style," Jackson said, rubbing at where the artificial leg met with his real one as he sat down. Losing the leg had been a parting gift from the first Phage Super Alpha he'd destroyed. "Maybe when this border dispute with the ESA settles down." Barton didn't say anything, but Jackson could see on his face that the Marine didn't think it was going to be that easy.

"General quarters! General quarters! All crew man your stations. Condition 2SS."

Jackson rolled out of his rack onto his feet. The younger, more fit Barton was already up and strapping on his weapon belt. When the admiral looked at the clock, he realized he'd only been asleep for a little over two hours. His mind was alert, but his eyes were gritty, and there was a weariness that he felt all the way to his bones.

"If this is a readiness drill, I'm going to have Captain Carmichael fired from mag-cannon turret number one," Jackson grumbled.

"Noted, Admiral," Barton said, waiting by the hatch as Jackson slipped on his black service coat and smoothed out his uniform.

"Let's go," Jackson nodded to him and followed the Marine out into the corridor.

"Where the fuck is the sentry?" Barton asked, his hand going to his weapon. Jackson hung back as the gunny cleared the area. "I don't like this, sir."

"Let's get to the bridge," Jackson said. "If this isn't just a mistake, then that's the best place to be."

"Yes, sir," Barton said, drawing his sidearm and holding it at a down-ready position in front of him.

The quarters that Jackson had been given were on the command deck so it was a short twenty meter walk up to the main corridor that led directly to the bridge. Along the way, they passed two enlisted spacers, rushing to their stations, who looked shocked at a Marine with his weapon drawn. The further they went, the more Jackson was convinced that the missing sentry was simply a mistake and not part of another plot on his life.

"Secure your sidearm, Gunny," he ordered as they approached the bridge hatchway. Barton wordlessly slammed the weapon back into the holster with an audible *click*. Jackson strode onto the hectic bridge and, seeing that nothing was amiss, waved Barton to his station near the hatchway.

"I'll talk to the detachment commander about this, sir."

"Later," Jackson said before raising his voice. "Report, if you please, Captain."

"Two ESA Striker-class missile frigates just appeared by the New Berlin jump point," Carmichael said. "Optics picked up their transition flashes, and CIC is tracking them via their RDS signatures now that they're underway. They appear to be heading straight for our resupply convoy."

"Unfortunate," Jackson said. "We're out of position to intercept."

"Exactly, sir," Carmichael agreed. "Orders?"

Jackson's mind was working furiously on different options that would allow him to save the helpless supply ships. He'd also like to prevent the Strikers from escaping and getting back to ESA space to report on his task force's position, erasing his advantage going into Odmena. There was a tickle at the back of his mind, something that told him these two frigates just appearing in an unoccupied system was not coincidence.

"Coms, order the convoy to abandon their intercept course for our position," he said. "Have them angle into the inner system and let them know we'll be doing the same. We'll cross their flightpath before the two enemy ships are within range. Once we've dealt with the immediate threat, we'll worry about rendezvousing for resupply."

"Aye, sir," the com officer said.

"Captain, break us out of this orbit," Jackson said. "I want to sharpen our descent so that we cross behind the orbit of the third planet to get around the primary star. OPS, broadcast our course change over the Link and order the task force into a loose column, twenty-thousand-kilometer intervals."

"Nav! Plot me a course downhill that kisses the orbit of the third planet," Carmichael barked. "Helm, come about on new course at your discretion...all ahead flank."

"Engines ahead flank, aye!"

The deck vibrated slightly as the cruiser's RDS was brought to full power. Jackson watched on the main display as the tracks for the enemy frigates were displayed in blue along with a dotted red line that was the predicted course along with countdown timers placed along the lines to let him know when they'd cross certain thresholds. The best guess of the tactical computer had them within range of the

ESA ships in sixty-eight hours, more if the Strikers decelerated or deviated from their current course.

"Full sensors, Captain," Jackson said. "This ship only."

"OPS?" Carmichael asked.

"High-power radar coming up now, sir," the OPS officer reported. "Instructing the rest of the task force to maintain passive posture."

"Fleet Intel isn't sure whether the ESA is aware of our ability to track RDS-equipped ships passively, but we may as well put up a show of trying to track them with radar," Jackson explained to Carmichael.

"A well-taken point, Admiral," the captain said.

The ESA was operating a version of reactionless drive that was a derivative of the first generation RDS pods the Federation was retrofitting onto its starships during the opening phase of the Expansion War. It was a rugged, functional gravimetric drive, but it lacked the sophistication of the newer, integrated RDSs that the Federation was fielding in its newest starships.

The new drive field emitters were so precise that they could accurately detect outside interference within their own fields, effectively allowing it to *see* any other gravimetric drives operating within an incredible range of just under ten billion kilometers. The system allowed Fleet ships to cut their detection time in half compared to traditional radar systems. It was highly unlikely the ESA was unaware of this capability given how good their intel was proving to be, but on the off chance they didn't know, Jackson felt it was prudent to keep up the ruse.

"OPS, stand down from general quarters," Carmichael ordered after studying the course plots and timers. "Tell the department heads that I want full coverage, but they're free to rotate the crew at their discretion."

"Aye, sir."

"Two missile frigates against a full task force?" Carmichael asked Jackson. "They can't be serious pressing this attack."

"Most likely they'll pull off well before we're within range...far enough out still that we can't pursue before they can get back to a jump point," Jackson said. "But there is a chance this is a ruse meant to pull us further down the well where a hidden force is sitting, waiting to jump us.

"We have no choice but to respect their attack and move to meet them before they can overtake our supply convoy, but I want our overall posture to be defensive. Expect that this isn't an attack that's meant to succeed. The ESA ships may lag behind ours in performance, but their commanders aren't foolish, and they know most of our standard responses from when we were still one big, happy family."

"Of course, Admiral," Carmichael agreed. "I'll make sure CIC is coordinating with the rest of the task force to provide overlapping sensor coverage."

"Very good," Jackson said. "You're in overall command of the task force while I'm not on the bridge. I'll be down in CIC. I want to know the instant we detect the *Jericho* arriving in-system. With any luck, we'll be able to spring a surprise of our own."

Jackson collected Barton and made his way to the lifts that would take him from the superstructure of the cruiser down into the bowels of the ship where CIC was located. He needed to report the incident to CENTCOM and see if there was any new intelligence from the Odmena System. The arrival of the two Strikers in the system confirmed that there was a high-level mole somewhere within either CENTCOM or Seventh Fleet that was feeding the ESA Task Force Vega's mission parameters and location. Neither prospect was particularly appealing, but as a point of personal pride, he hoped it wasn't someone within his office selling out the Federation.

"MP, welcome. It's an honor to see you again, sir."

"When did you become such a political kiss-ass, Pitt?" newly-elected MP Joseph Marcum walked into the office, extending his hand towards his old subordinate, who now held his previous job within CENTCOM.

"The same time you decided to become a politician, I suppose," Admiral Pitt said.

Marcum had served as the CENTCOM Chief of Staff during the Phage War and had been forcibly retired when a new administration came in and decided to clean out the old guard and bring in new leadership for Starfleet. After the new administration's approach had proved to be near-disastrous during the Expansion War, Marcum was lobbied to run for Parliament while Pitt was reinstated and promoted to Chief of Staff. Marcum was now the Chairman of the Fleet Oversight Committee.

"It really is a shit job," Marcum said, grunting as he sunk into a chair. "You think things move slowly at the command level of Starfleet? In Parliament, we have meetings to talk about the possibility of planning a meeting. So why did you ask me to fly up here for a personal briefing?"

"The number of high-level leaks in both the government and CENTCOM is…distressing," Pitt said. "At least here I know we can speak freely, and I thought you'd appreciate an informal heads up on this information before it became widely known."

"Regarding the attack on Eternis Pax?" Marcum guessed.

"The device that caused so much damage to the *Nemesis* wasn't nuclear...it was an antimatter bomb."

"Bullshit," Marcum scoffed.

"The analysis is conclusive," Pitt insisted. "If Wolfe hadn't pulled the *Nemesis* off her pursuit, we'd be missing a Valkyrie-class, not talking about moderate hull damage. From what they found on the ship, and the sensor logs, the eggheads at Fleet R&S are guessing anywhere between fifty to seventy-five kilos of antihydrogen was used with an equal amount of its hydrogen counterpart."

"Which means the ESA is lightyears ahead of us when it comes to producing and stabilizing antimatter," Marcum said. "We've barely been able to make any as a scientific oddity and they've already weaponized it. This is...not good news."

"It gets worse, I'm afraid," Pitt said. "This comes from my source within CIS, so I'd appreciate your discretion with what I'm about to tell you."

"Just get to the goddamn point, Pitt."

"An Agent that was embedded with one of our NOVA teams during the implementation of Operation Crimson Foil managed to pull a large amount of data off an ESA com drone platform that they turned over to a cracker team on a CIS cruiser. They're still working on it, but they've managed to decrypt enough information to begin seeing a pattern in the ESA fleet movement orders as well as the likely reason for the Eternis Pax attack." Pitt leaned back and steepled his fingers, staring at his old boss as if trying to decide if he should continue or not. "The intel analysts suspect that the ESA is after the *Nemesis* specifically."

"Interesting, if a bit implausible," Marcum said. "I know the ESA leadership is a bit...*odd*...but they're risking an all-out war with the Federation to snag a single starship? Just to shoot it down? The *Nemesis* is unique but not worth fighting a war over."

"The Phage found us because of the Asianic Union's illegal expansion and colonization beyond the Confederation's border," Pitt said. "To save face and offset blame away from the AU government, they pinned the entire Phage War on Wolfe. They claim he launched an unprovoked attack on a peaceful emissary, and the Phage destroyed Xi'an as retaliation. They might still think Wolfe is on the *Nemesis* and be after him."

"I've heard all that. I still have a hard time believing their people actually buy that horseshit."

"The AU and Warsaw Alliance more tightly control their media than the other enclaves." Pitt shrugged. "It was a simple matter of repressing the reports coming out of Haven and pushing their own version. The truth is that, even under the old Confederation, the AU and Warsaw Alliance were largely ignored— Well, maybe ignored isn't the right word. Perhaps culturally segregated would be more accurate."

"Whatever it is, it's irrelevant at this point. Not only do they know we're still trying to ramp up our enrichment capability for fissile material for weapons—something they controlled most of—but they now have something that makes nukes almost obsolete."

"We only know they have the capability of stabilizing antimatter for use in weapons, nothing about their production capabilities or how they're deploying it in their fleet."

"I'll act suitably surprised when the new CIS director briefs me on this," Marcum said. "This business about one of our officers being singled out and targeted by the ESA as a matter of strategy throws us off our game. We're countering their moves under the assumption they're preparing to secure important logistical and strategic assets, but you're telling me they're chasing around Wolfe because they're still embarrassed about the Phage War."

"Their alliance with the Darshik didn't help either," Pitt reminded him. "You were already a civilian at that point, but the ESA was providing intel *and* ships trying to help the Darshik topple the Federation."

"And the Tsuyo Corporation was playing all sides against each other," Marcum sighed. "What a fucking mess. Thanks for the heads up. I need to go down a few decks and talk with Admiral Wright about something so nobody will think twice about seeing me come out of your office. Make sure you get word to Wolfe that his old ship seems to be a target. That slippery bastard will probably find some way to use that to his advantage. You probably want to let Barrett know, too."

"Is that an order, sir?" Pitt said with a wry smile. Marcum may have been in charge of Fleet oversight, but he wasn't technically in the chain of command.

"Old habits," Marcum growled. "Just make sure our man knows that the ESA's reactions will be unpredictable."

"Of course."

The pair shook hands, and the MP stormed out of the office. In true Marcum fashion, he looked pissed off about something, and it caused people to dive out of his way and seek cover. When he was still an admiral in Starfleet, very few people crossed him and still had careers to speak of afterwards. Jackson Wolfe was the only person Pitt could recall that openly defied Marcum on more than one occasion and managed to keep his rank and position intact.

Pitt went back to his desk and began writing a Bluebird dispatch to let Admiral Wolfe know that the ESA had an interest in capturing or killing him personally and to adjust his tactics accordingly. He toyed with the idea of recalling the admiral and flying someone else out to take command of Task Force Vega but quickly spiked the idea. From a pragmatic point of view, keeping Wolfe in play near Odmena meant that the ESA might hold back from hitting other vulnerable Federation targets until they had him. He also knew that Wolfe would likely ignore any orders to come back to New Sierra.

Now that he was in Marcum's old position, he understood why the qualities he'd admired so much in the Earther starship commander were the same ones that made the old Chief of Staff throw furniture around in a rage.

"Hell...maybe Wolfe has one more magic trick up his sleeve, and we can stop this war before it starts," Pitt muttered to himself as he left his office so he could send the dispatch.

8

"They're still coming along the same course, Admiral," Carmichael said when Jackson walked back onto the bridge.

"Nothing they're doing makes me think they're trying to herd us towards something," Jackson said. "They've not made any significant velocity changes, so they're not trying to control the timing of the engagement. I think we'll most likely see them pull off on an escape vector within the next twelve hours. They know the range of our Shrikes and won't risk getting too close."

"I concur, sir. Orders?"

Jackson had read through a lengthy Bluebird dispatch from Admiral Pitt before coming up to the bridge and what he'd read made him rethink the intentions of the inbound ships. It was even odds that they knew which ship he was on and were willing to risk being fired on for a chance to take the cruiser out. The CENTCOM boss had also hinted at some sort of new *super weapon* the ESA might be deploying on their ships and to be careful. It was completely unhelpful advice without specifics, but it did make him wonder at the apparent confidence of the inbound Strikers. Did they have a nasty surprise for him loaded in their launch tubes?

"The Striker-class frigate doesn't have enough engine power to come about and cross in front of us heading back uphill for the outer system," Jackson said, pointing at the course plots on the display. "If they want to escape, they'll need to sharpen their descent even more and swing around the star to keep their gap on us and not bleed off too much relative velocity.

"I want the *Midway* and *Kestrel* to break formation now and begin angling for an intercept vector for where we think they'll be. I want to reclaim the initiative and let them react to our movements. We need to control the engagement instead of reacting to their moves."

"OPS, standby for orders to the task force," Carmichael said, relaying the orders from Jackson to peel off their two fast-attack frigates from the formation. Jackson made a mental note to try and streamline the process of disseminating orders to the other ships without having the captain of his flagship repeating everything he said.

The reactions to the redeployment of his ships would tell him a lot about both the intent of the ESA ships, as well as if they had stolen the Federation's gravimetric detection technology and implemented it in their mainline ships yet. Both Strikers were broadcasting tracking radar at full power, but so was Jackson as a way to mask his own capability.

The next few hours were tense despite the engagement still being over a full day away. His two fast-attack frigates had angled their course in sharply and now appeared to be steaming full bore towards the center of the system with no discernible goal. Jackson looked at the new timer on the display and saw it would only be another two hours before the Strikers' radar would let them know two ships had left the formation. He decided to stay on the bridge for the time being instead of hiding out in CIC. When he turned to get a refill on his coffee, he saw Barton trying to catch his eye from the hatchway and changed his course to see what he wanted.

"I talked to the detachment commander, a Major Elan Stiger," Barton said. "He seemed genuinely surprised and pissed that his Marines failed to report to their post. I pushed a little around the edges, but the major is convinced the orders just got lost in the shuffle and promised to make sure his people are where they're supposed to be from now on."

"I'm inclined to believe him," Jackson said. "There's normally never an admiral serving aboard this class of ship, and our just being here is disrupting the normal operations of the crew. Thanks for looking into this, Gunny. All the chatter coming from the CIS is making me paranoid."

"Just because you think you're paranoid doesn't mean some asshole traitor isn't trying to kill you," Barton said.

"I don't think that's how that quote goes, but point taken," Jackson said. "Carry on."

"A problem, Admiral?" Carmichael asked when Jackson rejoined him by the command chair.

"No problem, Captain," Jackson assured him. "It was merely a personal matter I was discussing with my security detail."

"About that, sir," Carmichael said hesitantly. "It's a bit... unorthodox...for even a flag officer to bring their own armed detail aboard a Federation vessel."

"Were you asking a question or merely making an observation, Captain?"

"If I might be so bold, some are wondering if you don't

trust the detachment Marines aboard my ship, or if there was some other purpose Gunnery Sergeant Barton served."

"The reasons for having my own security detail are classified," Jackson said. "Rest assured, they have nothing to do with your ship or crew."

"Of course, sir." Carmichael was clearly not satisfied with the non-answer, but Jackson wasn't about to divulge that for some inexplicable reason the ESA had decided that killing him was priority number one.

Both ESA frigates began to decelerate right about the time the computer estimated their radar would detect the deployment shift. It was nearly a full hour after that before they seemed to decide on a plan to deal with the split formation, and if anything, it confused Jackson even more than their initial appearance had.

"Striker One is coming about on a pursuit course after Vega Two," the tactical officer said, referring to the call sign of the split off task force ships. "Striker Two is...stopping."

"What?!"

"They're at full reverse power, sir."

"What the hell? Are they insane?" Carmichael asked.

"Let me know when Striker Two comes about onto a reciprocal course," Jackson said, ignoring the captain. "Begin plotting an intercept course for Striker One, and standby for course change."

"Aye, sir."

"Striker Two is reversing course. She's coming about, accelerating away at full power."

"Come onto new course now," Jackson said calmly.

"Sir! We can catch Striker Two!" Carmichael spluttered. "We need to—"

"You have your orders!" Jackson snapped.

"Aye-aye, Admiral," the captain said, struggling to maintain his composure as he executed his orders.

"Watch for Striker Two to decelerate now that we're not pursuing," Jackson said. "Tell Vega Two they're clear to maneuver at their discretion, but the rules of engagement stand. They are not to fire on any ESA ship without being fired upon."

"Task Force coming onto new course, Admiral," Carmichael said.

"Now, we wait to see what they do, Captain," Jackson said. "The RoE prohibits us from taking overtly aggressive action, so the best we can do is try provoke them early or avoid an engagement altogether."

"ESA ships have been hitting targets in Fed space for over a year now. You'd think that CENTCOM would loosen the leash a bit."

"Parliament still has hopes of heading off a full-scale war. A Federation task force running down two frigates that haven't shown any hostile intent won't play well in the press."

"You think they have a ship out there recording all this?" Carmichael asked, understanding seeming to dawn on him.

"I have to assume they do," Jackson said. "Otherwise, nobody would ever know what happened to these two hapless Strikers. The ESA doesn't have point-to-point com drones, and there's no platform in this system."

They fell silent as they waited for the ESA ships to react to Jackson's moves so they could better determine what their mission might be. Now that they were closing within half a billion kilometers, and the radar lag was decreasing, things were happening more quickly.

Despite all the advances, space battles still followed a

certain predictable pattern. Starships would close on each other within a system from great distances, taking days or weeks before they were within weapons range, and then they'd clash in a fast and furious burst of action before their relative velocities would send them streaking back apart. Each side would get a breather as their commanders tried to reposition their ships to gain an advantage on the enemy, then they'd come back at each other again. Normally by the second engagement one side was either eliminated or running for its life. It became more complicated the more ships you added, of course, but it was still a lot of waiting to see what the other side was going to do.

"Striker Two is flagging!" the tactical officer almost shouted. "Acceleration dropping. Engines appear to be offline. She's adrift."

"Trying to bait us back onto our original course," Jackson explained when Carmichael looked at him. He looked at where the supply convoy was, still plodding away from where they'd assumed the initial engagement would have been. "All ships, break off pursuit. Recall Vega Two and change course to rendezvous with our supply ships."

"OPS!" Carmichael barked.

"New orders going out over the Link, sir," the OPS officer said. Jackson pulled out his tile and began looking over the data they'd collected on the ESA frigates.

"OPS, I want a navigational hazard declared for grid coordinates five-alpha and five-echo," he said. "Tell all Federation ships to fly wide around that area."

"Sir?"

"A hunch, Captain," Jackson said. "I think our ESA friends may have left a present behind that we won't want to stumble blindly into."

"He suspects."

"So, it would seem."

"I warned you not to underestimate him. Your frigate commanders were clumsy, and their ploy transparent. Wolfe has not been victorious against two alien species because he is rash or foolish."

"I have already agreed with you. I see no point in further insulting our ship commanders."

The Yinying-class stealth penetrator was a small, uncomfortable ship. The observer, used to more plush accommodations aboard mainline ships, wasn't enjoying himself in the least. He'd been sent to observe Task Force Vega as the Alliance fleet provoked it, testing for reactions, and trying to verify a host of new technologies their spies claimed the Federation was fielding.

He'd watched the sensor footage from the Yinying that had been observing the task force's departure from the top secret Eternis Pax shipyards where the Federation was building *some* sort of new starship class that was confusing their experts. That team had deployed a Fox-class nano-ship in drone mode loaded with one of their largest ship-killer deployable antimatter charges. Unfortunately, Wolfe had sussed out that something was amiss and had pulled the *Nemesis* off course and kept the destroyer just outside the effective range of the weapon.

The observer, a political operative working for powerful people, took away two key points from that mistake; despite the propaganda about the man, Wolfe was not to be treated like some bumbling Earther who just fired mag-cannon shells at anything that moved. Secondly, the Federation was now likely aware of their new weapon technology and their newest stealth countermeasures.

The Alliance fielded a numerically superior fleet thanks to the Asianic Union and the Warsaw Alliance not having their fleets chewed up in the Phage War and completely sitting out their so-called Expansion War. The Council felt like that, along with their new technologies the Darshik had gifted them, would carry the day against the United Terran Federation and its beleaguered fleet.

But he knew better. While the Eastern Star Alliance had sat on the sidelines, playing spy games, and brokering backchannel deals with the Tsuyo Corporation and the Darshik, the Federation fleet had been in the trenches, fighting battle after desperate battle and winning. Their shipmasters were combat-hardened, confident, and skilled. He knew the reason the Council had put a priority on Admiral Wolfe and could agree with their reasoning, but he felt they might be missing the forest for the trees. Wolfe was unpredictable and difficult to corral. This was the second attempt to bait him into rash action, and they had come up with a second complete failure.

All hope to salvage things now rested on the Odmena operation.

"The Strikers are splitting up now, pushing for different jump points that aren't on the Federation charts," the commander said. "We'll wait and observe the refueling operations and see if our intelligence was correct and one of their *Juggernaut*-class battleships joins the formation."

"I'm aware of the plan, Commander," the observer said, hunching over on the cramped bridge. "Let's hope the frigate captains remember to trigger the antimatter mines they left in Wolfe's flightpath. It's obvious he knew something was amiss, but I doubt he knew exactly what."

"If not, we can send the trigger code before we leave."

"Lovely. Hopefully we'll be on our way to the Odmena System within the next few days. The sooner I can get onto a proper ship the better."

"Self-important parasite," the commander muttered after the bridge hatch had slid shut.

9

"Welcome aboard, Admiral!"

"Thank you, Captain," Jackson said, returning the salute. "This is quite a ship you have."

"She may not move like one of your destroyers, but she can deliver one hell of a punch, sir."

Jackson had never met Captain Alto Hardy before transferring over to the TFS *Jericho*, the ship that would fly his flag for the remainder of Task Force Vega's mission. Hardy had a stellar reputation but, somehow, he came off as...*slimy*...when he greeted Jackson at the shuttle hatch with a fake smile plastered onto his face. Maybe he didn't want an admiral aboard his ship, usurping his authority, maybe it was a problem with Wolfe personally. If there was a problem, he'd have to get over it. Task forces that were anchored by battleships would always have an admiral on the bridge going forward.

"The VIP quarters on the command deck have been prepared for you and your security detail," Hardy said after dismissing the honor guard that had been standing at attention in the hangar bay. "You did not bring an aide de camp, sir?"

"I'm between aides at the moment," Jackson said. "To be honest, Captain, when I'm not stuck behind a desk on the New Sierra Platform, I don't really need one."

"Of course, sir," Hardy said with another oily smile. "If you need someone, please have Commander Trane assign you someone from Admin." Jackson looked over and nodded politely to the *Jericho's* Executive Officer and second in command, now third since an admiral was aboard.

"I can find my way to my quarters, Captain," Jackson said when nobody showed any signs of moving. "I'm quite familiar with this class of ship. I'll meet you on the bridge shortly. In the meantime, please begin moving the task force on course for the Odmena jump point. We're quite behind schedule, and I want to be transitioning out of this system without delay."

"Aye-aye, Admiral," Hardy said, snapping to attention before walking off in a way that almost could have been mocking. Commander Trane looked at Jackson, and Barton and just shrugged slightly before following his CO.

"That was...interesting," Barton murmured.

"Keep your observations to yourself for now, Gunnery Sergeant," Jackson said. He went to retrieve his bag but apparently some enterprising young spacer had grabbed both his and Barton's while they'd been verbally jousting with Captain Hardy. "Let's go."

The pair moved quickly from the hanger bay into the main starboard access tube so they could move forward to the lifts that would take them all the way to the command deck. The crew they passed looked bright eyed, busy, and snapped to when Jackson walked by. The ship was also impeccably clean. While that might not seem like a big accomplishment on a ship that was barely four years old, Jackson knew how quickly the filth piled up on a ship that housed over two thousand spacers. From what he was seeing, he was forced to revise his initial poor opinion of Hardy. The man might come off as a slimy politician, but he ran a tight ship.

"You'll be sleeping here," Jackson said once they were in the VIP suite. "I don't want you all the way down in berthing with the rest of the Marine detachment wasting time running back and forth."

"Aye, sir," Barton said, not trying to hide his delight at being asked to stay in the smaller of the suite's two sleeping quarters. The furnishings were much posher than anything below where the detachment slept. He'd told Jackson before that the Marine Corps brass intentionally gave them broken down, garbage racks and poor food to keep them pissed off and ready to fight. Jackson was personal friends with Marine Corps Assistant Commandant Lieutenant General Jeza Ortiz, and he knew for a fact that wasn't true, but a high degree of suffering seemed to be central to a Marine's sense of self, so he let it be.

"Since you're my personal security detail, I'll make sure you're able to eat in the officers' mess on the command deck," Jackson said. "Don't make me regret that."

"Is it true that it's all you can eat steak and lobster and that there are champagne fountains, Admiral?"

"Of course," Jackson said, rolling his eyes and walking to the hatch when he heard someone knock.

"Admiral Wolfe, my name is Lieutenant Sam Trapp."

"And your reason for being here, Lieutenant?" Jackson asked after the young officer seemed to run out of steam.

"Sorry, sir," she said quickly. "I report to Commander

Omar in CIC. I'm your com and intel liaison while you're aboard the *Jericho*. I'm also Bluebird cleared so any—"

"Lieutenant, that doesn't explain why you're standing outside my quarters," Jackson said, cutting her off before she could say anything else. Bluebird was so highly classified that even mentioning it by codename outside of secure areas was a COMSEC violation. Lieutenant Trapp looked back and forth in the corridor before lowering her voice and continuing.

"I just wanted to introduce myself, sir," she said. "And suggest that it might be...prudent...if I were able to personally brief you in a more secure location."

"I see," Jackson said. His first instinct was to dress her down for wasting his time on something so trivial, but there was something about her furtive glances and hushed voice that stayed his intended tirade. For now, he'd give her the benefit of the doubt and assumed she wasn't pestering an admiral in his quarters to try and gain some type of personal favor, but because she had information she didn't trust her chain of command with. *Goddamn assassination attempts have me so paranoid I'm looking for conspiracies in every corner,* he thought angrily.

"I'll be down sometime on first watch to acclimate myself with the *Jericho's* CIC layout and staff," he said. "I assume you'll be there?"

"Yes, sir."

"You can brief me then."

"Of course, sir. I apologize for intruding."

"More mystery and intrigue, sir?" Barton asked once the hatch was closed.

"Probably just an overzealous young officer trying to get a jump on the competition," Jackson said, frowning. "But considering the fact we were intercepted during a secret resupply rendezvous, and the *Nemesis* was attacked deep in Federation space, I'm not willing to just ignore her."

"Prudent, sir," Barton approved. "It makes my job easier if you take these threats seriously."

The pair left the VIP quarters and made their way to the bridge where Barton took up his usual post outside the hatchway next to the bridge sentry while Jackson continued on. The bridge of a *Juggernaut*-class boomer was impressive. As was fitting of a ship her size, the *Jericho's* bridge was expansive with working space for at least forty crew. Most of the stations faced the immersive wrap-around main monitor, which began at the deck and curved upwards to take up a third of the ceiling. Clever acoustics kept the space quiet despite the multitude of simultaneous conversations taking place and Jackson noticed that everyone was wearing a wireless earpiece that was tied into the ship's internal coms.

He looked at the course plots on the main display and saw that the task force was now back in a column formation and spacing themselves out for transition at the Odmena jump point. The resupply convoy was lumbering around the sixth planet, building up to breakaway velocity so they could get back to Federation space. With two back-to-back wars and a new threat from an increasingly aggressive ESA, most of Logistic Commands fuelers and cargo haulers were still flying on the old magneto-plasma drives, the bright flare of their powerful thrust engines lighting up the thermal imagers as they fought against the pull of the gas giant.

Some of the older Fleet officers waxed nostalgic for the days of the monstrous thrust engines belching out plasma as they pushed starships around in real-space. Jackson wasn't one of them. He'd been the first human starship captain in the history of interstellar spaceflight to fight against a more advanced, alien ship when the Phage first entered Terran space. The disadvantage he'd been at when his MPD-powered Raptor-class destroyer went head-to-head with a Phage Super Alpha using a reactionless drive had been almost insurmountable. He'd trade the power and capability of the new RDS any day for the visceral rumble and pretty light show from MPD engines.

"Admiral, we're...forty-seven hours from transition," Commander Trane said when he noticed Jackson on the bridge. "Would you like me to give you a quick familiarization with our layout and procedures?"

"I'd appreciate it, Commander," Jackson said, thankful that Captain Hardy wasn't on the bridge.

Even though each starship was built to class specifications, and the crews went through the same training, once it was commissioned and entered into service, they all invariably developed their own cultures and ways of doing things that varied from ship to ship. Over the next four hours, the *Jericho's* XO gave him a quick rundown on their local procedures and how they had their bridge stations organized. After the overview, Jackson could see that the same orderliness he saw when walking though the battleship also applied to the bridge on Hardy's ship. The man might act like he was a politician trying to win votes, but the admiral couldn't find fault with how he ran his ship, arguably one of the most complex vessels in the Fleet with many new systems that no other ship yet had.

"An impressive, well run ship, Commander," Jackson complimented him once they'd covered all the major areas. "I know the task force concept is new to all of us and we'll be learning on the fly once we're in the Odmena System, but I'm sure your crew is up to the challenge."

"Most have never been in combat, sir, but they'll do their jobs," Trane said with obvious pride. "We were kept out of the last war for...a few reasons...but we're ready to show what a battleship can do in a real fight."

"Let's hope it doesn't come to that, Commander," Jackson said.

The *Juggernaut*-class ships were just coming into service towards the end of the Expansion War and a timid CENTCOM had held them back in the DeLonges System to protect the capital from a dangerous and unpredictable Darshik enemy. Now that the last vestiges of that leadership philosophy had been purged under Chief of Staff Pitt, the big boys were allowed to come out and play. Jackson was still a destroyerman at heart, but he had to admit he was intrigued by what might happen if an ESA cruiser tried to pick a fight with the *Jericho*.

"Greetings, Councilman Chan. What can I do for you?"

"A message just came in from one of our assets," Chan said. "Wolfe's task force has just transitioned out of system E-382 on the way to the Odmena System. The TFS *Jericho* has joined him and is now flying the flag. We may have been a tad premature in celebrating when you told us the *Nemesis* was left behind."

"Perhaps," the man behind the desk said. His name was Wei Zhang, an exceedingly common name for the planet he was on. When someone saw Zhang, they would be able to tell immediately that he was likely of Chinese descent and probably from one of the Asiatic Union worlds. They'd be half-right in their assessment. Zhang had originally been born and raised on a world in Britannia but had immigrated to Xi'an when his parents moved back to their home world. There, he finished his education and eventually headed the

AU's semi-secret expansion plans as they scoured space along their far border for resources and habitable worlds with which they could leverage concessions from the Terran Confederate Senate.

He'd been on Haven at a conference when the Phage had arrived and destroyed his adopted world, leveling every human-built structure, and killing every living organism. Three generations of Zhang's family had been wiped out in one inexplicable act of violence. When the AU found out that Starfleet R&S suspected it was their unauthorized expansion that had drawn the Phage in, Zhang was immediately recalled to the AU capital world of Xinjia, discreetly pulled off Haven so he could respond to the accusations leveled by the Senate.

What had started out as a simple inquiry had quickly become a fight for his life, the AU regional governor making it clear he'd like to see Zhang executed for treason if he found out the Phage had destroyed Xi'an by backtracking their scout ships. In the end, the AU Council decided in secret that they likely were initially responsible for the Phage attack, but in public they refused to take the blame and instead found a new target: some hapless Earther starship captain with a poor performance history and a reputation for being sloppy. The AU used Wolfe's recklessness as a rallying cry and, soon, their citizens were transitioning from shocked to enraged at the loss of Xi'an, demanding that the Council do something to hold the Earther accountable.

Zhang was able to exploit this to save his own neck, offering his contacts within the Confederate and Fleet establishments to help the Council further their agenda of demonizing Captain Wolfe to deflect blame. At first, it was an expedient way to save his own ass and just harmless politics as usual, but then the AU and Warsaw Alliance split from the Confederation to form the Eastern Star Alliance just as another enemy attacked human worlds. He began to have regrets at that point, but it was far too late to back out. He'd foolishly allowed himself to fall in love and start a new family. Now, there was something for the Council to use as leverage against him. Before long, he was back in a director's position, heading up a new secret project for the Alliance.

"Everything depends on what happens in Odmena," Chan said. "The Council seems to be split evenly still. We need something to shake loose more votes."

"I've made my reservations about this course of action clear," Zhang said carefully. "However, I will do as I am required."

"I'm here to ensure you do." The menace in Chan's voice was unmistakable. Zhang had made the mistake of thinking he'd been brought into the inner circle of the powerful Committee for Military Affairs for his opinion and expertise on the cultural differences in Britannia and New America. He'd told them that an escalation of tensions, leading to an all-out war with the Terran Federation, would be a grave mistake that would cost both sides dearly.

They'd not appreciated his candor. All he'd managed to do was get himself labeled as a Fed sympathizer and watched constantly by agents of the State Security Directorate, an innocuous name for an organization that had a reputation for ruthlessly enforcing the will of its government on the people.

"I know most of the Federation's new weapons technologies and have helped devise countermeasures for them," Zhang said. "It's highly unlikely there's anything we missed given from how high up the information came. Your forces will be ready. Why are you really here?"

"Assurances," Chan said, seemingly taken aback by Zhang's directness. "A lot of faith has been placed in your team's new weapon—too much, in my opinion—and I want to know if you think it's ready to take on the might of a Federation task force."

"If your fleet masters do as we've instructed, the plan will succeed," Zhang said with a confidence he didn't feel.

"I hope you're right, Director."

10

"The full decrypt is coming along quicker than we thought, Agent. Most of the stuff is low-level junk, just routine com traffic, but some of the higher-level stuff is proving interesting."

"How interesting?" Pike asked the analyst. He'd rendezvoused with a CIS support cruiser, one of three the service had, to offload his NOVA team and refuel the Broadhead. While he was there, he decided to give the tech team a crack at the data core rather than fly it all the way back to New Sierra himself.

"There's some reference to a semi-autonomous ship called a Fox that Alliance Fleet Command deployed to the Eternis System," the analyst said. "It was sent to look for a target of opportunity they reference as 'Gridlock.' We have two people trying to figure out what that codename is attached to. They've tentatively said it likely is the Alliance codename for the *Nemesis*."

"The *Nemesis was* at Eternis Pax recently. The ship was

there for an extensive refit," Pike said. "It's plausible. Go ahead and begin cross-referencing everything that's decrypted for instances of Gridlock and see if we can figure out what the ESA was so interested in that they were willing to risk sending military hardware into Fed space."

"We'll stay on it," she assured him. Pike nodded and walked back out the hatch. Analysts were a funny group and a full Agent hovering over them seemed to make them nervous, Pike especially so.

He was one of the most decorated Agents within the intelligence service and, unfortunately, his growing legend had made him nearly useless for covert work. He was too easily recognizable thanks to his exploits during the previous two wars, so now he was forced to spend the rest of his career as a tactical asset for the CIS unless he wanted to run the clock out serving as an administrator behind a desk. Although he didn't necessarily enjoy all the running and gunning that came with being an operator, it beat dying of boredom while signing off on field reports.

"Agent, you have a Bluebird waiting for you in coms."

"On my way," Pike told the orderly. Since it was a CIS ship, all of the spacers were dressed in either civilian attire or merchant marine uniforms. There were a few Starfleet officers walking around in utilities, probably Fleet Intel types but, overall, the cruiser had a much more relaxed feel than an actual military ship. It was a nice change of pace for Pike given how much time he'd been forced to spend with regular Fleet units over the last five years.

The com center aboard the support cruiser was impressive. At any given time, there were a couple dozen operators on duty managing the flow of information through either the new Bluebird system or the ship's complement of GenIII point-to-point com drones. While the new CIC package being installed on the newer warships for Starfleet were impressive, the cruiser had enough command and control capacity to manage anything from a single-system skirmish to a medium-sized war.

"Agent, you can use terminal four," a com specialist said, pointing to a bank of unoccupied stations without looking.

"Thanks," Pike said, walking over and logging in with his CIS credentials and a quick biometric scan. Since everyone serving aboard a CIS ship was vetted much more stringently than in Starfleet, the secondary and tertiary security protocols were a bit laxer.

AGENT PIKE—CIS OPERATIONS AND CENTCOM HAVE RCVD CONFIRMATION OF PACKAGE DELIVERY. GOOD WORK. ONLY 1 TEAM FAILED DUE TO A CORRUPTED UPLOAD. ORDERS: REMAIN ABOARD GUARDIAN AND STANDBY FOR NEW ASSIGNMENT.

The brevity of the Bluebird messages from CIS Operations always made him chuckle. Sure, the system had piss-poor bandwidth, but there was no constraint on message length other than it would take time to be received and compiled in the buffer. He frowned at his new orders. Cooling his heels aboard the cruiser wasn't exactly what he thought he'd be doing as the cold war with the ESA threatened to kick off into a hot one at any time.

The only thing that could mean is they didn't have anything for him to do other than likely fly back out to some contested system to sit and watch. Given that Wolfe was heading to the place he'd just come from, odds were good he'd be going right back.

"Oh, how the mighty have fallen," he mumbled to himself, signing the read receipt and deleting the message before bringing up the next one. At one point in his career, he'd been the right-hand man of sitting presidents and wielded so much influence that even the director of the CIS would tread carefully around him. Now that Augustus Wellington had died and his own infamy made him useless as a covert asset, Pike felt like his waning years would be spent as a glorified observer, only tolerated because nobody in upper management wanted to be the guy who force-retired a legend.

"Huh...this could be interesting," he said, looking at a message header from a contact of his within Fleet Intel.

DIRTBAG—I'VE BEEN AUTHORIZED BY MY SUPERIORS TO GIVE YOU A COURTESY HEADS-UP ON THE ETERNIS SYSTEM ATTACK. DEVICE USED ABOARD THE UNMANNED CRAFT WAS AN ANTI-MATTER BOMB OF SIGNIFICANT POWER. RADIATION DAMAGE ON THE HULL OF THE *NEMESIS* CONFIRMED BY FLEET R&S. EGGHEADS THINK A BOMB THIS SIZE WOULD TAKE OUT A STARSHIP IN A SINGLE SHOT FROM EVEN A CLOSE DETONATION. CENTCOM WANTS SECONDARY CONFIRMATION ON FINDINGS BEFORE DISSEMINATING TO THE REST OF THE FLEET. THIS WILL BE GOING OUT IN A FLEETWIDE BRIEF SOON... IF YOU RUN ACROSS ANY FED TASK FORCES HEADING TO ESA SPACE YOU MIGHT WANT TO GIVE THEM A FRIENDLY WARNING. HUGHES OUT.

. . .

Pike leaned back and let that bit of news sink in. Antimatter weapons were still theoretical according to what his friends at Fleet R&S had told him, but now that shit-heel Hughes was telling him that the ESA had not only managed to produce it, but they've weaponized it. From the admittedly little he knew about it, Tsuyo Science Division had only produced the stuff in miniscule amounts at huge expense while experimenting with it as a power source. In the end, it was decided that modern fusion reactors were safer and cheaper so the project was archived.

He and Hughes weren't friends. In fact, the two fairly despised each other. The only way the Fleet spook would be sharing information with him through backchannels was so that Pike would read between the lines and get the information where it needed to go. As far as he knew, there was only one full Federation task force heading out to the border systems and that was Vega. Given that his relationship with Admiral Wolfe was widely known he had to assume that someone in CENTCOM wanted Wolfe to know about the threat of antimatter-tipped ship busters before the official word went out to the entire fleet.

"Bullshit politics as usual," he sighed before flagging down one of the specialists in the com center. "Do we have a current roster?"

"Updated last watch, Agent," she said.

"What ship is heading up Task Force Vega?"

"The TFS *Jericho* is currently the flagship for Task Force Vega," she said, scrolling through the data on her tile. "Admiral Wolfe is commanding."

"Wolfe is on the *Jericho*?" Pike asked.

"Transferred over before they entered warp heading for the Odmena System," she confirmed. "I'm very busy, Agent. Is this going somewhere?"

"I need the Bluebird address for the *Jericho*," he said. "And the name of a com operator aboard we trust to deliver a message."

"Warp emitter hatches closing, clearing the jump point now."

"We're the first ship through, Admiral," Captain Hardy reported.

"Very good, Captain. Move us off and maintain strict EMSEC protocols. I don't want—"

"Sir! Something big has happened here," Lieutenant Orr interrupted from the OPS station. "The com drone platform has apparently had a catastrophic malfunction. CIC is intercepting heavy radio traffic from the planet and ships in the area about a massive explosion that took it out nearly fifteen days ago. The ESA ships in the system are denying having anything to do with it, and the Odmena government is claiming that it was destroyed when they began arriving in the system."

"Anything else, Lieutenant?" Jackson asked.

"There are a lot of ESA military ships here, Admiral," Orr said. "We're getting ident beacons from seventeen ships. They're all mainline warships, but the newest hull was commissioned nearly seventeen years ago."

"Keep on it, OPS. The com drone platform being gone works in our favor," Jackson said. "The ESA doesn't have point-to-point drones that we know of, so they'll need to dispatch a ship out of the system to communicate with their own command."

"Which takes time because ships are so much slower than drones," Hardy finished. Jackson looked at him with mild disgust. Filling the air with needless words just to state the obvious wasn't a trait he admired for an officer.

"Tell CIC I want them sifting through the noise and letting me know what happened to the platform within the next two hours," Jackson said, frowning. Com drone platforms were some of the oldest structures in existence, so it's plausible that one had a critical failure with its powerplant, but something about it seemed suspicious. Even aboard a starship at the edge of the system, Jackson could swear he felt a palpable tension. He would need to proceed carefully to avoid lighting a fuse that couldn't be snuffed out.

Over the next twelve hours, two more task force ships transitioned in, and the com chatter in the system indicated that either they'd been unobserved or nobody cared that more ships were arriving to the party. Jackson debated broadcasting their ident codes loud and proud and flying straight down the well to take up position over Odmena Prime rather than slinking around the edge of the system but, in the end, decided that it would be better to remain on more passive footing. The *Juggernaut*-class boomer he was aboard was a political statement all her own, a terrifying war machine meant to impose the Federation's will on a system. It stood unopposed among the other classes of Terran ships when it came to raw firepower, something Jackson hoped wouldn't be a factor in the coming weeks. He was acutely aware of the message CENTCOM was sending to the ESA by deploying a true battleship into the Odmena System.

"Hopefully, the *Jericho* truly will be the deterrent her designers claimed she'd be, Admiral." Jackson turned and saw the ship's CO, Commander Trane, standing a few steps away.

"An interesting observation, Commander," Jackson said. "Is there something I can help you with?"

"I wanted to take the opportunity to congratulate you on the Mickeys," Trane said. "Before I was assigned to the *Jericho*, I served on a Fleet R&D test crew that did the shakedown runs on the Frigate-2 and -3 configurations."

"There are a lot of people who deserve to be congratulated for the program, Commander, but I don't believe that I am one of them."

"I respectfully disagree, sir. Without your weight behind them, many wouldn't have taken the new proposal seriously enough to even prototype them. I believe this is a necessary move if the Fleet is expected to defend the Federation from a potential ESA attack."

"You're one of the few who think that way, apparently," Jackson said. "I appreciate the sentiment, Commander. I'm hoping that the entire program will amount to nothing more than an interesting engineering exercise."

"Ah!" Trane said after a moment, catching on to Jackson's meaning. "As do I, Admiral. The idea of fighting humans? It's certainly not what I expected to be doing after the end of the Expansion War."

"Where were you serving—"

A blaring alarm cut Jackson off, and the words "EMSEC Protocol Breach" flashed on the main display.

"Report!" Trane demanded.

"Our beacon came on momentarily," the second watch OPS officer said, his hands flying over his controls while he tried to determine what went wrong. "We're locked down again, but it looks like a full ident stream was broadcast three times before it was shut off."

"There's no way they missed that down there," Trane said. "Orders, Admiral?"

"Light us up," Jackson sighed. "Instruct the other ships in the task force to remain silent and to hold position. I want the *Jericho* being the only ship squawking. Commander, please move us further away from the jump point. Coms, kindly locate Captain Hardy and have him report to the bridge."

"Helm, move us off on our current course, all ahead two thirds. OPS, bring our beacon up, full ident package."

"Engines ahead two thirds, aye!"

"I want to know how that beacon activated, and I want it ASAP," Trane said.

"Aye, sir. Com backshop is working on it now." The OPS officer had slipped his headset back on and was in an animated conversation with the technicians below deck to find answers.

Jackson forced his face to remain impassive as he stalked the bridge, his hands clasped behind his back. An ident beacon didn't just come on by itself. The only question in his mind was whether it was inadvertently activated through gross incompetence, or he had a traitor onboard his flagship that was warning the ESA fleet that the task force had arrived. If it was the latter, it would have to be someone up on the command deck since the individual shops didn't have any way of knowing the ship's position or status. All they'd know is that the ship had transitioned from warp flight and that there were no alerts.

As he looked around the bridge, some spacers and officers staring back, he suddenly felt alone. He was aboard an unfamiliar ship with a command crew he only knew by reputation, and all he'd brought with him was one Marine NCO for protection. If the *Jericho* harbored ESA sympathizers in any kind of numbers, he could be in for a really bad time.

His thoughts flitted briefly back to his first command, the TCS *Blue Jacket*, and how he'd been forced to put down a mutiny by blowing an engineering mate's brains out. It was something that still gave him nightmares despite all he'd been through and definitely something he'd rather not repeat. For a captain, having your crew turn against you was possibly one of the worst things one could experience.

"Report!" Hardy almost shouted as he stormed onto the bridge.

"Our ident beacon was activated...somehow...and now we're steaming away from the jump point since we've almost certainly been spotted, Captain," Trane reported. "Or at least we will be once the signal makes its way to the inner system in another three and half hours."

"OPS?"

"It wasn't anyone at a bridge station, sir," the ensign said. "Backshop is still tracing the command path that brought up the transmitter."

"That should only take a few seconds," Hardy said. "Tell them they have five minutes to figure it out and give me an answer."

"Yes, sir."

"Admiral," Hardy acknowledged Jackson for the first time since walking onto the bridge. "I see we're steaming away from the jump point at a fair clip...too quickly for some of our ships to easily catch up."

"The rest of our ships have been instructed to stay silent until we're able to further ascertain the situation down by the planet, Captain," Jackson said. "Hopefully, their crews will be able to handle those orders." He ignored the ship's captain as he struggled to contain himself after such a pointed insult aimed at his crew.

"Of course, Admiral," Hardy finally managed to get out. "Will there be anything else, sir?"

"That will be all, Captain," Jackson said, turning away as a dismissal.

Having his orders questioned in front of the crew was not something he would tolerate. Admiral Pitt and Joseph Marcum had both pulled him aside when he'd pinned on the second star and before he'd been given command of an entire task force to impress upon him the need for a flag officer to be an absolute dictator when on the bridge of a starship. If Hardy had a question or concern, he should have held his tongue until they were in private unless it was a dire emergency.

The time waiting for the transmission lag seemed to drag on without end while the crew continued to monitor the area via the passive optics and gravimetric drive detection system. Jackson ordered the high-power tracking radar array brought up so that the *Jericho* was the noisiest, brightest object in the region to provide cover for the rest of the task force that was still arriving. As good as the newest generation of Terran warp drives were, it would still be a number of days before all of the ships had arrived and could be deployed throughout the system.

"We're receiving a query from a ship identifying itself as the formation lead in the ESA delegation," the com officer said. "From the time stamp, it looks like it broadcast the message as soon as we appeared in the system. CIC puts the ship almost halfway between us and Odmena Prime."

Jackson checked the mission clock and saw they were some hours from expecting a reply from the planet and the Federation representative there. He could feel the tension on the bridge as everyone was waiting on him to decide on a direction other than *wait and see* as they'd been doing since transitioning in.

"Coms, I want a tight-beam transmission to the *Blake* instructing Captain Carmichael to hold position until the rest of the task force arrives," Jackson said. "Once they do, I want the formation moved into a heliocentric orbit in the shadow of the fifth planet. They're not to break com silence."

"Aye-aye, Admiral."

"Captain Hardy, I want the *Jericho* repositioned near Odmena Prime," Jackson continued. "This mission is about communication and averting hostilities. I can't do that parked out in the outer system with a twelve-hour communication lag. Maintain our passive posture for the time being, but make sure she's ready to defend herself if someone on the other side does something foolish. Commander Trane, I want a senior staff meeting in one hour. Make sure CIC sends someone from intel to brief the group on all the com traffic we're picking up in the system."

"Right away, sir," Commander Trane said, moving to an auxiliary terminal at the back of the bridge.

"Nav, plot us a course down the well that steers us around the Alliance fleet formations in the inner system," Hardy ordered. "Helm, once you have your new course, let's light the fires...all ahead full."

"Coming onto new course, engines ahead full, aye!"

"We'll try to play nice as long as we can, but I have no intention of letting the Alliance ships try to deny us free navigation or corral us away from the planet," Jackson said softly to Hardy. "Go ahead and bring up the WEPS reactors and keep them at low-power."

"Prudent decision, sir," Hardy nodded and walked over to his tactical officers to relay the order.

The *Juggernaut*-class ships were equipped with weapons

that had such a heavy draw that the ships were fitted with two additional, smaller fusion powerplants that could be brought up to make sure there was enough power to keep the engines and weapons fully operational in a fight. One issue with WEPS—short for Weapons Express Power System—was that the helium exhaust wasn't routed through baffles to cool it before venting into space, so they greatly increased the ship's thermal signature, but with the *Jericho* already spotted and broadcasting her ident beacon, it wasn't like they were trying to hide.

As everyone scurried about to execute his orders, and the deck rumbled as the RDS came up to full power, Jackson walked over to the com station and asked to see the communique that came in from the ESA ship. He doubted it would be anything more than meaningless posturing since they transmitted it as soon as they saw a transition flash, but it might still tell him what the ESA's ultimate goal in the Odmena System was.

Unidentified United Terran Federation warship; your presence here is neither requested nor desired. We will permit you to navigate within the system to the jump point of your choosing that will allow you to fly back into Federation space. You are instructed not to interfere with the ongoing negotiations the Eastern Star Alliance is conducting with the regional government of Odmena Prime. End transmission.

Jackson almost laughed aloud when he read the boilerplate message. The transmission didn't tell him whether or not ESA's intelligence service knew the *Jericho* was coming to Odmena, but it did tell him that their intentions were to try and pressure the planet into leaving the Federation. He wished the Diplomatic Corps had been able to send a civilian representative of the government to speak on their behalf in cases like this, but there hadn't been any time to transfer someone to the Eternis System before Task Force Vega had had to depart. Hopefully, New Sierra had loaded someone up on a Broadhead and was flying them out. He made a mental note to check during his next Bluebird session.

"The *Jericho* is on course for an Odmena Prime orbital intercept in just over one-hundred hours, Admiral," Hardy interrupted Jackson's ruminations. "We can shave a bit more off that if you'd like, sir, but it will force us to decelerate hard enough that the artificial gravity won't be able to fully nullify our inertia."

"There's no need, Captain," Jackson said. "I doubt we'll ever make it into orbit over the planet before something happens to force us into action."

"Sounds ominous."

"Just a gut feeling," Jackson said, walking towards the hatchway. "Please let me know if anything changes, Captain. I'll be in my quarters until the staff meeting."

"Yes, sir."

"Talk to me."

"We've managed to unpack enough of the data dump you grabbed to say with certainty we know what Gridlock is referring to. It wasn't easy, either. The data you stole from the com drone queue wasn't organized in any logical manner."

"From this extended lead up I'm assuming you're going

to give me something good," Pike said, leaning over the table to try and peek at the tile the analyst held in her hands.

"It's good enough that I want a favor before showing you," she said. "This is the type of information that really should be passed up the chain *before* being shown to anyone else, much less an Agent with a reputation for poor impulse control."

"What do you want?"

"Off this fucking cruiser and into a dirtside assignment, preferably on New Sierra or Arcadia, but I'll take anything that isn't a metal tube sitting in deep space," she said.

"I can probably swing that," Pike said. "Now, come on... out with it." She stared at him a moment as if trying to judge whether or not he was being sincere, and then weighing that against her tenuous position of withholding information from a full Agent.

"Gridlock refers to none other than your old buddy, Admiral Jackson Wolfe," she said, sliding the tile over to him. "At first, we were convinced it was the *Nemesis*, but some of the context was odd if they were referring to a ship. We cracked two high-level messages being routed to Alliance Fleet Command through the Odmena System platform that verified they've been tracking the admiral's movements, and they want him pretty badly. There's been some chatter about the Nemesis and Wolfe that we've been picking up for some time, but this is the first time he's mentioned in specific orders."

"The ESA is launching attacks into Fed space to get one Fleet officer?" Pike asked skeptically.

"It has something to do with the lead-up to a possible incursion into Federation space. We haven't been able to determine the targets, but there are three strategic goals they've mapped out that they think, if destroyed, will cripple

Starfleet enough that the Federation Parliament will come to the table and accept terms...but they'll still need to sell the idea of even a short war to their people. Wolfe has long been painted as a loose cannon and a war criminal by the ESA propagandists, so I'm guessing capturing or killing him will give them the spark they think they need to get the people behind the attacks."

"Remind them of the Phage War and everything that was lost during it, not to mention the fact the old Confederation blamed the Asianic Union for the whole thing." Pike nodded while reading her report synopsis. "You came up with this based on just the data grab I gave you?"

"My team and I did, but yes, it's just from what you gave us," she said.

"What's your name?"

"Analyst Harper. *Bryce* Harper."

"Okay then, Analyst Harper Bryce Harper, let's go and take this to the big boys back home," Pike said. "I think it's safe to say I won't have any trouble holding up my end of the bargain. If what you're saying is true, Starfleet just delivered Admiral Wolfe right into the ESA's hands. Your report might be just in time."

"Let's hope so," Harper said.

11

"That's four ships now moving to intercept, sir."

"How close will we get to the planet before the leader is within weapons range?" Jackson asked.

"No closer than sixty-five million kilometers before the leading ship could turn in and get a firing solution," Commander Trane said. It was just into second watch, and Captain Hardy had left the bridge to walk the ship and look in on the different work centers.

The trip down into the inner system had been oddly quiet. There had been a handful of blustering threats from the ESA ships. They'd been transmitting each message from a different ship in order to confuse them and hide which Alliance cruiser was flying the flag. Unfortunately for them, the CIS had already provided Jackson a full roster of ships, and from the ident beacons, he knew that his counterpart would likely be aboard the Saber-class heavy cruiser, *Heart of Xi'an*.

Jackson had been briefed when the Heart had been

commissioned and Fleet Intel had shown him the propaganda the ESA was providing its citizens about the new class of heavy cruiser. They claimed that it was capable of taking on a Federation Valkyrie-class destroyer, a claim that was obviously taking aim at the only active ship in the class: the *Nemesis*. The ESA knew that the destroyer had killed the Darshik *Specter*, but they weren't clear on exactly how. In the absence of facts, they applied their own tactical outlook onto the incident and assumed that Jackson had somehow overpowered his foe with his ship. This badly rattled the top brass within the ESA's fleet and elevated the *Nemesis* to almost mythical proportions in their minds. Even though he'd gotten no official word on the investigation he assumed that the attack in the Eternis System had been designed specifically for her.

"Time to intercept?" he asked, turning away from the main display.

"Forty-six hours, sir."

"Now, it's time to begin moving our own pieces around on the board," Jackson said. "OPS, inform CIC I want a message sent to the *Robert Blake*, priority Bluebird. Instruct Captain Carmichael that I want the rest of the task force to change course and approach Odmena Prime on a vector that puts them behind the ships moving to intercept us."

"CIC would like to know if you would like to transmit specific navigation data with the message, Admiral Wolfe," Lieutenant Orr asked.

"Captain Carmichael has my full confidence. Tell him to use his best judgement."

"Aye, sir."

"If the task force veers in towards the planet the rest of their picket ships will be completely out of position," Trane said, nodding.

"And the ships that are at full-burn to intercept the *Jericho* wouldn't be able to reverse course and have any hope of matching their movements," Jackson said. "But this is a transparent ploy. The Alliance fleet commander will have seen this as an obvious move. How he reacts to this will tell me more about what their goal here is and how willing they are to engage our bigger guns before we're in close with each other."

"Do we know who is commanding the opposing ships, sir?"

"We do not, and that worries me," Jackson admitted. "I know most of the ESA's flag officers since they served in Starfleet during the Phage War, but they've been oddly tightlipped about who they've sent to run their Odmena operation."

During the flight, the *Jericho* had been bombarded with messages from high-ranking officials on the planet demanding to know what Jackson was going to do about the ESA destroying their com drone platform. He'd calmly told them he would make sure New Sierra sent out a com ship to replace the platform until a new one could be brought in. In the meantime, he offered the use of his task force's point-to-point com drones so that the planet wasn't cut off from the Federation's network. He didn't need them thanks to Bluebird, of course, but he had to keep the ruse up. The ESA knew that Fed ships carried point-to-point drones, but they likely had no idea that the task force had near-instantaneous communication with the capital.

"Another incoming message from the planet, Admiral," the com officer called out. "It's the assistant governor, and she's asking to speak to you directly."

"Sir! The ships moving to intercept are decelerating... hard!" the tactical officer said, clearly confused.

"Get Captain Hardy up here," Trane said over his shoulder to the com officer.

Jackson looked at the plot courses on the main display, trying to figure out why the ships would suddenly begin braking so far outside of the *Jericho's* known effective weapons range. Even more concerning was that they'd executed the maneuver in unison, something that should have been impossible if their intelligence was correct and the ESA was still using radio-based communications for ship-to-ship.

"What are you up to?" Jackson murmured before raising his voice. "Tell the assistant governor I will be with her as soon as I can."

"Aye, sir."

Thanks to their ability to use their own RDS drive to track other ships in the system, Jackson had a pretty good picture of what was happening with the rest of the ESA armada as a sizable number broke off to pursue the rest of Task Force Vega, and from the timestamps on the course tracks, it looked like they began decelerating at the same time the first four did.

"OPS, ask CIC to analyze the sensor logs and give us a spread on when each ship began braking," he said. "I want to know how closely synchronized this maneuver was."

"They've already sent the data up, sir," Orr said. "It's a fourteen-point-oh-two second delay from the time the first ship slowed to when the last ship began braking."

Jackson just nodded his head, impressed with whoever was running CIC and sending up relevant data before it was even asked for. So, the ships were closely synched, but not perfectly. He breathed a sigh of relief as it was obvious this was a preplanned action coordinated from individual mission timers on each ship and not the result of orders passed down via their own superluminal com system. He was certain of the *how* but was still not sure about the *why*.

"OPS, have CIC send another Bluebird message to the *Blake*. Tell Captain Carmichael I want the task force steaming on a direct course for an Odmena Prime orbital intercept," Jackson said.

"Aye, sir."

"Orders for the *Jericho*, sir?" Captain Hardy asked. Jackson had missed him coming onto the bridge. He studied the main display a moment more before deciding.

"Steady as she goes," he said. "Maintain course and speed. They're trying to draw a reaction out of us, so let's just ignore them for now. I'll be in my office talking to planetary officials if I'm needed."

"Yes, sir," Hardy said and began relaying orders.

Jackson felt like he was being herded and wasn't certain where or to what purpose. It wasn't a pleasant feeling when the ones doing the herding were warships with nuclear warheads mounted to ship buster missiles. He was confident the *Jericho* could defend herself against the four cruisers that were ahead of them, but he was missing the overall strategy so far and that was making him more than a little nervous.

"Your office, Admiral?" Barton asked when Jackson crossed the threshold of the hatchway.

"Yes. I'll be secured inside for a while if you want to go grab chow."

"Much appreciated, sir."

The office Jackson had commandeered was on the command deck a short walk from the bridge. It had hardwired access to CIC as well as a complete secure com suite. The space was so well-equipped, Jackson could almost manage his entire task force from the comfort of the plush leather chair. The VIP quarters he'd been provided also had a well-appointed work space, but it wasn't as connected to the ship's nerve center as the one he was currently in.

He'd just settled into the seat to prerecord a series of messages to be transmitted to Odmena Prime to answer the slew of requests that had come from planetary government officials when there was a soft knock on the hatch. Assuming it was Barton needing something, he walked over and opened it without thinking, surprised to see the short, female intelligence officer that had met him when he'd first boarded.

"Lieutenant...Trapp, wasn't it?"

"Yes, sir."

"I apologize for not getting back to you like I said I would," Jackson said. "We've been a bit busy. What can I do for you?"

"I've brought up a tile from CIC that has been coded for your biometric signature only and can directly access both of our Bluebird transceivers, sir," she held up a ruggedized version of the ubiquitous tablet computers that people carried around. "We set the link up so that it only works in places that have a hardline connection to the com center like the bridge or this office."

"Why don't you step in and brief me on it," Jackson said, stepping into the office to allow her in. She seemed to hesitate before walking through the hatchway, looking around the corridor first. "You seem unusually nervous, Lieutenant."

"The Bluebird tile is the official reason I'm up here in Officer Country," Trapp said, handing the tile to Jackson. "But the *real* reason I had wanted to talk to you was to brief you on some...*odd*...occurrences within the com section and CIC prior to you coming aboard."

"Lieutenant, I know that some commanders pay lip service to having an *open door policy* for people to come to them with issues...I am not one of them. If you're coming directly to me—going over the heads of a dozen people within the chain of command—I'm afraid you'll not likely be happy with the answer you'll get from me. Whatever issues you're having in your section it would be best if you—"

"I'm not talking about petty grievances, sir," she said forcefully. "I'm talking about possible treason and a threat to this task force."

"You have my full attention," Jackson said. She took a deep breath before plunging ahead with her story.

"Around seven weeks ago I was in CIC and became aware that the *Jericho* had launched two point-to-point com drones without clearing it through us," she began. "I thought it was just an oversight by the OPS station on the bridge but when I went into the logs to make sure we had the drone serial number and flightpath recorded, I found that there were no entries for the launches in the bridge log or the com backshop's records."

"Highly unusual and sloppy but hardly treasonous."

"I didn't think so either...at first. But when I began asking around to see why standard procedure for any drone launch hadn't been followed, I was told by my section chief that if I cared about my career, I'd drop it. And, at first, I did. But then, two weeks later, there was another unauthorized com drone launch. This time, when I went to check the logs, not only was the launch data scrubbed but the manifests had been altered to make it appear as if the three com drones were never aboard the ship in the first place."

"That *is* something," Jackson said. "Secret com drone launches could be explained away, but this is effectively trying to erase the fact the drones even existed at all."

"It's more than that, sir," Trapp said. "I used my Bluebird

access to reach out to a CIS associate on New Sierra and asked them to discreetly look into the loadout manifest for the *Jericho*. Someone altered the database there as well. The number of drones Starfleet has record of this ship having matches the number that's aboard right now; three less than we actually left port with."

"This isn't proof of anything other than shoddy bookkeeping at the moment," Jackson said, watching her face fall. "But...I think your instincts are good. Something is happening on this ship right now that is being kept quiet for reasons that don't seem to be aboveboard. Do you have any theories?"

"I'd rather not—"

"Nothing you say here goes any further than this room," Jackson assured her. "I'm interested in hearing your speculation as someone who has been on the ship much longer than I have and understands her internal politics."

"One interesting coincidence I was able to find: each launch was within an hour after the *Jericho* received move orders," she said. "The first was when we received word we were replacing the *Nemesis* in the task force, the second was after we were given confirmation of our destination, and the third was after the updated rendezvous order came in directly from you. Since these orders were all either from CENTCOM or with their knowledge, I'm thinking that the drone launches were to alert someone outside of Starfleet as to our movements and schedule."

"A serious but plausible accusation," Jackson said, now very troubled by what he was hearing. "Do you have any idea who might be taking these actions or why?"

"I don't, sir. The list of officers with the necessary clearance across multiple systems to manipulate records and order launches is small and insulated. They're not officers I would want to wrongly accuse of something so serious and the reason I felt the need to come to you directly."

"Smart," Jackson nodded. "You can relax knowing I'm not going to be discussing this with any of your superiors about this conversation. You did the right thing by coming to me. I'm going to take a bit to think about how I want to proceed on this, but I'll make sure you're insulated from any blowback. Now, in the meantime, give me a quick brief on how this tile is setup, and then you can get back to CIC."

"Yes, sir," she said. "And thank you for not dismissing this out of hand."

As she went over the simple command structure of the Bluebird-linked tile, Jackson's mind began to wander, and he imagined all sorts of horrible scenarios regarding the secret com drone launches. Nothing he could come up with explained why someone would be launching drones and doctoring official ship logs to make sure nobody could backtrack them.

Once Jackson was certain all of his credentials were properly working on the device, and they'd verified that connecting the tile didn't violate COMSEC regulations regarding Bluebird usage, he dismissed the intel officer. He'd promised he'd take her findings seriously, and he did. Never one to entertain baseless conspiracy theories, he found himself believing that Lieutenant Trapp had stumbled onto a credible threat.

With the attempts on his life and the attack on the *Nemesis* while she was deep in Federation territory at a secret production facility, Jackson knew the ESA was exploiting traitors within Starfleet with far more success than the CIS or Fleet Intel was able to do reciprocally. It wasn't outside the realm of possibility to think there was a high-ranked officer aboard the *Jericho* who was taking orders from an Alliance handler to turn over sensitive intel. He simply didn't have the time or the training to ferret out security leaks aboard a ship he didn't know while also commanding the task force. He needed help. With that in mind, he opened a window on his terminal.

Captain Hardy,

I've found that I need additional personnel assigned directly to me. I require someone who is cleared for both incoming intelligence reports and Bluebird dispatches. I'd like to have Lieutenant Samantha Trapp put on detached duty, assigned directly to my staff, for the duration of the Odmena operation or until I no longer need her expertise. She has all the requisite clearances and training for this task.

Admiral Wolfe

The message was short and to the point. He didn't want to spin Hardy a complicated story that would raise eyebrows. He intended to use Trapp to push around the edges of what was happening on the *Jericho*—if anything actually was—and he didn't want to handicap her movements by claiming he needed her for something that would keep her stuck in Officer Country or on the bridge.

Once he'd taken care of that, he straightened out his dress blacks and powered through a series of six messages that would be sent out to both the ESA ships in the system and the planet. The mission so far had an unfocused quality to it, like he was trying to hold on to sand by squeezing even harder and it wasn't working. The Phage and the Darshik were enemies that came right at you leaving no ambiguity as to what they wanted.

Not only were the ESA's intentions murky, they were also humans who had only recently separated themselves from the whole. He felt like he was in a no-win situation and didn't know the right thing to do while the Alliance ships seemed to have a definite goal, thus having the advantage of clarity when devising tactics.

"I have a feeling that no matter what I do, it's going to turn out horribly," he muttered to nobody. "Like I've already lost simply by showing up."

12

"You've seen the preliminary brief?"

"I have, Director, and I'm a little concerned at how long it's taken for this intel to get from the field, to your headquarters, through your analysts, and now a *preliminary* brief finally makes it to Starfleet. Things are happening along the Fed/Alliance border that require agility and speed. The usual plodding and territorial pissing matches just won't do."

"Admiral Pitt I can assure you that—"

"Furthermore, I am recommending to the president that steps be taken to bridge this separation between Fleet and CIS in certain cases so that my commanders in the field have the most up to date information available. What's the point of having instantaneous superluminal com capability if we don't streamline our bureaucratic holdups to get the information where it needs to be?"

Admiral Celesta Wright was tense as she watched the

exchange. Admiral Pitt was beginning to understand the political power he wielded as CENTCOM Chief of Staff, but the man was still so direct and brutal in his approach that she feared for his professional life. Even a president as pro-military as Cornell Stark would cringe if he saw his appointee dressing down CIS Director Jair Perez.

Perez was the intelligence service's new director, and he was widely regarded as an up and coming political powerhouse. He was young, ruthless, and, shockingly enough, a native of Earth. Whereas Jackson Wolfe downplayed and hid the fact he was an *Earther*, Perez used it as a bludgeon, daring people to use a slur or make assumptions based on his birthplace.

"Admiral Pitt," Perez said, no hint of agitation in his smooth baritone voice. "I can assure you we're not intentionally withholding information. What we *are* doing is vetting field reports before they're passed on to CENTCOM. In my experience, bad intel is just as dangerous as late intel."

"Let's not forget the point of this meeting," PM Joseph Marcum said from the head of the table. He was there in his capacity as Chairman of the Fleet Oversight Committee, and even though the committee actually dealt more with the logistical side of the Federation's military, Marcum's experience and expertise in matters of war were welcome. "Director Perez, let's please focus on the guts of your report, and then we'll deal with the office politics of it once we've addressed the important part."

"Thank you, sir," Perez said respectfully, shooting Pitt another death-glare before continuing. "During the execution of Operation Crimson Foil, an Agent was able to secure a data dump of encrypted Alliance Command communiques that were being routed through that com drone platform. What's not widely known is that the Odmena System platform was unique. It was one of three platforms that still had connected routes to other platforms within Federation space *and* the ESA. We think that's how they've been able to communicate with their operatives and assets within our territory.

"During the decryption process, we became aware of a massive covert operation centering around a Fed target they'd codenamed 'Gridlock.' At first, the context of the messages pointed to it being a ship; specifically, the TFS *Nemesis*. Our analysts began to operating on the theory that the ESA was planning to try and steal or destroy the ship while she was at the Eternis Pax facility receiving repairs for damage caused by one of their antimatter warheads."

"You now think differently?" Celesta asked, aware of the theory that the *Nemesis* was a priority ESA target.

"We do," Perez nodded. "Given what we've uncovered so far, the codename Gridlock is referring to a person: Rear Admiral Jackson Wolfe. We have conflicting information as to the specifics, but whatever the goal of this operation they have going is, it hinges on him."

"Son of a bitch," Marcum bit out. "We just deployed his task force right into their laps. If they're after him specifically, they won't have a better opportunity than right now in a remote system like Odmena."

"I'm not privy to Operation Crimson Foil," Pitt said. "But can you tell me if that had something to do with the destruction of the Odmena com drone platform? Reports from Task Force Vega indicate the situation in the system is tense, and that the planetary government is blaming the ESA fleet." Perez looked away and shifted in his seat.

"I can tell you that the destruction was a decision by our

Agent on site, but that the reactor overload wasn't actually part of the mission," he finally said. "It was done to cover up the fact they'd been there. Agent Pike didn't want to risk the entire op being blown because his team had been caught by a maintenance crew."

"Fucking Pike," Marcum growled, causing Perez to flinch and his eyes to widen in confusion. "Why am I not surprised that little prick had something to do with this debacle?"

"Sir, I can—"

"Rhetorical question, Director." Marcum waved him off and stood to pace the cramped room. "Pitt, I think it'd be smart to recall Wolfe and leave the task force in the hands of Captain Hardy. The *Jericho* is carrying two warp-capable courier ships in her hangar, he can get out of there while the getting is good." He paused and looked over at the CENTCOM Chief of Staff a bit sheepishly, seeming to remember his new title didn't include a military rank. "That's just a suggestion, of course."

"I'll pull him out," Pitt said. "Given the ESA's propaganda war against the Federation that centered around Wolfe being responsible for the loss of Xi'an and the entire damn Phage War it probably wasn't wise to send him there in the first place."

"We also believe that this operation is being executed by a small, secret cabal within the ESA military," Perez went on. "There are three names we've mined out of the data that appear to be the people who conceived and planned the operation. One of them we're quite familiar with, he was the man who was in charge of the Asiatic Union's colonization program that we now know alerted the Phage to our presence. We also know where he is and are getting ready to launch a mission into ESA space to… recover him."

"Isn't that needlessly provocative?" Marcum asked. "What if your agent is caught?"

"He won't be," Perez said confidently. "He actually has legitimate citizenship on the planet he'll be going to from when he operated there in the Confederation days. It's a world with immigrant populations from all over, so its ethnic makeup is too varied for him to stand out."

Celesta swallowed a hard lump as she realized who would likely be deployed deep into ESA space if for no other reason than he was already in the border region. Her and Pike's relationship was complicated, but it was something they both wanted to make work. She'd thought his days of infiltrating enemy space and running one-man operations in their backyard were over. He still held the rank and title of Agent, something the CIS never had in abundance due to the expense and difficulty of the training, but Pike was older and had lost a step or two since he was busting up interplanetary smuggling rings and putting down coups as he did in the pre-Phage War days.

"Admiral Wright, do you have anything to add?" Marcum was asking. She shook her head to clear out the extraneous fluff and looked down at her tile.

"Two *StarWraith*-class Prowlers have been dispatched to Odmena and an additional four *Sentinel*-class Prowlers will be repositioned to the Eternis System to provide fill-in where needed," she said. "We have autonomous drones shadowing Fleet units in the other three major hot areas along the border, but given what we've recently found out about the ESA's fixation on Admiral Wolfe, we feel like these are likely distractions. I don't want to tie up too many of my crews there since we're still actively monitoring the Ushin/Darshik reconciliation."

"You, your boss, and I will talk about Prowler Fleet's

budget offline later, Admiral," Marcum promised. "Right now, I want everyone focused—and working *together*—on defusing this Odmena powder keg. I don't need to tell anyone in this room that the Federation cannot afford a prolonged shooting war with the ESA. The numbers are not on our side even with our more advanced starships."

"Understood, sir," Pitt said. Perez just nodded, looking at Pitt distastefully.

Celesta was decidedly uncomfortable given the dynamic shift her new position created. She had been a Starfleet officer—and a damn good one—for most of her military career. When she'd bucked CENTCOM and let then-Captain Wolfe take the TFS *Nemesis* against orders and hunt down the Darshik *Specter*, she'd been drummed out of the service. She didn't stay unemployed for long, however.

CIS grabbed her to head up their Prowler program the same day Starfleet processed her *retirement*. This meant that her direct boss wasn't Chief of Staff Pitt, it was Director Perez. It made for a few tense meetings when she was asked her opinion and sided with Admiral Pitt over the CIS Director.

"A word, Admiral," Perez said, nodding his head back to the table.

"Of course, sir," Celesta said, retaking her seat. Perez waited until Pitt and Marcum had left and closed the door behind them. When light over the door went from red to green, indicating that the anti-snooping countermeasures were active, he turned to her.

"I need your help with this Odmena situation, Admiral. CIS is somewhat less affected by the high-level leaks that is plaguing CENTCOM, but I still need someone I can trust implicitly."

"I'll do whatever is required of me, Director," Celesta said carefully. She'd been expecting a lecture about not showing a unified front when talking to CENTCOM and the civilian oversight, so this was a turn in the conversation she wasn't prepared for.

"I'd expect no less of you," Perez said, smiling humorlessly. "Admiral Pitt and I have been working on something together, and it's nearing fruition, we just need a qualified officer to head things up."

"You and...Pitt?"

"I'm glad to see that our ruse of openly disliking each other has fooled even you," Perez said with another of his enigmatic half smiles. "The admiral is a shrewd and perceptive man. Much more so than his demeanor would indicate. He came to me after we learned the extent of the ESA's treachery concerning the Darshik and proposed an idea to keep some assets off the books, so to speak. We've been building a small strike force that's at a location so secret it makes Eternis Pax seem like HEI Ironworks."

HEI was one of the Federation's biggest contractors for building new hulls. It was in the Columbiana System, the New America enclave's seat of power and the sprawling, gleaming orbital facility was probably the least covert installation next to the New Sierra Platform.

"I'm intrigued," Celesta said. She was still trying to wrap her head around the fact that his and Pitt's public combativeness had all been for show.

"It's a sort of quick reaction force," Perez went on. "The ships were completed at a Fleet R&S black site, and we've been working closely with CENTCOM to get the crews cleared and moved out there. We'd been planning on keeping it in reserve in case the shit hit the fan, but now we think it might be prudent to reposition the force in anticipation of the Odmena situation deteriorating."

"Where would I come in, sir?"

"Finding flag officers without deep political connections that might compromise them has been damn near impossible," Perez said. "The person we assumed would be heading up this strike force is sitting on a battleship right now, completely ignorant that the ESA is actively targeting him in this operation. You're another, but you're no longer a Fleet officer.

"Pitt stretched the regulations to near breaking when he pitched the idea of putting you in overall command, but we've found a loophole that will keep it all aboveboard."

"Me...command a Starfleet strike force?" Celesta asked. "Sir, I've never commanded in the field as a flag officer. My rank came with a desk job, and at CIS, I'm little more than a glorified administrator."

"While it pains me to hear you speak of yourself in those terms, I think we both know you're being needlessly modest. As a senior captain, you commanded a squadron of destroyers for the duration of the Expansion War, coming out as one of the most decorated starship captains of the conflict. You're imminently suited for this job and don't worry, it's a temporary billeting. I'm not letting Fleet steal you back after how quickly you whipped Prowler Fleet into shape."

"And the nature of this new unit? Is this the first operational unit flying Mickeys?"

"No, no, no." Perez waved her off. "The first Mickeys are close to being activated, but that's a high-profile program under close scrutiny. We're calling the strike force we've built the Wolfpack."

"Cute," she said. "I'm assuming there's some connection to the admiral of the same name?"

"Tell me, Admiral, how many Valkyrie-class destroyers are currently in service?"

"One," Celesta said confidently. "The TFS *Nemesis* was completed in a rush, and then the *Valkyrie* Program was shelved because the ships were deemed unnecessary and too expensive. It was the poster child of runaway costs and the main reason Parliament signed off on Wolfe's mickey proposal."

"There are six operational *Valkyrie* ships currently," Perez said. "One famous ship that Captain Barrett drove into a bomb, and five that make up our new strike force. In the confusion following the Expansion War, and Merchant Fleet's rush to begin moving people and materials to our newly acquired planets, we had the five unfinished *Valkyrie* hulls moved to the aforementioned black location and completed in secret with slush funds. Officially, they don't exist. We publicly stated that the program was halted and the hulls recycled."

"You have *five* fully operational *Valkyrie*-class destroyers just sitting back in reserve?!" Celesta could hardly believe what she was hearing. The *Nemesis* was one of the most feared ships in the Federation's arsenal, even more so than the new battleships. Six of them could have rattled the ESA leadership enough that they wouldn't have left the negotiating table.

"Operational and markedly more advanced than the *Nemesis*," Perez said. "You remember when Wolfe commanded her during the end of the war and the ship was able to make intra-system warp flights?"

"Yes," Celesta said carefully. The details of Wolfe's final battles were highly classified, but since Perez brought it up, she had to assume he was cleared. "But the...computer...that allowed him to do those warp hops was lost in the mission."

"I know all about Project Prometheus and the sentient alien computer that was the program principle, Admiral. Before Wolfe destroyed the Cube, it had uploaded everything we'd need to duplicate its method onto one of the *Nemesis's* servers. We've been able to refine the process with some interesting results that you'll learn about once you're on your way."

"I'd heard the *Nemesis* is no longer authorized to make intra-system hops," Celesta said. "You're saying these new ships are?"

"We purged and reloaded the original warp drive field equations on the *Nemesis* so that she is incapable of short warp hops," Perez said. "CENTCOM's paranoia about ESA infiltration has them distrusting even their own crews...and they're not entirely wrong there. If someone managed to get a copy of new field equations to the other side, it's likely they'd be able to figure out how to perform the short hops themselves. There were quite a few Tsuyo scientists that defected when we began prosecuting the company's management."

"I remember."

"Anyway, that's a little background on why we never implemented the new capability on the rest of the Gen V hulls even though their drives are capable of performing the same maneuvers. There's no advantage to be gained deploying that capability where it could be compromised before the fighting even begins. Your liaison will give you the rundown on the rest of the upgrades."

"I'm leaving immediately, I take it?" Celesta asked.

"Effective immediately, you're on detached duty to CENTCOM Special Warfare Command," Perez said.

"There's a Broadhead docked below that will take you to your new command. I've already informed your office that Captain Elliot will be standing in for you until you return. With any luck, it'll be soon and without any shots being fired in anger."

"Let's hope, sir," Celesta said.

"A word of advice, perhaps even a bit of a warning." Perez raised his hand, stopping her from getting up. "I agreed to let Fleet take you for this assignment because I agree with their assessment that you're the best for the job, but I'm also aware that you have a history of going rogue and using your political connections to avoid punishment." Celesta seethed at his words but decided not to press the issue. She felt his characterization was unfair but couldn't deny there was some truth to what he said.

"Excuse my bluntness, Admiral, but I want to make sure there is no misunderstanding between us," he went on. "There can be no mistakes on this mission. If one of these ships were to be disabled and captured, the consequences for the Federation would be immense."

"I understand, Mr. Director," Celesta ground out.

"If you operate outside the parameters of your mission orders, there will be no forced retirement this time. It'll be a court martial, and then whatever appropriate punishment they decide. Please keep that in mind. You're a great asset to the CIS, and I'd hate to lose you." Perez stood and looked at the clock on the wall. Comlinks were strictly prohibited inside the secure room as were wristwatches so Celesta was surprised when she looked herself and saw they'd been there for over four hours.

"You'd better grab any personal effects you want from your office and get down to your ship. Sorry, but I can't let you go back to your planetside office or home for security reasons."

"I have a go-bag in my office here on the Platform," Celesta said, rising. "When will I get my mission brief and orders?"

"They're waiting for you on the Broadhead. Good luck, Admiral."

13

CIS HAS DISCOVERED CREDIBLE EVIDENCE OF ESA OPERATION TO CAPTURE REAR ADMIRAL JACKSON WOLFE.

ADM WOLFE IS ORDERED TO RELENQUISH COMMAND OF TASK FORCE VEGA TO CAPTAIN HARDY AND DEPART THE ODMENA SYSTEM UPON RECEIPT OF THIS MESSAGE. FAILURE TO DO SO COULD COMPROMISE DIPLOMATIC AND STRATEGIC GOALS WITHIN SYSTEM.

PLEASE REPLY WITH CONFIRMATION OF ORDERS AND ESTIMATED DEPARTURE TIME.

-CENTCOM CHIEF OF STAFF PITT

Jackson stared at the message with disgust, then closed down the tile before he was tempted to respond rashly. His first instinct was to simply ignore the order. As the on-site commander of all Federation forces in the system, he could legally claim that he was unable to follow the order. Starfleet's charter hadn't been updated to reflect that

CENTCOM had the capability of communicating with officers in the field in real-time. The regulations still assumed that an order would be traveling days or weeks by com drone, and that the issuing official would have no way of knowing what was actually happening. With that in mind, Starfleet gave their field commanders a lot of leeway when it came to this sort of thing.

That wiggle room wasn't infinite, however, and Jackson didn't think that he could reasonably apply it to the order Pitt had sent him. This was the highest-ranking person in the Federation military, not some overzealous administrator in CENTCOM. Ignoring or openly disobeying Pitt was something he wasn't willing to do, so his only option was to reason with him. He'd had varying degrees of success with that in the past. Pitt didn't dislike Jackson like a lot of CENTCOM brass did, but nor was he necessarily a fan. He would ruthlessly use Jackson's legend and past exploits like a bludgeon when politically convenient, but Jackson wasn't foolish enough to mistake that for admiration or friendship.

"Problem, sir?" Lieutenant Trapp asked. She'd been working in the secure office space he'd taken over on the command deck once Jackson had successfully pulled her out of CIC.

"Nothing that I can't—"

"General Quarters, General Quarters, General Quarters! All hands to stations and in your restraints! Repeat, all hands to stations and in restraints! Set condition 1SS!"

Jackson leapt from his desk, the servos in his prosthetic's ankle whining in protest, and ran for the hatch. His mind raced with the possible scenarios based on the last tactical snapshot CIC had sent to him, and he could think of nothing that would cause Captain Hardy to put his crew in restraints, something that only happened when the ship was about to receive incoming fire.

"We had a small ship sneak in on us, Admiral," Hardy said as Jackson walked onto the bridge. "CIC doesn't know how it was able to get so close without being detected. Range is just under two-hundred thousand kilos range, quartering into us from the port side."

"How did we detect it?" Jackson asked, not bothering to take his seat and strap in just yet.

"High-power array painted what the tactical computers is labeling as an engine thrust nozzle. The ship is small, barely bigger than a Broadhead, and we still don't have a real good lock on it. The stealth they're employing is impressive."

Jackson walked over to the tactical station and looked at the rotating three-dimensional model the computer had generated from the high-resolution radar array. The detail was quite good at such a close range. It didn't take him more than a second to recognize what he was seeing.

"It's a bit larger, but it's strikingly similar to the ship that very nearly destroyed the *Nemesis*, Captain," he said. "I would normally recommend firing before it can close the range, but our rules of engagement are explicit...we cannot fire first."

"Yes, sir," Hardy said. "Helm! Hard to starboard, all ahead full...angle us away from the incoming ship. "Nav, give the helm a running update of course corrections that will put us back on our orbital intercept vector when I order it. Tactical! Keep sharp. The closer they get, the less effective our point defense will be."

There was a chorus of affirmatives and a flurry of activity as the *Jericho* turned onto her new course and the powerful multi-phase RDS surged with power, pushing her away from an Odmena intercept and towards the innermost planets. Jackson found his seat and pulled the Bluebird-connected tile from a utility pocket, firing off a quick message to Captain Carmichael to tell him to be alert for the small attack craft and to maintain his stately approach to the planet.

He looked up to see that even though the *Jericho* wasn't the fastest ship in the fleet, she was easily putting distance on the small stealth ship and would be well past it in time to come back onto their original course. Once he was sure Hardy had the situation well in hand, he replied to Admiral Pitt, telling him that the window of opportunity for his departure had passed and that the task force was now being engaged. If they really were after him, trying to flee in a small, unarmed courier ship seemed riskier than staying on the bridge of a battleship.

"Do you think this was a serious attempt?" Commander Trane asked from just behind Jackson. The admiral had not heard the XO walk up. He slipped the tile back into his pocket and stood back up.

"I have no doubt that they'd have taken a shot at us if we let them get close or repeated the same mistake from the Eternis Pax attack," he said. "But this was just a feeler...the opening moves to find out if they can goad us into shooting at shadows, turning tail and running, or blindly driving our ships into obvious ambushes. I am concerned, however, that they seem to be able to sneak in close on us at will."

"The tactical computers will look at all the sensor data leading up to the encounter and begin building a model based on any anomalous readings it finds that were initially ignored," Trane said confidently. "They shouldn't be able to pull the same trick twice." Jackson found it mildly comical that the younger officer thought he needed to have the ship's predictive modeling capability explained to him. The computers that performed that task were an output of Project Prometheus, an emergent AI program he'd been heading up before being dragged back into Starfleet.

In the two days prior to the recent encounter, the Alliance fleet ships seemed content to shadow them from a distance and allow them to navigate where they wanted. Jackson had used the time to communicate with the local government and Federation representatives on the surface but, so far, all attempts to talk to the ESA commander in the system had been ignored. He hadn't felt like they were being herded or led around by the nose, but now they'd just dodged an ESA attack boat that just happened in along their flightpath. Seemed a bit too coincidental.

"Captain, please stop the ship," Jackson said conversationally as he looked at the enemy ship tracks along the main display.

"Helm, full stop...full reverse!" Hardy barked without hesitation.

"Engines answering all astern, aye!" The deck began to vibrate harshly as the RDS reversed its fields and worked to drag the massive battleship to a relative stop in space.

"Admiral?" Hardy asked as crew began grabbing loose items during the increasingly violent maneuver. Despite the near-magical capabilities of the gravimetric drives it would still take nearly two and half hours to bring the ship to a stop...less if they didn't care about the wellbeing of the crew.

"Now, we wait, Captain," Jackson said. "Keep scanning local space and make sure CIC is looking for any new RDS signatures popping up in the system. After that last encounter, I think the odds are good that we're flying into something worse further in."

"Turning in to get behind the approaching ship would

have been the most logical course of action," Hardy nodded. "They'll have anticipated that."

"It was the only logical move to avoid fending off a close-range missile shot, Captain," Jackson assured him. "One problem at a time, as they come to us."

"Admiral! CIC is reporting multiple new RDS contacts," the tactical officer said. "Eighteen so far."

"*Eighteen!?*" Hardy spun to stare at the main display.

"Yes, Captain. Now there are twenty-three. Five smaller ships have just powered drives dead ahead at a range of three-hundred and sixty thousand kilos."

"Coms! Tell CIC I want a Bluebird message sent to Captain Carmichael," Jackson ordered, the horror of his situation slowly dawning on him. "I want a full status update from the task force. Ask him if he sees a way for the formation to break contact and escape."

"Aye, sir," the com officer looked like he'd just swallowed poison and made no move to comply. He just stared at the main display.

"*NOW*, Lieutenant!"

"You're sending the task force away, sir?" Hardy asked.

"I'm going to try to, but I don't think they'll find open space to a known jump point."

"We'll be isolated and cut off!"

"We already are, Captain," Jackson said. "Don't you see it? This was the trap...and we just sprung it." He waved to the main display where RDS signatures were still popping up.

"What are we going to do, sir?"

"Our damned best to not have a mistake on our part lead to a war that will kill millions."

"Oh, God," Hardy muttered as the full implication of their situation made itself known over the panic and chaos of having a few dozen enemy ships appear on his scopes.

The Alliance fleet had been prepared for them and had played their role perfectly. Now, Task Force Vega was trapped without relief forces in range to do any good. Damn the luck.

"You asked to see me, Administrator?"

"Yes, Captain Barrett. Please, come in and have a seat."

Barrett walked in and sat down in the plush chair, looking across the desk at the civilian administrator of the Eternis Pax Shipyards that, inexplicably, was holding his ship in dock and not allowing them to leave.

"The repairs to the *Nemesis* have been completed for over two weeks now. I'm guessing you want to know why you're still here," Administrator Nakamura said.

"It's crossed my mind, sir."

"I was asked to hold the ship here while CENTCOM made up its mind about what to do with you," Nakamura said bluntly. "My guess is that because of your war hero status, they've run into some political turbulence over the idea of replacing you as captain of the Federation's most infamous ship."

"I'd guessed much the same," Barrett admitted. "They normally would never let a CO keep their ship after a blunder like mine, but they also don't have anybody ready to step into such a high-profile role just yet, so their answer to appease certain politicians is to just store us here. I've become accustomed to these games in my short time as a captain, but this isn't fair to my crew."

"An unfortunate turn of events, for sure. I'm privy to

certain channels of information over Bluebird, and I've learned that your mentor's task force has been engaged by a numerically superior force in the Odmena System. We've also learned that the ESA is targeting him specifically."

"And we're stuck here," Barrett fumed. "This is...infuriating."

"I agree," Nakamura said. "Unfortunately, I have no Starfleet rank so I can't really tell you what to do one way or the other."

"Perhaps if I try to contact CENTCOM directly and—"

"I don't think you understand what I'm saying, Captain," Nakamura leaned in. "This is *not* a Starfleet facility and I do *not* have any rank within your chain of command, assimilated or otherwise." Barrett just blinked a moment until his anger-addled brain could catch up with what the civilian administrator was saying.

"Son of a bitch," he muttered, leaping from the chair. "Excuse me, Administrator."

"Of course," Nakamura said calmly as the young captain knocked the chair over and charged from his office, the ghost of a smile playing across his lips before he reached over and keyed his intercom.

"*Yes, sir?*"

"Inform the Transient Docks supervisor that the TFS *Nemesis* will be throwing off lines and departing the station. She's to do nothing to interfere with the ship's departure."

"*Yes, sir.*"

Under United Terran Federation maritime law, a civilian is not allowed to hinder or prohibit the free navigation of a registered ship of war. Eternis Pax was a defense contractor, but not technically a military owned or operated installation. It was a technicality, but the law thrived on technicalities. Where CENTCOM had royally screwed up was in not wanting to directly confront Captain Barrett about the attack on his ship until they knew they were on firm political ground to have him replaced.

Instead, they thought they'd be clever and ask the shipyard to hold his ship hostage, unaware that Eternis Pax wasn't legally able to do so. Nakamura had hoped that Barrett would calm down enough to figure that out for himself, but with the ESA getting ready to rout Admiral Wolfe's task force at Odmena he figured the brash captain needed a little coaxing in the right direction.

Nakamura busied himself again with his work until, barely six hours after his conversation with Barrett, he heard the intercom *ping* with a departure announcement.

"All personnel in sections eight-alpha, nine alpha, and eight bravo, standby. TFS *Nemesis* departing Transient Docks."

The announcement repeated twice more, something Nakamura normally ignored as part of the routine background noise of a busy shipyard. This time, however, he spun his chair around so he could look out the porthole of his office out over the sprawling docking complex. He picked up a pair of high-powered binoculars and peered down where the Transient Docks were located some four kilometers away and could just make out the shiny sliver of a Valkyrie-class destroyer gliding gracefully from berth. He figured it wouldn't take long for the ship to depart since the crew was staying aboard, and he'd ordered his harbormaster to keep her topped off on fuel and consumables.

He sighed and put aside his optics, now worried about how he'd craft his message to CENTCOM without losing his own job or making it sound like Captain Barrett had just stolen a very expensive bit of Federation property.

14

"We're ready on your order, ma'am."

"Execute transition," Admiral Celesta Wright ordered from the bridge of the *Broadsword*, one of the five Super Valkyrie-class destroyers that were part of the Wolfpack, her new temporary command.

"Engaging warp drive in 5...4...3...2...now!"

The transition to warp flight was anticlimactic except for where the ship was in the star system when it happened: inside the orbit of the sixth planet in a system designated XB-801. The nameless black site was a joint effort between Starfleet and CIS, kept so secret that even Chief of Staff Pitt wasn't certain exactly what all they did there.

"All ships reporting in, ma'am," Captain Risher reported. Celesta had never heard of him, but her Fleet liaison during the trip out, Jillian Wolfe, assured her he was as good as they come.

"Amazing, isn't it, Captain?" she asked. "Five years ago,

this was unheard of, transitioning deep within a system and communicating with other ships while in warp."

"Very effective tools, Admiral," Mansk said. "The newer drives fitted to the Wolfpack ships will allow us to get to Odmena within eight days by bypassing all the normal stops within other systems to utilize the jump points. All the ships will arrive within three hours of each other, give or take an hour."

"And no transition flashes?" Celesta asked. She'd been amazed by that when Jillian had told her they'd eliminated that old vulnerability with the new drives.

"Correct, ma'am. The new drive field controllers are so accurate there's no longer the dissipation of wasted energy when the fields collapse." Celesta just shook her head, not wanting to sound like a yokel by raving on and on about the new technologies represented in the newly-finished destroyer hulls.

The trip from XB-801 to the Odmena System would normally take three and a half weeks, the bulk of that transiting the two systems in between if they stuck to the established warp lanes and jump points. The Wolfpack would be doing the same trip on a direct line in less than a third of that time.

Her last Bluebird dispatch said that the shooting still hadn't yet started in the system, but Wolfe was now pinned down by a much larger ESA force and unable to break away. Celesta had confidence he'd be able to hold them at bay for the short time it would take for her to get her ships out there.

Wolfe had been told that a relief force was on the way, but in order to protect the secrecy of the program and the nature of the Wolfpack ships, he hadn't been given specifics details despite repeatedly asking which ships and captains were being sent. She'd also caught word that one of her Prowlers had tracked the *Nemesis* steaming full bore out of the Eternis System, on the way to the Odmena jump point despite CENTCOM's effort to keep Barrett on ice until they decided what to do with him.

She was painfully aware that President Stark was trying to avoid open hostilities with the ESA at all costs, and had even been ignoring raids into Federation territory in order to keep the peace, but Celesta knew it was in vain. The game was beginning to speed up, and all the pieces were either already in Odmena or hurtling towards it faster than light. The coming conflict had been inevitable the moment the ESA had cut a deal with an alien power that had been slaughtering civilians on human worlds, and it seemed that the ESA had decided that Odmena would be the catalyst. If they were able to corner the *Jericho* and swarm Wolfe under, there would be no stopping a full-blown war. The ESA would be emboldened by defeating the legendary Starfleet officer, and the Federation would demand blood for his death.

"Warp fields are stabilized," the OPS officer reported. "Engineering will begin ramping up the power and be at full output in seventy-four minutes."

"Excellent," Captain Risher said. "Maintain normal watch schedule. Inform the department heads they can train their people at their discretion for the next five days."

"Aye, sir."

"Captain, I'll be in CIC," Celesta said. "I don't expect you'll need anything from me until we get ready to transition back into real space."

"No, ma'am," Risher said. "We'll be running proficiency drills for the next week, and then the strike force will get its first taste of real action. Our crews won't disappoint, Admiral."

"I'm already impressed, Captain," Celesta assured him. "With the crews and your ships. I have no doubt they're up to the task ahead of them."

"Admiral." Risher nodded to her, and then went back to his discussion with the first watch tactical officer.

Celesta walked off the bridge, her stomach in knots. She'd been there at the beginning with Jackson Wolfe when they first encountered the Phage. A young, ambitious officer, woefully unqualified for the position she'd been thrust into. She survived that war—and the one after that—and now it looked like before she was done there would be one more fight. The idea of turning the weapons of war they'd built to protect humanity from alien threats on each other sickened her. Had they learned nothing in the last twelve years?

"The *Robert Blake* has broadcast the visual data they collected on one of the new bogeys over the Link. They say the new ships are smaller than a frigate and appear to have some sort of retractable shrouds CIC thinks may be radar absorbent."

"That's how they did it," Jackson said. "They peppered the system with these smaller attack boats that have been sitting out there powerless until they'd chased us down into the inner system. It's a brilliant move...simple and effective."

"It also creates a major issue," Commander Trane said. "Not only are we badly outnumbered, but we had no idea this class of ship even existed. We have zero intelligence on its capabilities or even basic specs."

"We have to assume they all have the same antimatter

armament the ship that attacked the *Nemesis* was sporting," Jackson said. "But are these also suicide drones, or will they have guided missiles they're firing in on us? Tell CIC that I want their initial workup immediately. By now, they should have a good idea what sort of tracking and targeting arrays these ships are equipped with."

"Coms!" Trane barked over his shoulder.

"On it, sir. CIC is sending up everything they have."

Jackson reflected on the brutal simplicity of the ships he now faced. Hiding an object—even one as large as a starship—wasn't especially difficult, but nor was it especially useful. Normally. A Starship's radar cross-section is only one aspect of its visibility on sensors, and since they operate in an environment full of enormous radar-reflecting objects like nickel-iron asteroids and derelict hulks, it's not normally focused on by designers.

Active ships have gravimetric wake if they're flying with RDS drives, belch out huge plumes of super-heated exhaust from their fusion reactors, and have a significant thermal signature from dissipating heat from their internal systems. They're not subtle machines. Also, radar absorbent coatings are fragile and normally are peeled away after less than a year in space from micrometeor impacts and the friction of aero-braking during orbit.

The ESA, lagging badly behind the Federation in technological prowess but making up for it with manufacturing capacity, had been forced to come up with a clever workaround for their shortcomings...and they'd caught Jackson completely flat-footed. By positioning their ships ahead of time and equipping them with deployable stealth panels, they were able to hide a sizable assault force and allow the Federation task force to blunder into the inner system, overconfident and oblivious.

"Where is Captain Hardy?" Jackson asked the com officer while Trane talked to OPS.

"I haven't seen in him since I came on watch, Admiral. It's not like him to not be on the bridge when the ship is at quarters. Would you like me to try and find him?"

"Please do."

"Full stop, relative!" the helmsman called out. "Drives to station keeping." Jackson looked up at the main display in the corner where the *Jericho's* telemetry was and saw that all of their velocities relative to the system's star were zeroed out.

"Maintain position and continue to monitor local space," Jackson said, injecting himself into the ship's operations without waiting for Commander Trane. "Any word on Captain Hardy?"

"Sir he's not answering his comlink or the intercom in his quarters," the com officer said.

"The computer says he's in his quarters, Admiral," Orr reported from the OPS station.

"Commander, would you please see what's keeping the captain?" Jackson asked the XO. "Have teams from security and medical meet you there."

"Aye, sir," Trane said. If he was irritated about Jackson stepping in and assuming command, he didn't show it. Jackson turned back in time to see a highly animated conversation between Lieutenant Orr at OPS and Lieutenant Commander Easton at Tactical.

"You have something to report?" he asked forcefully.

"Sir, the *Tangiers* and the *Brighton* are...missing," Orr said, his face ashen.

Jackson frowned but said nothing at first. The *Tangiers* and *Brighton* were his task force's two supply ships, assigned to him from Logistics Command. They were non-combatants and, as per normal operating procedure, were deployed along the system boundary to stay out of the way. It was an unspoken rule of interstellar warfare that the medical and supply ships, usually ungainly and slower than the mainline warships, were left unmolested unless they interjected themselves into a battle. Even as ruthless as the Phage were, they would normally fly right by unarmed ships without so much as slowing down.

"Do we have confirmation or did they just drop off the Link?" Jackson asked.

"CIC is working on an answer now, sir, but there were explosions caught by the optics within the area the two ships were assumed to be," Allgood said. "Secondary explosions were consistent with a stricken ship, but no distress calls were made by either."

"Coms! Have CIC call over to the *Robert Blake* and see what they know," Jackson said.

"If the ESA actually just took out two of our supply frigates what—"

"Let's not speculate until we have something more solid, Mr. Easton," Jackson said. "OPS, you're handling this issue with CIC. Tactical, you're to concentrate on making sure a stealth ship doesn't sneak up on us."

"Aye, sir," they said in unison.

In truth, Jackson was as concerned as they were about the possibility that the ESA was ignoring centuries of warfare doctrine and attacking support vessels as an opening move. It would be a marked departure from the accepted standards of decency and force the Federation to respond in kind. What then? Bombarding civilian populations from orbit?

The atrocities that could be committed with even a single starship and the will to fully unleash it was almost unimaginable. While his speculating might be a bit far ranging at the moment, he knew from personal experience that once one hard, fast rule was broken, it was much easier to break the next one.

"Sir! Admiral! Commander Trane has just checked in... and...it's—"

"What did he find, Lieutenant?"

"Captain Hardy is dead, sir. Suicide."

Nobody spoke. In the absence of human noises, the sounds from the ship seemed oppressively loud. It was finally broken when Lieutenant Orr spoke up.

"OPS, tell Commander Trane that he will need to handle the situation with Captain Hardy himself," he finally said. "Please note in the log that as of 1611 ship's time I am assuming command of the TFS *Jericho*."

15

"We've heard from our operative. Admiral Kohl has just destroyed Wolfe's supply ships."

"Needlessly reckless," Zhang said. "The point of this is to provoke Wolfe into rash action that can be used against the Federation, not justify his actions if he wipes out Kohl's entire armada."

"Kohl has forty-three ships at his disposal," the visitor scoffed. "Wolfe's thirteen ship task force is woefully outgunned. He will not be able to escape this."

"Perhaps," Zhang said doubtfully. "Tell me, how is our contact getting this information so quickly?"

"He's vaguely calling it leftover alien tech from the Phage War." The visitor shrugged. "We think it's not quite instantaneous, but damn close. We have no idea if it's something they have wider access to, if it really is just old Vruahn hardware, or if the Fed has cracked the code for superluminal communication. For right now, we're letting him keep his secrets as long as the useful intel keeps rolling in."

"It might be prudent to inform Alliance Fleet Command that the Federation could possibly have faster-than-light communications deployed on their ships," Zhang said. "Withholding that type of information is dangerous. If it leads to the loss of ships and they find out we knew about it..." Zhang left the rest of his sentence dangling, certain that his guest could put the pieces together himself.

"They'll have us imprisoned, likely killed." The man shrugged. "It's the game we're playing. You're having second thoughts?"

"No." Zhang hesitated but decided now wasn't the time to voice his doubts...at least not to *this* man. He didn't even know his real name. He just knew the reputation he had for eliminating problems when necessary. "The plan will proceed as we've lain out. We're committed to this course of action regardless, and now our fate is tied to Admiral Kohl and his ability to execute."

"Be sure you're ready to do your part when it's time."

"Save your threats. Everything on my end was put in place over a year ago and is ready to be implemented anytime it needs to be. Tell your handlers their time would be better spent making sure the Council will vote accordingly once it's time."

"Just be ready," the man growled before slinking out of the office. Zhang let out an explosive breath, his shoulders still bunched up and tense. Dealing with him always felt like trying to move a sleeping cobra: at any moment, it could wake up and kill you for reasons you'd never really understand. After taking a few breaths to center himself, he turned his desktop terminal back on and read through the message that had come through the civilian com system.

. . .

I'll be in your vicinity within the next week...would love to get together to talk about your latest proposal.
W. Anders

Zhang knew Anders was an alias for the man he'd met a few times when he was on Haven. Through some discreet poking about, he'd learned he also was known as Aston Lynch, personal aide to then-Senator Augustus Wellington. Zhang had cultivated the relationship, thinking he was so clever and intended to use Lynch's proximity to Wellington as a source of inside information.

Little did he know Lynch had also been an alias and, before he knew it, he found himself as an informant to a CIS Agent. Lynch—or whoever the hell he really was—had promised to keep Zhang's names off any official reports or mission logs as long as he agreed to feed him intel about certain programs within the Asianic Union.

Now, Anders was coming there in person. This was very, very bad timing. If the others in the cabal found out a CIS Agent was coming to see him, his life would be forfeit. They wouldn't even bother asking him for an explanation. He doubted the message being sent just as they were rolling major plans into action was a mere coincidence. Somehow, the Fed's intelligence service had caught wind of what they were doing.

"This is not good," he moaned. He was a glorified project administrator at heart. He simply didn't have the stomach for the political intrigue he found himself caught up in.

"Looks like he hung himself with that tie-down strap," Trane said, pointing to one of the common self-cinching web straps that were used on starships to secure cargo.

"No note, but no signs of a struggle either," Barton said quietly to Jackson. "This whole thing seems...strange."

"Agreed," Jackson said. "But it's not something I have the luxury of dwelling on. Commander Trane, turn the investigation over to the master at arms and return your people to their post."

"Aye, sir," Trane said and began ushering people out of Captain Hardy's quarters, stepping around the sheet that covered his former CO's body. Jackson nudged Barton and made his own way to the exit, anxious to get back on the bridge.

He had risked a few minutes away in order to see Hardy's body and the scene of his demise in person before the *Jericho's* master at arms began cleaning everything up. The *Jericho* was still sitting at a full stop in space, and there seemed to be a lull as the ESA fleet master tried to figure out exactly what he was up to.

The truth was that Jackson wasn't sure himself. He knew the whole situation seemed...off...somehow. The amount of firepower and preplanning the Alliance had brought to bear for a system that wasn't of critical strategic of logistical value made him suspicious, like there was a much larger picture he just wasn't seeing from his vantage. Since he couldn't be sure exactly what the rules of the game were, he decided to simply not play. The Alliance fleet's next moves would hopefully let him know what their intentions were.

"Sir, CIC confirms that the *Tangiers* and *Brighton* have been destroyed," Lieutenant Orr reported when Jackson walked back onto the bridge. "They say it looks like a nuclear strike on both, coordinated to hit simultaneously."

Jackson's stomach dropped at the news. This was it. The ESA had drawn first blood, and now the leashes were off his task force according to the rules of engagement imposed upon him by CENTCOM. He'd be within his right to begin running down and eliminating every Alliance ship he could put a missile into. But is that what they wanted? The fact he still wasn't sure what their overall goal in the system was made him hesitate to answer force with force.

"Coms! Have your backshop continue trying to make contact with the Alliance fleet," he ordered. "I want you talking to officials on the planet letting them know that we've had an unprovoked attack on our ships and that we demand answers from the ESA rep on the surface."

"Aye, sir."

"OPS! Tell Captain Carmichael he is clear to engage any ships that demonstrate hostile intent. Make sure the task force has all the intel we've collected on the stealth ships in the system. Helm, set a course down to Odmena Prime... ahead full."

"All engines ahead full, aye!" the helmswoman said. "Coming back onto original course for Odmena Prime orbital intercept."

"Tactical, call out anything we have in front of us," Jackson said, sitting in the command chair. "I don't think they're going to give us a free pass all the way down to the planet."

"Aye, sir."

The deck vibrated as power from the *Jericho's* four main reactors poured into the drive generators and the massive battleship leapt ahead at over sixty G's of acceleration. She wasn't an especially fast ship despite her awesome power, but she was quick enough that Jackson felt like he could get them down over the planet into a holding orbit before any of the Alliance ships would have a chance to intercept them. He felt like once he was flying above Odmena, the game would change, and he'd be able to secure the beachhead with the powerful ship despite his opponent's numerical advantage.

"Odmena orbital intercept in...thirty-eight hours, Admiral."

"Acknowledged," Jackson said. "OPS, send out a more detailed message to all the department heads letting them know the change in command and the death of Captain Hardy. Leave out the cause for now, but let's try to head off the scuttlebutt on the lower decks before it becomes a problem."

"Doing it now, sir."

"For now, we will remain at quarters, but I want normal watch schedules," Jackson continued. "Look alive, everyone! We've already lost two ships, and we don't even know what the enemy's goals are. Our actions here could determine whether or not we get dragged into a shooting war with the ESA, so let's make sure we do everything right."

That seemed to shake some of the lethargy from the crew, and they went about their tasks with a new edge to their actions. The shock of losing their captain on top of having two of their ships blown out of the sky by another human fleet had them looking a little lost. Task Force Vega had flown out here to wave the flag and be a presence ahead of a diplomatic delegation that would do the real work of securing the system for the Federation. He had to admit he'd been caught flatfooted by the sheer volume of ESA ships and by their willingness to fire on him in such an open, messy way. They'd been sending covert strike teams into Fed space for some time now, but this was an entirely new, brazen direction they were going.

"Enemy ships are redeploying, sir," Lieutenant Erikson reported from Tactical. "Five cruisers are breaking off to pursue us. CIC says they're at full power but will not be able to close within weapons range before we're in orbit over the planet."

"Coms, send another message to the planetary authority and let them know we intend to move into the area and establish orbital superiority. I'm not asking permission. If they have any commercial ships in their skies over an altitude of one thousand kilometers, we strongly suggest they order them out of the area."

"Yes, sir."

"The master at arms is now handling the investigation into Captain Hardy's death, Admiral," Commander Trane said, breathing heavily as if he'd run the whole way to the bridge. "They'll report their findings directly to you."

"Very good, Commander," Jackson stood up. "You have the bridge for now. We're making way for the planet. If a ship tries to deny us navigation, destroy it."

"Aye-aye, sir." Trane said grimly. "I have the bridge."

Jackson made his way back to his office so that he could inform CENTCOM of their change in status. When he walked in, however, Lieutenant Trapp looked agitated and appeared to have been waiting for him.

"Admiral," she said, her words tumbling out. "I've made some progress with that matter you had me investigating. You're not going to like this."

"Oh, good...more bad news."

"We were able to reconstruct the altered records to figure out who had authorized the point-to-point com drone launches as well as the access override to activate the beacons when we first arrived here," she said. "It was

Captain Hardy's command codes that were used in each instance."

"And now Captain Hardy is dead from apparent suicide," Jackson said. "How convenient."

"Yes, sir. We're still working on it to try and pin down exactly where and when the authorizations came from, as well as the data that was loaded onto the drones."

"You're not making a big splash down in the intel section with this investigation, are you?"

"No, sir. Only two people helping, and they're technicians I trust completely. They understand this is being done in absolute secrecy," she said.

"Good. Keep digging then, and if you find anything more, make sure you come to me immediately, unless you feel the ship taking hits. I don't believe that Hardy was doing all of this alone. With that in mind...be careful when you're poking around."

"I will, sir."

Once she disappeared, he was able to pull the secure tile out and log in to the Bluebird system and check his incoming messages. The first one he read was a welcome bit of good news, finally.

ADMIRAL WOLFE... THE NEMESIS HAS DEPARTED ETERNIS PAX EN ROUTE TO THE ODMENA SYSTEM. EXPECT HER WITHIN SEVEN DAYS TIME OF RECIPT OF THIS MESSAGE. GOOD LUCK. ADMINISTRATOR NAKAMURA

So, it looked like Captain Barrett had bucked CENTCOM—again—and was bringing his Valkyrie-class destroyer to

Odmena. It was the best bit of news he'd gotten since arriving to the border system. With the *Nemesis* there, the Alliance fleet would have to completely retool their strategy, no longer able to focus so completely on the *Jericho*. Bolstered by the news that he was being reinforced, he sat down and composed a series of communiques to CENTCOM and Seventh Fleet HQ letting them know that the ESA had destroyed two Federation ships and that the captain of the flagship had apparently hung himself in his quarters. He could imagine the staff having to peel Admiral Pitt off the ceiling when he read how badly a simple force projection mission was going.

"They're still quartering into us, sir. Range is eighty-thousand kilometers and closing."

"Firing solution is locked on!"

"OPS, tell the rest of the task force to hold course. Helm! Put our bow on the incoming ship, maintain current velocity," Carmichael ordered.

"Coming about, aye!"

The *Robert Blake* swung to port off her original course to meet the incoming enemy ship head-on. After the admiral's warning to treat any encounter as a threat, he wasn't taking any chances on letting it get closer to the rest of the task force where it could get off multiple shots. The Alliance ships had been pushing close to their maximum weapons range since the *Jericho* had broken off, testing their reactions, and trying to goad Carmichael into doing something rash. Now that they'd taken out the resupply ships, it looked like they were about to make a run on the task force formation in earnest.

The cruiser that had been approaching them from a

parallel heliocentric orbit further up the well had angled in on them and began painting the formation with her targeting radar. It might have been another feint, but Carmichael wasn't taking that chance.

"Forty-four thousand kilometers and closing!"

"Arm Shrikes, tubes one and three," Carmichael ordered.

"Tubes one and three ready," the tactical officer said. "Firing solution uploaded, missiles locked on."

"Your board is green. You're clear to fire when we close to within twenty thousand and she hasn't veered off." Carmichael pressed his palm to the terminal at his seat and entered his authorization code to arm the warheads and launch tubes for the *Blake*'s primary ship-to-ship weapons: the Shrike II nuclear ship-buster missile.

The bridge was tense as they watched the Alliance cruiser bear down on them without showing any sign that it was going to pull off at the last minute. At such a close range, the sensor updates were coming in virtual real-time, and Carmichael felt the cold lump in his stomach as he realized he would be the one to fire the first shots in anger from the Federation side of a war that looked to now be inevitable.

"Firing! Tubes one and three away. Missiles tracking clean. Tubes two and four armed, one and three reloading."

"Full reverse!" Carmichael barked. "Hard to starboard. Put us on course to move back to the formation lead."

"Engines all reverse, aye!" the helmsman practically shouted. "Coming about on new course."

Carmichael split his attention between watching the telemetry stream from his weapons and his ship bleeding off velocity as she came back on course. He saw that the enemy ship had also angled to starboard to put as much distance as they could on the incoming missiles.

"Helm, engines ahead full," he said once he saw they'd completed their turn and were no longer closing to within enemy weapons range.

"Ahead full, aye!"

"Tactical, make sure we're—"

"Incoming! Enemy ship has fired two— No, three missiles!"

"Settle down and focus, everyone!" Carmichael said. "Time to range?"

"Missiles will close within point defense range in...forty-seven minutes."

"Missiles appear to be a variant of the Shrike, sir," his OPS officer said. "CIC says the telemetry stream is encrypted, but the tracking radar signatures are the same."

"Start jamming them, maybe we'll get lucky," Carmichael said. "Activate point defense batteries and authorize the computer for autonomous fire."

"Point defense is armed and ready, Captain. ECM active but no effect."

Carmichael felt a sudden, inexplicable calm come over him. The two ships had traded shots and were now separating. Either his missiles would get through, theirs would get through, or both would be successful, but now there was nothing left to do but wait.

"One of their missiles has lost guidance...it's going ballistic," the tactical officer said. "The other two are still tracking for us."

"They got one of our missiles, sir," OPS said. "Still tracking the second for— Impact! Second missile hit her amidships!"

"Tell CIC I want battle damage assessment immediately,"

Carmichael said. "Helm, all ahead emergency and shallow out our course. Let her run."

"Safety locks disengaged, engines to full power, aye."

The deck rumbled in warning as the engines were pushed up past their maximum rated power input to take as much as the reactors could deliver. The number on the main display said they were currently running at one hundred and twelve percent of maximum. He couldn't risk running her this hard for too long so early in the battle, but he also didn't think getting hit with one or two nuclear missiles would do them any good either.

"CIC confirms kill," OPS said. "The enemy ship has broken up into three pieces. Fourteen lifeboats were launched." Carmichael had a momentary sadistic thought to target the lifeboats in retaliation for the ESA taking out two unarmed supply barges, but quickly stuffed it back down. The crew watched tensely as all but one of the missiles chasing them failed, detonating well short. The last was easily collected by the *Blake*'s aft point defense batteries.

"Coms! Tell CIC I want a Bluebird dispatch sent to the *Jericho* letting Admiral Wolfe know we've been engaged and were forced to defend ourselves," he said. "Tell him the task force is still intact and patrolling outside the orbit of the fourth planet, awaiting further orders."

"Aye, sir."

"So, this is happening," his XO said quietly. "We're going to war with the ESA so soon after the Darshik."

"It would appear so, Commander," Carmichael said. "What happens after this is up to the policy makers. We need to focus on what we can control."

"That being?"

"Winning this battle...at all costs."

16

"The provincial governor would like a word with you, Admiral. He's waiting on an open video channel right now."

"Commander Trane, you have the bridge until I get back," Jackson sighed, annoyed at the timing of the governor finally getting back to him. "Keep an eye on Captain Carmichael's formation and interrupt me if anything else happens there."

"Aye, sir."

The *Jericho* had made it down to orbit over the planet Odmena without too much issue, only having to alter course once to avoid one of the small stealth attack ships that popped up on their radar but didn't pursue them. Now that the *Blake* had drawn blood, the ESA fleet was acting more cautious despite having such large numerical advantage. The smaller attack boats seemed to be corralling the *Jericho* rather than moving in to attack, while the cruisers that had been moving to intercept them were now on a pursuit course, flogging their primitive RDS drives to try and match the battleship's impressive acceleration down to the planet.

CENTCOM had been adamant that Task Force Vega maintain its defensive posture even in the face of having two ships destroyed without provocation. Jackson had respectfully told Chief of Staff Pitt and Fleet Admiral Lazonic, the Starfleet Chief of Operations, that he wouldn't allow them to run his mission via Bluebird dispatches. He was the ranking officer in the system, and it was his call on how they would proceed. He's assured them he currently had no intention of actively pursuing ESA ships, but he also wouldn't let another Federation ship sit passively while attacked.

"Governor Novak," Jackson greeted the scowling face on the monitor in his office. "Thank you for agreeing to discuss the situation face to face."

"Admiral Wolfe, your reputation proceeds you," Novak said. "You've been here less than two weeks and already starships are burning in space above us."

"Governor, I'm not a politician nor am I a diplomat. I've been tasked with maintaining a Federation presence in this system until our diplomatic envoy arrives or you officially secede and declare Odmena a member system of the Eastern Star Alliance. To that end, I will defend both my own ships and the civilians of Odmena against any further ESA aggression. As you no doubt already know, we've already lost two ships in an unprovoked attack. So, unless you are officially informing me that this is ESA sovereign space, I'm afraid my task force is here to stay."

"Blunt," Novak grunted. It was obvious to Wolfe that the locals had been playing the Fed against the ESA to see what sort of sweetheart deal they could get. When he called that bluff, the governor had become visibly uncomfortable, obviously not authorized to declare the system as an ESA protectorate and, therefore, still a member of the United Terran Federation. As such, he had no authority to ask a Federation military ship to leave.

"I'm not authorized or willing to discuss our current negotiations with you, Admiral," he continued. "The purpose of this talk is to impress upon you our desire to not have any more bloodshed in our skies. We've asked Admiral Kohl to do the same and hope that during this tense time, you'll both keep your missiles and guns pointed away from each other."

"As I said, Governor, I wish nothing more than a peaceful resolution to this, handled by the civilian representatives," Jackson said. "However, I will not tolerate any further attacks upon my ships. Be sure to pass that on to the ESA representative."

"Good day, Admiral," Novak said, not quite sneering, and killed the channel. Jackson stared at the blank monitor for a moment, running the conversation through his mind.

"Trapp!" he shouted.

"Yes, sir?" The intel analyst had been hovering in the small foyer attached to the workspace.

"Take a break and have your intel friends in CIC look up an ESA admiral named Kohl. Tell them they're authorized to use Bluebird if they need to contact the New Sierra Archives for the information. I need it ASAP."

"Admiral Kohl...got it," she said, punching notes on her tile. "Is this for your eyes only, sir?"

"No," Jackson said. "Once you get a summary report ready, send it up to the bridge and then disseminate it to the task force. Kohl is the officer commanding the Alliance fleet in this system. Novak let it slip while he was putting me in my place."

"I'll start right away, Admiral." She took a second to log out of the terminal she'd been working at and rushed out of the office.

Now that he had a name, he could likely run through the archives and make an educated guess which ship Kohl was on since the Alliance fleet now had their ident beacons chirping away. All of the cruisers they'd brought were once Terran Confederation ships, now modified with RDS and upgraded weapons, and the full build specs of each were sitting in the *Jericho's* servers.

Being able to directly threaten the flagship or focus communication efforts on a single, specific person would be much more effective than broadcasting vague messages to the entire system, but Jackson wanted to know more about Kohl before he went about it. Thanks to Bluebird, he could try and reach out to the few active officers in Starfleet who had been around long enough that might know him and give some insight into his command style, reactions, and general psychological makeup.

"Admiral Wolfe to the bridge. Admiral Wolfe to the bridge."

Jackson stabbed the intercom button embedded in his desk. "On my way."

"Sir, Captain Carmichael is concerned he may be swarmed under if he maintains their current course," Trane said when Jackson walked back onto the bridge. "He's asking what you want him to do."

Jackson studied the main display for a moment, the left side having a top-down representation of the Odmena System with the planetary orbits in blue, enemy ships in red, and his own forces in green. Carmichael had correctly bunched his ships up into a tight diamond formation so that they'd be able to overlap point-defense coverage and not leave the rear as exposed as a traditional phalanx would. He'd been cruising along just inside the orbit of the fifth planet while Alliance ships herded them along, keeping just out of range to their aft.

The problem was that the enemy was already deployed, so Carmichael was flying into formations of ships that were sitting ahead, waiting on him. He'd still been trying to avoid direct engagement, and each time he'd opted to move his ships further down the well. Jackson understood that Carmichael wouldn't want to move further out because it would make it that much harder for him to provide protection for the flagship, but at the distances they were dealing with, he'd not be able to arrive in time to offer any sort of help anyway.

He looked at the telemetry streams coming in over the Link and saw that his subordinate wasn't pushing his ships too hard, leaving plenty of engine power in reserve for emergency maneuvering. Smart. Now, Jackson had to decide if he wanted to move his ships further away from most of the danger, or bring them down to the planet through a gauntlet of ESA attack boats and an enemy commander with unknown goals.

"Tell him to move the task force up and away from the engagement," he said finally. "Push out near the orbit of the seventh planet and loiter there. Make sure he's maintaining enough relative velocity that if I need him down here, I'm not waiting on him to accelerate back up to speed. I don't want to precipitate anything while we're in orbit over the planet and any aggressive moves on his part may cause them to try and take out the *Jericho* first."

"Relaying orders, sir," the second watch OPS officer said when Trane nodded to her.

"We'll be completely isolated from the rest of our forces, sir," Trane said quietly.

"We already are, Commander," Jackson said. "Reinforcements are inbound as we speak, so let's not precipitate a full-scale battle before they arrive."

"Reinforcements?" Trane frowned. "I wasn't aware CENTCOM was deploying any other ships to this system."

"The move orders didn't come through normal channels," Jackson said. "Is that a problem?"

"I... No, of course not, sir." Trane flushed and seemed irritated that he was out of the loop. "When will they arrive?"

"Soon. Probably," Jackson said, watching Trane closely. "As I said...not normal channels."

"Yes, sir," Trane said, now composed.

Jackson didn't say anything further, but his mind was firmly on the fact that he had a suicided captain on a slab down in the infirmary and a young intelligence officer telling him that someone aboard the *Jericho* had secretly been firing off com drones before he'd arrived. For all he knew, it could have been Hardy communicating with a mistress on some other ship or planet. That *had* been known to happen from time to time in the Fleet. Or, more concerning, Hardy could have been a traitor that was communicating his plans and movements to the enemy. If that was the case, what was the likelihood he was working alone?

Lieutenant Samantha Trapp was completely absorbed with her own thoughts as she walked down the port access tube on her way to CIC. So much so that she didn't notice when someone walked up behind her and grabbed her by the elbow.

"You have a minute?"

She yelped and yanked her arm away, turning to see Ensign Weiskel standing there. He was a med tech that had been pursuing her from practically the moment she boarded the *Jericho* back on New Sierra. She'd tried to make it clear—nicely at first—that she had no interest, but he was dogged.

"Now isn't a good time," she said. "I'm busy and—"

"You're working as Admiral Wolfe's aide now, right?" Weiskel asked, looking around the tube and trying to pull her aside. She looked closer at him and realized he might not be there to try and proposition her. "You can get information to him directly?"

"I can," she said carefully.

"Tell him that Captain Hardy wasn't a suicide," Weiskel whispered. "Commander Jeong found that the ligature marks from the strap were done postmortem. I overheard him discussing it with the XO. I think Trane has convinced him to just go ahead report it as the captain killed himself."

"Why?" Trapp asked.

"I don't know," Weiskel hissed. "But I could tell it was a conversation that wasn't meant to be overheard. I couldn't hear everything they were saying, but Commander Jeong didn't seem too happy once the XO had left."

"And the official report?"

"Being delayed per Jeong's orders. I don't think he wants to go against Trane, but his ethics won't let him falsify his findings. So, he's just going to sit on it and do nothing."

"Why are you telling me this?"

"Seriously?" Weiskel asked. "If the captain wasn't a suicide, but someone made it look like it was—"

"Then someone murdered Captain Hardy," she finished, now understanding why Weiskel looked so scared. "This is serious."

"You'll tell the admiral to look into it? Some shady shit has been happening on this boat since before we made dock at New Sierra last, and it could have something to do with this Odmena mess."

"I'll tell him," Trapp promised, making a mental note to begin pinging her contacts on the lower decks to see what else others may have seen lately that looked out of place.

"I have to go. I'm back on duty in a few. Be careful."

Weiskel disappeared leaving her feeling both nervous and paranoid. If Hardy was murdered, could it have been for something personal or did it have something to do with all the falsified records she'd been finding with his access codes? She continued down the tube to the lifts, now feeling like she had a target on her back.

Trapp cleared her way through CIC quickly and made her way back to one of the dedicated Bluebird coffins that also had a local network terminal so she could access the *Jericho's* archive. Her initial search on the local servers showed that Admiral Vadim Kohl had been a lieutenant serving in Eighth Fleet, the numbered fleet operated by the old Warsaw Alliance, as a tactical officer on a Nimrod-class heavy cruiser during the Phage War. By the end of the conflict, he'd been promoted to captain and given command of the TFS *Huntsman*, an aging destroyer that had predated the Raptor-class ships flown by Seventh Fleet.

Like the Asianic Union's Third Fleet, Eighth Fleet had spent most of the war in a logistical or reserve role since their ships were considered too outdated to risk in a fight with the powerful Phage combat units. Despite his quick promotion to commanding his own vessel, there was little regarding Kohl's exploits other than a generic list of assignments and ship deployments.

The rest of the entries in the ship's archive for Vadim Kohl were just as unhelpful. He was listed in half a dozen after-action reports as having also been in the area, but nothing regarding his specific role in battles or what tactics he was known to employ. Trapp dutifully read through each one before logging into the Bluebird terminal with the credentials Admiral Wolfe had given her—credentials that would make the people at CENTCOM answer her request much more quickly than if she'd used her own—and sent a series of queries out about how someone as relatively unknown as Kohl ended up commanding an entire ESA armada.

"I wonder," she murmured to herself, using the higher tier command credentials she'd been provided to try and look at the Bluebird access logs. As she'd assumed, it also wanted a biometric reading for full access, which she couldn't provide. But it did give her a level of access beyond what her own analyst login did. She could look at the time stamps for each outbound message and whose credentials had been used to send them, but the message body, length, and recipient were all still masked.

She started specific searches in the log, looking at when Admiral Wolfe had sent outbound messages, Commander Trane, the *Jericho's* Chief Engineer, Commander McKenna, and the expected large number of entries for Captain Hardy. What wasn't expected, however, was that Hardy had apparently sent over thirty-six messages over the system *after* his death. Trapp double checked to confirm that they were from Hardy's personal access codes and not some generic ship-wide code that had his name attached. She pursed her lips and looked at the damning evidence sitting in the log. She'd been unaware that the higher access levels would have system information not available to all users.

The incoming message alert pinged on her terminal, interrupting her ruminations, and giving her something to focus on other than her immediate problems. As he'd predicted, Wolfe's access codes had made CENTCOM Central Archives jump through hoops to get the information she'd wanted. It was slow going through the low-bandwidth Bluebird connection, but the more complete background of Admiral Vadim Kohl came streaming across thousands of lightyears and onto her terminal. What she read there didn't fill her with hope that the Odmena situation would be resolved peacefully. She took one last look at the log before backing out of the terminal and closing it down.

One problem at a time, working big to small. She could come back to this later. Hardy was dead so the problem wasn't going anywhere.

17

"One of Wolfe's ships just took out a cruiser, but it was after Kohl had destroyed two of his supply ships *and* the cruiser was making overtly aggressive moves towards Task Force Vega's formation. I'm not sure it's anything we can use."

"I read the report as well," Zhang said. "I'm afraid our original strategy may well be off the table now thanks to Admiral Kohl's overly-aggressive execution."

"It's frustrating that the flow of information is one-way. We can get reports from the battlefield, but there's no way for us to send word to Kohl to instruct him to temper his tactics and get back on mission."

"Councilman, I think we may have to begin making plans for a graceful exit strategy," Zhang said delicately. "If Kohl ends up making the ESA look like the aggressor in a system that is still technically part of the United Terran Federation, we will have failed utterly, no matter if Jackson Wolfe survives or not."

"Nonsense!" Councilman Makov almost shouted. He quickly regained his composure. "This can still be salvaged, but more extreme measure will need to be taken. I think you know what I mean."

"There will be no going back from this," Zhang warned. "I feel that it's too risky at this juncture. We can abandon the Odmena operations and approach this from a different angle without wasting so many lives and ships."

"We've been trying half-measures now for years, and it's gotten us nowhere. We can't afford to wait any longer. Every day the Federation is regaining its strength and, soon, we will have nothing to threaten them with. The time is now."

"Very well," Zhang sighed. "I will send word."

"I'll be in touch."

The councilman left Zhang's office, leaving the administrator feeling sick and defeated. When he'd first been approached about the plan, he'd been hesitant. Only once they'd threatened his new family had he given the cabal access to his network of contacts and his knowledge of the internal workings on New Sierra. Now that the Odmena operation seemed to be leaking out from around the edges, and they were losing control of their carefully scripted plan, he wondered how much longer they could go on before the Council caught wind and began inquiries into who authorized such aggressive actions against a Fed system.

Once it came to light that a small number of Councilmembers and a few bureaucrats took it upon themselves to launch a military campaign that cost the Alliance ships and standing at the negotiating table, there would be no place for him to hide. The more politically connected members of the cabal would throw people like him to the wolves. He would be the public face of a conspiracy while the ones actually pulling the levers would, at worst, be forced to resign their seats. Zhang, on the other hand, would be lucky if he just spent the rest of his life in prison.

"Maybe Mr. Anders is bringing me an escape option," Zhang said to the ceiling, laughing bitterly as he realized he was screwed no matter what he did. He allowed things to go too far, for too long, to alert the Council of what was actually happening so now he had little choice but to ride the storm out to the end. He hoped in vain that sociopath, Kohl, didn't kill too many more before it was all said and done.

"You have ten minutes, Lieutenant," Jackson said as he sat down.

"Yes, sir," Lieutenant Trapp said.

It was late into second watch and Jackson had called her to the small meeting room that was directly off the bridge. The battleship was in high orbit over the planet Odmena and was being shadowed by three ESA cruisers above and behind them. It seemed the reality of three destroyed military starships in their system had just sunk in for the local government, and they were now demanding a cessation of hostilities and asking the Alliance ships to break off and disengage from the Federation fleet for the time being. Predictably, the Alliance fleet ignored these requests and continued to harass Wolfe's task force. In fact, half a dozen of the small attack boats that had been hidden in the system were converging on the Alliance formation.

"I've compiled a short brief about Admiral Vadim Kohl as you asked," she began, flicking a gesture on her tile and sending a picture of a younger officer in an old Confederation uniform on the wall monitor.

"Kohl graduated from the Pinnacle Starfleet Academy on the planet Waygate in the Warsaw Alliance enclave, that's the same planet where he was born and raised. He accepted a commission into Eighth Fleet and served in what his performance reviews indicate was an adequate, bordering on mediocre capacity. During the Phage War, Eighth Fleet was mostly sidelined since their ships could neither keep up with the more modern First and Fourth Fleet ships, nor did they pack much of a punch. Kohl spent the entire war sitting on the bridge of a ship that never saw combat."

"If the Phage had never showed up, it's likely an underachiever like that would have been pawned off on Black Fleet, such as the custom was back then," Jackson said, looking at the below average performance evals that were scrolling across the monitor.

"Once the Warsaw Alliance worlds broke off along with the Asianic Union," Trapp continued. "Kohl saw an opportunity to make a fresh start and reinvented himself as a student of war, writing paper after paper for the Kocyk War College on New Berlin...his favorite topic being an analytical look at the tactics and philosophy of Captain Jackson Wolfe."

"I think I see why you asked to brief me in private."

"Since your name was a hot topic within the newly minted ESA government, Kohl was asked to come to the capital and give talks. He began rubbing elbows with the right people and, before long, started getting promotions and opportunities from those connections. Even while he was providing the Alliance Council red meat about your exploits, many of which he fabricated, he was also modeling himself as a commanding officer in your image. The end result has been a fleet master that tries to emulate the caricature of you that the ESA has spent years building. He's needlessly aggressive, he throws away ships and spacers recklessly to forward non-critical mission goals, and he routinely ignores orders and guidance from Alliance Fleet Command to pursue his own agenda."

"That almost sounds like what the Federation fleet brass thinks of me," Jackson said sourly. "So, how does someone like this keep his command? The ESA is not a pack of incompetent fools, why hasn't he been removed? It's not like it would take much digging to figure out he's a fraud."

"Part of it is the power of his political connections, part of it is that he was propped up early as a hero to the people," Trapp said. "By the time their command caught wind that he might not have been the expert he billed himself as, he was already embedded into the capital's power structure to the point they couldn't conveniently remove him. He's become a figurehead to the public for the Alliance military, their own Jackson Wolfe who makes the Federation quake in their boots."

"What a pile of shit!" Jackson groaned, leaning back and rubbing his temples. Trapp jumped at the rare outburst from the normally stoic admiral, seeming to be unsure if she should press on or wait for him to tell her to continue.

"Okay, I have a good handle on who this guy is now," Jackson said. "Let's move on. What else do you have?"

"The two people I pulled out of intel that I trust still haven't determined who was using the captain's Bluebird access codes, but we've figured out who they've been talking to," she said. "It's to a Bluebird station that's registered to the CIS. I can't really reach out to them and ask who it is and what they're doing without throwing up dozens of red flags, sir."

"Give me the information, and I'll take care of that,"

Jackson promised. He stood up and smoothed out his uniform. Since he was taking video channel requests from various officials on the planet, he was wearing dress blacks complete with all ribbons and devices rather than utilities like the rest of the crew.

"We'll keep on it, sir,"

"You'd better. I need something actionable, and soon. This system is about to blow, and I need to know if I have a traitor on my ship before it does."

Jackson stalked out of the conference room and back onto the bridge, nodding to Commander Trane and checking the main display for any changes in the enemy's posture.

"Captain Carmichael reports that he's moved into open, uncontested space, Admiral," Trane yawned. "The enemy cruisers have given up pursuit and are now paralleling the task force further down the well."

"They'll run hard to keep up so that if Carmichael begins to come back down into the system, they'll be in position for an intercept," Jackson said. "Go get some rack time, Commander. You can relieve me at the start of first watch. I have two more scheduled vid-cons with representatives from the planetary government and the Fed delegation here."

"Hopefully, they begin dropping off with burnt out RDS field emitters trying to chase the *Blake* around the outer orbits," Trane said. "Hope it's a quiet watch, sir."

"Get some rest, Commander."

Jackson took his seat, checked the ship's vitals and the enemy positions one more time, and then began entering a series of messages on his tile to go out over a Bluebird channel. He took the station identification that Lieutenant Trapp had given him and plugged it in to a message going to both Pike and Celesta Wright. Both would understand his desire for discretion and would try to get him the information without alerting CIS that he suspected one of theirs. The fact that a dead man's access codes were being used to send messages to someone in the CIS *and* that person was deleting the logs afterwards made it clear to Jackson that something was amiss on the ship.

His ship.

Should he even be commanding the *Jericho* right now? Would it be smarter for him to remain distant from the operations of a single ship and spend his time in CIC directing the task force? Maybe Jillian was right, and he was unwilling to accept the fact that as an admiral his role had changed. Commanding a single ship was what captains did, not flag officers. Logically, he knew what the right thing to do was, so why was he so hesitant to turn over the ship to Commander Trane? Pride? Fear?

"Sir, the smaller attack boats are closing in on the formation of enemy cruisers. There are...eight of them now," Lieutenant Easton reported from tactical. "CIC says that there is a lot of encrypted com traffic happening up there."

"Com traffic, or could it be a command and control signal?" Jackson asked. "Are those smaller ships manned, or are we looking at a bunch of drones?"

"Unclear, Admiral," Easton said after a moment of talking on his headset. "Intel thinks you could be right given the nature of the signal, but they've not been able to crack the encryption yet."

"Have them analyzing the movements of the smaller ships. Lots of minute course and speed corrections would indicate it's not a human driving it," Jackson said, putting away his tile and looking at the main display with renewed interest. He'd spent some time as the director of a project that dealt with AI systems, and while the project principle was a computer of alien origins, all of the machines humans designed all seemed to have similar telltale attributes. Some were more obvious than others, but he suspected the ESA was far behind the Federation when it came to deployable AI systems, and that the boats he was looking at on the radar returns were probably semi-autonomous.

The tension of the prolonged engagement was beginning to wear him down. They'd been in the system for weeks, had lost two ships already to suspected enemy fire, and now the waiting was fraying nerves. Jackson felt himself becoming numb to it as he did those many years ago when the Phage had chased the *Blue Jacket* for days on end, toying with him.

CENTCOM had been clear that they wanted him to remain on defensive footing. When he'd told them that he had strong evidence the Alliance fleet had taken out two noncombatants, they had expressed the expected perfunctory sympathy but told him not to needlessly engage. Each time Task Force Vega's ships ignored aggression or tried to flee, the enemy seemed to become more emboldened. The cruisers pacing the *Jericho* had little hope of taking the battleship down on their own, but they seemed confident Jackson wouldn't turn his guns on them just for chasing him too closely.

Then there was the odd silence from the opposing fleet. The *Heart of Xian* had stopped squawking its ident beacon and had disappeared among the other ESA ships in the area, so Jackson had no idea where the Saber-class heavy cruiser was other than *not* one of the ships pursuing him.

The ship going silent only reinforced his suspicion that Kohl was aboard that ship.

"CIC says they've caught some atmospheric venting from the smaller ships, Admiral," Easton broke into his thoughts. "They also say they analyzed the ships' flight patterns and feel confident stating that they're manned vessels."

"That's preferable, at least," Jackson said. "The enemy will be less likely to send swarms of them in on a suicide run at us if there is crew aboard. Keep trying to jam the encrypted streams and let's see where this goes."

"Aye, sir...ECM active."

"Sir the cruisers are starting to fan out and are closing the gap to get in above us," Ensign Flynn reported from the OPS station. "The smaller attack boats are bunching up and moving down into a lower orbit, still trailing behind us." Jackson's gut clenched as he watched the formation shift, recognizing it for what it was.

"This is it," he said. "Sound the general alert. Tactical, bring WEPS up to full power and—"

"WEPS reactors are cold, sir," Easton said, looking confused. "They were shut down. It says two days ago."

"On whose authority?!"

"No annotation, sir. I didn't get turnover on a change so I assumed they were still hot. My apolo—"

"No time for that," Jackson said. "Get missile firing solutions for the three cruisers and activate the point defense batteries."

"They're moving into a higher orbit directly above us. We'll have to shift our orientation to bring the missile tubes to bear, sir. The Shrikes can't fire and reverse course away from the planet to get at them."

"Just make sure you have a hard target lock, and then

we'll worry about putting iron on them," Jackson said. Now that it was apparent Kohl was about to make a move on the *Jericho*, all of the tension and uncertainty evaporated and calm feeling poured down his neck like cool water. This he understood. This he was good at.

"Nav! I want running course corrections fed to the helm in case we need to run. Make sure he has a vector for a transfer orbit on his display at all times. Helm, we may need to inertially decouple and move the ship independent of her trajectory to fire the forward tubes. Be ready when I call for it."

"Aye, sir!"

"OPS, tell Engineering I want WEPS at full power ASAP and then let Chief Engineer McKenna know that I will want to know who authorized the shutdown. As soon as the reactors are hot start pumping plasma into the containment cells," Jackson said. He paced the bridge slowly, confident they had a few hours until Kohl's ships were in position and they tried to spring their attack. Normally, he'd try and outrun them, lead them away from the planet so that there was no collateral damage to the surface, but the cruisers above him had cut off that course of action. Now, he'd have to wait for their opening move and then react.

"Coms, tell the defense force coordinator on the surface that the ESA fleet is becoming increasingly aggressive and that we'll try to make sure they don't fire towards the planet. Send the same message to the Federation reps down there, too."

"Yes, sir."

"Admiral, the attack boats are stacking up behind us, one on top of the other," Easton said.

"It's an outdated and obvious tactic," Jackson said. "The

cruisers will keep us pinned down while the gun boats come at us one at a time, never giving us a shot at anything other than the one at the bottom of the stack. Fortunately for us, the Hornet missiles we carry make this an obsolete maneuver. Get me firing solutions for each individual small ship, and then let the computer assign a missile to each."

"Aye, sir."

"OPS, get everyone in their restraints and tell first watch to stand fast. We don't have time for a personnel change. This is happening quick if it's happening at all. Let's just hope this is just another feint this close to the planet."

The klaxons began wailing, and the automated instructions telling the crew where to be echoed through the ship. Jackson split his attention between the smaller ships stacking up for an attack run and the three cruisers keeping pace above him, making plans for how to get the big battleship away from it all if the shooting started.

The *Jericho's* drives were immensely powerful, but they were still being asked to push four-hundred *thousand* tons of starship up away from the pull of a planet. She couldn't just pull straight away at their current velocity and would need to accelerate around at least twice to gain enough altitude to break orbit. The cruisers sitting thirty thousand kilometers above them, however, had more options to maneuver and block any moves he might make.

He'd moved the *Jericho* down into low orbit over Odmena because he wanted to make sure the Federation had a presence over the planet rather than hanging back while Alliance ships flew through its sky. It was a subtle psychological reminder for the government on the surface who they were still beholden to and who was stronger in spite of the ESA's entreaties for them to break off.

What Jackson hadn't counted on was an Alliance Fleet

commander that was willing to put civilians in harm's way and fire on noncombatants, erasing centuries of unspoken agreement when it came to interstellar warfare. Now, instead of projecting strength, he looked reckless and callous as the *Jericho* was now putting the population at risk. All he could do was wait them out and see how serious they were.

"WEPS reactors have been restarted, sir," Flynn said. "Engineering says they'll be clear to ramp to full power within the hour."

"Sir, Odmena Orbital Authority is demanding we break orbit and vacate the area," the com officer said over the noise of everyone talking at once. "They're making the same request of the ESA ships." Jackson thought it over for a moment, about to tell his com officer to remind the Odmena government they didn't have the authority to demand that he leave. But he was here to represent the Federation *and* protect civilians, and staying where he was conflicted with both of those goals.

"New plan," he said. "Helm! All ahead flank. Get us out of here. Bounce to transfer orbit Bravo-Two and hold there until you have breakaway velocity. Tactical! Coordinate with the DSO and look alive. We'll be coming up right into those cruisers."

"Engines ahead flank, aye!" the helmsman called out, pushing the engines up to full power. The battleship shuddered slightly as the RDS shoved her ahead, quickly running out from under the three cruisers above them. Jackson knew that if they were at all competent, they'd simply come about and wait for him as the *Jericho* came around the planet.

"The smaller ships are reacting," Easton said. "They're trying to— Collision! One of the ships descended into the one below it!" Jackson watched as the part of the main display showing the formation enlarged so he could see the enhanced visual and radar data. It had been a hard hit, and the ships were piled too closely together.

"Another impact! The second ship has collided with the one below it...three ships total damaged. The others are peeling off and thrusting for higher orbit."

"The damaged ships?" Jackson asked.

"Two are adrift and still descending, the other is still under power, but the engines appear to be damaged," Flynn said. "The third is also venting reactor coolant."

"Coms, tell the planet they have incoming. Make sure they're aware of those ships," Jackson said. "Tactical, focus on the cruisers above us. Those smaller ships are no longer a threat."

"Sir, the cruisers are clearing the area," Easton said. "They're shifting up to a polar orbit that will make it difficult to hit them, but also make it just as hard for them to fire down on us."

"What are they up to?" Jackson mused.

He watched as escape capsules began firing out and away from the three stricken ships as the *Jericho's* powerful optics tracked their descent. The crew members were doomed. The small pods weren't as robust as full-sized lifeboats and didn't have the necessary heat shielding or landing system to survive atmospheric entry. They were designed to be recovered in space, which might have been possible if the crew had ejected as soon as the mishap had occurred. Now, they were going to burn up once Odmena's gravity pulled them into the atmosphere.

"One of the cruisers is sending out a wideband transmission, Admiral," the com officer reported. "They're claiming we shot at their ships before departing the area."

"Ignore them," Jackson ordered. "We'll be losing contact soon as we cross around the other side of the planet. I want everything reacquired quickly when we come back around. Make sure we're recording this whole incident on optics and radar."

Within the hour, the *Jericho* was over the horizon and lost line of sight with the Alliance ships. They were still getting telemetry streams from Odmena's automated orbital control satellites so they were able to observe the smaller attack ships hitting the upper atmosphere in near-real time. Jackson hoped against hope that the ships might sharpen their descent once they slammed into the denser stratosphere and splashed down into the planet's single, enormous ocean. From what he was seeing on the main display, however, it didn't look like they'd get that lucky.

"First ship is breaking up in the upper atmosphere, sir," Flynn said. "CIC is in contact with one of the dirtside observation posts. The Odmenans are saying the third is going to enter at a shallower angle."

"Coms, broadcast a wideband message to every ship in this system. Tell Admiral Kohl that I want his ships to disengage and retreat back past the orbit of the fourth planet immediately," Jackson seethed. It was now clear there were going to be civilian casualties when the debris from the three ships began hitting the continent. Odmena had some dense population zones, so there was a chance the death toll could be high.

When they flew back around the terminator, however, nothing could have prepared them for what they'd see.

The optics washed out for a split second, and then the multi-spectral imagers showed an explosion on a scale Jackson didn't think was possible, and it was within Odmena's atmosphere. That explosion was followed by two more in quick succession, so violent that the shock waves could be clearly seen as clouds were burned away and everything was flattened before it. Jackson couldn't comprehend what he was seeing and the silence on the bridge told him his crew felt much the same.

"That was no nuke. What the fuck was that?" he asked hoarsely.

"It's...it's...uh... CIC says they're not sure," Easton said. Ensign Flynn had leaned over and was retching onto the deck. "They don't think it was a nuke either. They...they're working on it."

"OPS!"

More retching and gagging.

"Ensign Flynn! I need you at your post and functional!" Jackson barked. He felt for the kid, but he couldn't afford to have him freeze up.

"I'm here, sir."

"Where did...whatever the hell that was...where did they hit?"

"One ocean impact, two inland," Flynn read off the running report being piped up to his station from CIC and Intel Section. "One of the inland detonations was only two kilometers outside of Odmena's third largest city...four million people. The ocean hit sent up a tsunami that will wipe out three coastal settlements. No time for them to evacuate."

"Those *motherfuckers!!*" Lieutenant Easton raged.

"Calm yourself or be relieved, Mr. Easton," Jackson said. "Where are the Alliance cruisers now?"

He was so enraged that he felt as if he was having an out-of-body experience. The general sense of numbness was so complete even tactile sensations seemed dulled. He'd witnessed entire planets being devoured by the Phage, but this seemed an atrocity on a whole new level somehow.

"They're still coming onto a polar orbit, Admiral," Easton said. "They're at full power and gaining altitude. I think they're going to try and break away once they're on the far side of the planet."

"Coms, any response from the Alliance fleet?"

"No, sir.

"The other attack boats?"

"Already cleared the area, sir," Flynn said. "They began to withdraw right after the first ship-to-ship collision in their formation."

"I know what you think we should do right now," Jackson said to the faces looking at him, "but we can't. If we bring down those three cruisers while they're still in orbit, the wreckage will fall to the surface. Let's not compound this problem. Helm, get us into a high elliptical orbit. I need speed and altitude to work with. Coms! Tell CIC I want a Bluebird dispatch sent to Captain Carmichael. Tell him it's open season on any Alliance ship in this system. He's clear to execute at his discretion, but I want him working his way back downhill to us. After that, I want a detailed report sent to CENTCOM letting them know what's happened here. Understood?"

"Understood, Admiral!"

Jackson compartmentalized things in his mind so that he could focus on his responsibilities. There was nothing he could do for Odmena. His task force consisted of only warships with a limited number of ship-to-surface shuttles and no resources to speak of that would be of any help.

His comlink chirped in his pocket, distracting him for a moment. He read through the message on the screen twice before looking up and waving Gunnery Sergeant Barton onto the bridge.

"Sir?"

"Do you have any new friends in the detachment that you trust?" Jackson whispered to his only real confidant aboard the ship.

"A few," Barton whispered back.

"Go get them, and then I want you to come up to Officer Country and arrest Commander Trane," Jackson said, pulling off a physical encrypted passkey that had been hanging around his neck and discreetly handed it to Barton. "This will let you bypass any of the hatch locks on this ship. Grab him quickly and quietly. Don't let him get to a terminal or even his comlink. Put him down in the detachment's holding cell. Once I talk to the master at arms, we can move him to the brig." To his credit, and displaying one of the traits Jackson liked most about Barton, the gunnery sergeant just nodded without wasting time with questions or acting shocked.

"I'll ping your comlink when we have him secured, sir," he said. He looked around to make sure the rest of the bridge crew was minding its own business before unholstering his sidearm and passing it to the admiral. "I'll grab my backup on the way below deck. You keep this one on you, sir."

"Get going," Jackson said, pocketing the heavy pistol. It didn't fit worth a damn in his dress blacks, but he doubted anyone would notice or care.

"Sir, there are people on the orbital platforms around Odmena who are asking what's happening," Flynn said.

"Can we broadcast from here?" Jackson asked, not quite familiar with every aspect of the *Juggernaut*-class's bridge com suite.

"Yes, sir," the com officer spoke up. She pointed to a green circle that appeared illuminated on the deck in front of the command chair. "Stand there, and we can begin when you're ready." Jackson moved to the indicated spot and nodded to her.

"You're live, sir...system-wide broadcast," she said softly.

"This is Admiral Wolfe, broadcasting live from the TFS *Jericho* currently in orbit over the planet Odmena," he began, his mind racing to corral his flitting thoughts into a coherent message. "We've just witnessed an atrocity unlike any we've seen since the days of the Phage War. The Eastern Star Alliance has, through design or negligence, hit the planet with an unknown weapon of immense power. To those on the planet who can hear me, to those civilians on ships and orbital platforms still in the system...we will do everything we can to provide help. The Federation will dispatch ships from nearby systems capable of pulling survivors off the surface and rendering aid as needed.

"Unfortunately, none of my ships have much to offer you in the immediate aftermath. That won't stop us from trying, but be aware that our capabilities in that regard are limited." He paused for a moment to collect himself.

"To Admiral Vadim Kohl and the rest of the Alliance Fleet...you would be wise to withdraw from this system. You have committed an act of aggression that can only be interpreted as a declaration of war. You will get no further warning. Admiral Wolfe, out."

"You're clear, Admiral."

"Thank you. Please have Lieutenant Trapp come up to the bridge," Jackson said.

"Right away, sir."

It was twenty minutes later when Barton messaged him.

. . .

XO secure in detachment holding cell. He's pissed.

Wolfe realized he couldn't leave the bridge since he'd just had the only other person he could leave in command with enemy ships so close arrested. The only option was to have the ship's XO dragged all the way up to the bridge in front of the crew, or keep him on ice in the Marine detachment's holding pen until the *Jericho* was clear of the immediate threat. Neither option was particularly appealing.

If Trane really was working for the other side, it was unlikely he did so alone aboard a ship as big as the *Jericho*. Jackson had already gone through one mutiny with open fighting in the corridors in his career, and he wasn't in a big hurry to repeat the experience. The first time he'd been forced to shoot a spacer with a replica of an ancient Colt 1911 .45 pistol his friend had made him...not a pleasant memory.

"You needed to see me, Admiral?"

"Yes, Lieutenant. I've just had Commander Trane detained based largely on the info you provided," Jackson said, watching her closely. "You don't look pleased by this."

"I'm just...surprised, sir," Lieutenant Trapp said. "The information I gave you was preliminary—"

"I have no time for this," Jackson cut her off, waving to the main monitor where scenes of the devastation on Odmena were shown in individual windows. Trapp gasped as she looked upon the reality of the ESA's attack. "You need to get your evidence together so I can turn all this over to the master at arms. You also need to get a statement from Chief Engineer McKenna regarding Trane authorizing the shutdown of the WEPS reactors without clearing it with me."

"I'll do that, sir," she said to Jackson's retreating back.

He had to shake off the shock of what he'd just witnessed and get a workable strategy for the rest of the operation. Barring word from CENTCOM telling him to retreat, he had to assume the Odmena System was still in play despite Kohl's attempt to depopulate the planet itself. All pretense of finding a peaceful solution were out. It was now a gunfight, and Jackson was badly outnumbered.

18

Lieutenant Trapp broke into a run as soon as she was clear of the bridge, racing for the lifts that would take her below deck so she could have a face-to-face meeting with Commander Trane. She checked her tile on the way down to the main access tubes to make sure she had everything she needed. It all needed to be wrapped up before the next time she talked to Admiral Wolfe.

She made her way to the Marine detachment, the section of the ship set aside for shipboard Marines to train, live, and eat. On a ship the size of a *Juggernaut*-class, it was a big space since the Marines serving aboard her would be tasked with fending off borders as well as participating in boarding actions of their own. Once she'd been cleared through by the Marine corporal manning the CQ desk, she found the security center without much issue.

"Lieutenant Trapp," Gunnery Sergeant Barton greeted her. Wolfe's personal security guard had never taken much of a liking to her. She could feel his eyes boring into her while she worked in the shared office on the command deck, and it definitely wasn't the type of look she normally garnered from men.

"Gunny," she said. "Where's he at?"

"Cell four, down by himself," Barton said. "We have him long-cuffed to the desk in there for interrogation. If the admiral tells us to hold him much longer, we'll need to reconfigure the cell or move him to the brig."

"I just came from the bridge," she said, waving her tile as if that were some sort of proof of her claim. "Admiral Wolfe wants me to question Commander Trane regarding the WEPS reactor shutdown."

"You want us to bring him out here? The cell isn't really big enough for more than two people comfortably."

"I'll be fine with him by myself." She gave what she hoped was a disarming smile, trying to sway the hard-bitten NCO to her side. "The XO is accused of inappropriate com usage at this point. I don't see him being a danger."

"We'll be out here if you need us," Barton finally said. He seemed ready to deny her request at first, but she was still an officer, and he didn't really have the authority to tell her where she couldn't go in the execution of her duties.

After Barton had searched her and checked over her belongings, she was buzzed through. The hatch was already open to Trane's cell, so she slipped inside and closed it behind her.

"What the hell are *you* doing here?" Trane demanded. "Did Wolfe actually send his aide down to interrogate me? What's the meaning of all this?!"

Barton watched on the monitor as Trane argued with Trapp. When he went to turn the sound up, however, the image flickered. A moment later, the camera feeds to all the detention cells began to flicker just before they all winked out.

"What the hell?" He tried to reboot the cell monitoring system from the security desk, but nothing was working. "Corporal! Go down and check on the lieutenant and make sure she's okay. We just lost the video feed to all the cells."

"You've got it, Gunny." The Marine corporal was gone for less than two minutes before he came back through the checkpoint, shrugging. "Everything's okay in there. I looked in on the other two detainees and nothing looks odd."

It was only a few minutes later when Lieutenant Trapp came back up the corridor looking slightly frazzled. He buzzed her through the security door and waited while she put away the tile she'd been carrying.

"What happened?" Barton asked. "The camera in the cell went crazy right after you entered. Now, none of them are working at all. Did he say anything?"

"Weird about the cameras," Trapp said. "I got nothing. He's claiming he has no idea what I'm talking about, and that he's going to see you all court martialed for manhandling him. I tried to pry a little and let him see what we had on him, but he's not budging. I'd just let him stew for a bit until Admiral Wolfe can come down and put some real fear into him."

"He's good at that," Barton laughed. "Okay, we'll let him sit in there for a while longer. These men will make sure nobody enters the cell without permission from the bridge."

"You're not staying?"

"I've got to get back to my post, ma'am. They're more than capable of babysitting one officer chained to a desk."

"Very well." She smiled again. "You can accompany me if you don't mind."

"Delighted," Barton said, his voice indicating he was anything but.

"No, no, no, no, *NO, NO!!!*"

Zhang was in a panic. The latest dispatch had come in from his source within the Federation fleet, and it wasn't good. Apparently, Kohl had made a grave miscalculation, and the planet of Odmena had been hit with three high-yield antimatter warheads that had been aboard Dagger-class attack ships. The death toll was expected to be in the millions, and it was all because that psychopath they'd found to command their battlegroup had been too aggressive in how he approached Wolfe.

"Bad news?" Mr. Anders asked. The sardonic Fed spook had arrived the previous day, and they'd spent most of the evening negotiating and figuring out a way for Zhang to extract himself from the mess he was in. In the end, Anders had seemed unenthusiastic about helping him defect, but he seemed open to getting his family to safety. That was something, at least.

Wordlessly, Zhang handed him the tile with the latest dispatch from Odmena. Anders read it once, then twice, then once more. His normal half-bored, half-amused expression evaporated, and his visage turned dark, frightening Zhang. He had to remind himself that beneath the sarcastic wit and polished personas, Anders was a full Agent. He was an assassin when the Fed needed him to be, and he could kill Zhang in ways that would leave no evidence of foul play...or Zhang would simply disappear altogether.

"It would appear the nature of our negotiations has

taken a rather dramatic turn," Anders said. "There's no chance I can offer you asylum given that you were tangentially involved in a plot that has resulted in a slaughter like this on a Federation world. I already know who your contact is with the stolen alien tech, and I'll deal with him soon enough. What else do you have to offer?"

"I swear! This was never part of the plan!" Zhang was trying his best not to just break down into tears as he blubbered out the words. He was a lifelong mid-level bureaucrat. To even imply that he had anything to do with this ripped at the core of his being.

"Give me something." Anders shrugged. "A whole night of talking, and all I've gotten so far is that you were forced into it and a list of names I'd already figured out for myself. Why do you want to kill Admiral Wolfe?"

"Kill him?"

"Isn't that the point of the Odmena operation?" Anders pressed. "We have intel that indicates he was baited there so that Kohl could trap his task force and eliminate him."

"You've misunderstood." Zhang shook his head. "We need Wolfe alive. He's the key to starting the war those I work for so desperately need. Contrary to what your politicians believe, most of the Council is content to leave the Federation alone. The small excursions into your territory have been on local authority, and the orders always filter down out of Admiral Kohl's office."

"Keep going," Anders prompted.

"Kohl's mission was to try and pin Wolfe down, make him feel trapped, and let him strike first. There are dozens of observation craft throughout the system watching the engagement and waiting for the *Jericho* to open fire and start destroying Alliance ships, thus giving the cabal what it needed to goad the Council into moving against the Federation. If an ESA armada was attacked by an already-despised Starfleet officer while they were there as invited guests, the public would put tremendous pressure on the Council to respond."

"Why did you assume Wolfe would take the bait and just start blasting ships out of the sky?"

"The psychological profile Kohl had worked up on him along with years of study regarding his previous engagements," Zhang said uncomfortably.

"But you knew better," Anders guessed.

"I know that Wolfe isn't the caricature that is popular among the Alliance elite right now," Zhang said. "He's no bumbling fool, nor a mindlessly aggressive animal. I tried to voice those concerns once I'd been roped into this fiasco, but the people in charge are convinced Kohl is the subject matter expert."

"You realize that once the news of Kohl's actions at Odmena comes out, you'll likely be executed." It wasn't a question. "The ESA Council has little tolerance for rogue elements."

"Hence why I reached out to you," Zhang said. "Of course, I'd like asylum within the Federation, and I have a lot of inside knowledge to offer. But if I can get my family out, that will be enough, and I will fully cooperate."

"We'll see," Anders said coldly. "Let's not forget that many on my side still think your irresponsible program within the AU is what brought the Phage to our doorstep. If they find out you were also instrumental in the massacre at Odmena, they may order me to just kill you while I'm here. So, this entire debacle was designed to get Wolfe to blow a few of your ships up so you could convince the Council to go to war with us?"

"In a nutshell," Zhang said, eager to push past the

previous topic. "Some think that the war is inevitable, and that it would be wiser to come at the Federation while you're weakened from the Darshik."

"Why is it inevitable?"

"The ESA doesn't have the resources to self-sustain much past the next ten to fifteen years," Zhang admitted after a long pause. "Our production facilities are woefully outdated, and we're running out of room from population booms on most worlds. We didn't get a couple dozen beautiful new worlds from the Ushin, so we're stuck where we are unless we begin pushing past the outer boundary again, but there are no guarantees there and exploratory missions take precious resources.

"The planets will survive individually, of course, but as a space-faring empire, the ESA will wither and die without access to Federation production and resources. The two major sides of this argument currently are: take it by force while we have the numbers, or come to the table, hat in hand, and negotiate a trade agreement."

"Nobody is talking about reconciliation and unification?"

"A few, but they're quickly shouted down and often physically assaulted in the Grand Council Hall."

"Promising," Anders grunted. "I'd better leave now. With the news you just got, I'm sure you're about to have a stream of visitors looking to be reassured. I'll see what I can do about getting you out...but I don't expect much."

"I understand," Zhang said.

"That's it...we can't avoid it now," Joseph Marcum said with a weary sigh. "Parliament will hold a special session, and within the day, they'll almost certainly vote in a war resolution for President Stark to sign."

"You don't think they should?" Pitt was incredulous. The Odmena incident was the largest loss of life attack since the Phage had completely destroyed the planet Haven.

"I'm not sure we're ready for it," Marcum said. "Starfleet is still depleted, our personnel are exhausted after two back-to-back wars, and now we're going to be asking them to fight their own kind. Humans haven't been at war with each other for nearly five centuries not counting the small squabbles between enclaves."

Pitt didn't answer right away. As CENTCOM Chief of Staff, he was privy to a lot of intelligence even the admiralty wasn't trusted with, and the ESA wasn't quite the technological backwater many in Starfleet liked to claim. They'd negotiated for a lot of tech trade from the Darshik, and they'd managed to spirit away more than a few high-level Tsuyo scientists before the Federation had moved to seize all that company's assets. There were some weapon designs that had been given to the Alliance Fleet that could be a real problem for Starfleet in a head-to-head battle. It would just depend on what scale they'd been able to integrate them on.

"We made a serious mistake keeping the knowledge of their antimatter weapons from the people who needed to know it," he said finally. "If Wolfe had known those smaller ships might be packing such a devastating weapon, he could have focused on keeping them away from the planet."

"And in the process, giving the ESA exactly what they were there for: ultra-high-resolution footage of the *Jericho* blasting Alliance boats out of the sky," Marcum said. "The end result would have been the same except it would be the ESA Council voting on a war resolution."

"The end result might have been different for the people

of Odmena," Pitt spat back. "Don't tell me you've been in the capital for such a short time and already no longer see the value in fighting for every life."

"You're out of line, *Admiral*," Marcum growled. "I'm just looking at this issue from every side before I go and add my vote to send more young men and women to die and who knows how many civilians before this is all over."

"I'm sorry, Joseph," Pitt said. "This is just happening all at once despite knowing it was coming for years."

"Any word on reinforcements for Wolfe?" Marcum changed the subject.

"The *Nemesis* disobeyed a stay order and is on the way right now, as is some extra super-secret strike package the CIS has been spearheading. Barrett should get there first, then Wright with her ships."

"The old Blue Jacket Mafia is reuniting for one more ass-kicking party, huh?" Marcum said, actually smiling. "I hope that dipshit, Kohl, is ready for the level of violence those three together can bring to bear."

"Kohl outnumbers them nearly four to one still," Pitt pointed out.

"He'll need it."

19

"Second cruiser is coming up from under us!"

"Status on the MACs?" Jackson asked.

"Twenty minutes until the first charges are ready to fire."

"You're clear to engage with laser batteries when they're in range, Tactical, no missile shots over the planet. Shoot to disable."

"Aye, sir."

The *Jericho* was still clawing her way up out of Odmena's gravity well, and the smaller, more nimble Alliance cruisers had decided to use that to their advantage. The three ships shifted out of their polar orbit and broke formation, getting ahead of, behind, and underneath the battleship to harass them. The remaining attack boats already cleared the area, but now the rest of the ESA's forces in the system were mobilizing and converging on the planet and Captain Carmichael's formation.

Jackson needed distance from the planet and relative velocity before he could begin to engage the threat. All he could do while they cleared the orbit was wait for the enemy ships to fire and hope their point defense systems were up to the task. So far, it looked like the ESA hadn't made any significant upgrades to their missiles' countermeasure capability, so the *Jericho's* ECM suite and laser batteries had kept the ship from taking any hits from the half-dozen shots sent their way, but Jackson knew that no defensive system was absolute. If the enemy lobbed enough incoming missiles at them, eventually, something was going to get through. He could easily take out all three cruisers around him with his more advanced Shrike II series ship-buster missiles, but he didn't dare while still so close to the planet, and Admiral Kohl was well aware of that.

"Still no response from anyone in the capital on the planet, sir."

"Keep trying," Jackson said to his com officer. "Have CIC put someone on the task. I need you free up here."

"Incoming!" Easton called. "Four missiles fired from the ship ahead of us!"

"DSO!" Jackson barked at the *Jericho's* defensive systems officer.

"Tracking all inbound, sir!" she said. "Point defense is—"

"Three more incoming from the ship below us!"

"How long until we can return fire without endangering the planet any further?" Jackson asked.

"Forward ship will be clear in ninety-one minutes, the other two in three and five hours respectively," Lieutenant Orr said from OPS.

"Tactical, in ninety-two minutes, I want two Shrikes launched at the leading ship," Jackson said. "Keep the other two bracketed, but once we're in open space, I'm going to try and outrun them. We need to get back uphill and rejoin the rest of the task force. Kohl is going to understand this as well and do everything in his power to prevent that. He'll want to keep us divided so that his slower, smaller ships can swarm us under one at a time."

"Point defense firing!" the DSO called out.

On the main display, Jackson watched as blue lines lanced out from the *Jericho's* icon, representing the forward laser batteries that would try to knock down the incoming missiles. It wasn't as straight forward as it sounded. Missiles were comparatively miniscule, travelling at blistering velocities, and their laser emitters were mounted to a moving, shaking starship. Rather than trying to destroy the missile outright, the point defense mode would defocus the beams to cover a bigger patch of sky. It diminished their destructive capability, but it greatly increased their odds of scoring a hit.

Two missiles winked out on the main display quickly as the beams converged and destroyed the munitions. The remaining two continued their charge as the guns were redirected and stagger fired to keep from overheating the emitters. Jackson watched as his cannons took out one more missile, and then the last seemed to veer off course before detonating on its own well out of effective range.

"Forward threats clear, point defense standing by for the three coming up aft."

"Helm, bring us to bear on the cruiser dead ahead, all ahead emergency," Jackson ordered. "Tactical, stand by to fire Shrikes, simultaneous launch."

"Disengaging safeties," the helmsman said. "All engines ahead emergency, aye."

Over the next hour, the *Jericho* slowly reeled in the cruiser that was now fleeing at full power. After having four of their missiles intercepted or destroyed, the captain wasn't wasting any more of his munitions at such an extreme range. While the three ships rightly thought they had the battleship pinned down, what they hadn't counted on was that, despite her bulk, the *Jericho* had a significant acceleration advantage on the aging cruisers. They were slipping out of range of the pursuing ships and would quickly be able to fire on the lead ship. The point defense batteries never had a chance to fire on the pursuing missiles as the ECM suite scrambled their sensors, all three detonating once they were blinded.

"Tactical, how long until we're at our maximum effective range for the One Fifties?" Jackson asked.

"Seventeen minutes assuming no acceleration changes for us or them, sir," Easton said. "All four of the One Fifties are energized and ready."

"Set up for a max range shot, all four cannons," Jackson said. "Keep the missiles ready to launch as a backup."

The One Fifties were four next-generation tactical lasers that were specific to the *Juggernaut*-class. The name referred to the one-hundred-and-fifty-millimeter final optic diameter. The four projectors were mounted in precision turrets and, in theory, were capable of hitting a target at a range of just over four hundred and fifty thousand kilometers and still have enough punch to boil away hull armor. Laser weapons had proven to be impractical compared to missiles and even good old kinetic weapons, so most warships employed them primarily as a defensive measure. The engineers at Fleet R&D had promised Jackson that the One Fifties would be a nasty surprise for anyone he turned them on. The beauty of lasers, in addition to the fact they worked at the speed of light, was that they couldn't be intercepted, jammed, or even detected until it was too late.

"Projectors refocused for a long-range shot, targeting RDS drive pod at her aft," Easton said. "Guns are hot and ready, nine minutes and counting."

"You are clear to engage at your discretion, Mr. Easton," Jackson said, using his biometric print to authorize weapon release at his station. "DSO! Coordinate with CIC to track incoming threats."

"Aye, sir."

Jackson had seen the test data on the One Fifty laser system and was cautiously optimistic that he could score a disabling shot at extreme range, then take the cruiser out once they closed. He stole a glance at the Link data displayed on the right side of the main display and saw that Carmichael had a force of fifteen closing in on his formation, and that Kohl, as he predicted, was moving his swarm of smaller attack boats to clog the lower orbits and force him to run a gauntlet to recombine the task force.

Once he was away from the planet and had some breathing room, he had to confer with CENTCOM and find out just how critical it was that he risk losing his entire command for a system the ESA was now going scorched earth on. Kohl may well have depopulated Odmena with his clumsy mistake, so there seemed to be little gained in staying other than a strong urge for revenge. But throwing away an entire task force against a numerically superior enemy wouldn't do anything to strengthen the Federation's position.

"One Fifties locked...firing!"

The massive capacitor banks discharged with a thrum that could be felt through the deck as the four cannons disgorged trillions of watts of power, each firing a fifteen-millisecond burst, resetting, and firing again until they'd discharged the entire volley bank. Less than ten seconds later, they observed the leading cruiser break apart like an egg.

"Direct hit!" Easton said. "CIC confirms the first shots

took out their drive...the subsequent hits got much better penetration than we expected at this range. Initial BDS indicates we hit the powerplant."

"Helm, angle our course nine degrees to port to avoid the debris," Jackson said, the adrenaline shock still hitting him from the engagement despite having fought dozens of more harrowing battles in the past. "What are our pursuers doing?"

"They've cut power and are falling back, Admiral," Orr said.

"Watching their other ship get dusted by laser fire from so far off probably rattled them," Easton said. "One Fifty volley banks are recharging from WEPS reactors, standing down Shrikes."

"OPS, tell CIC I want some options for getting the *Jericho* up to where the task force will be," Jackson said. "I want multiple options, and I want it within the hour."

"Aye, sir."

"Admiral, Chief Petty Officer Wilkins is asking to meet with you," the com officer said. It took Jackson a moment to remember that was the *Jericho's* master at arms.

"We're a little busy right now," he said. "Ask him if it can wait."

"It's urgent, sir." The catch in the ensign's voice made Jackson turn and look at him questioningly. "Sir... Commander Trane...h--he committed suicide, sir." Jackson swallowed hard and looked at the main display again, gauging which enemy ships could possibly threaten the *Jericho* and how far out they were.

"Tell him I'm on my way to him," he said finally. "Mr. Easton, you have the bridge in my absence. Remain at Tactical and keep her steady as she bears."

"Aye-aye, sir," Easton said, his voice barely above a whisper.

Jackson looked around at the shell-shocked expressions of his bridge crew. He admitted he may have royally screwed up by having Trane grabbed. The crew had already lost Captain Hardy, now their XO appeared to have killed himself, as well. When it inevitably came out that he did so while being detained on Jackson's orders, the shock and sadness would likely turn to resentment and anger. It was a potentially explosive dynamic he could scarcely afford at a time when he was cutoff and outnumbered by an enemy fleet that seemed intent on killing him.

"Coms, make sure Gunnery Sergeant Barton meets me there."

"Aye, sir."

"How the fuck did he have a knife in here? Wasn't he searched?"

"Yes, sir," Corporal Stevens said. "By myself and Gunny Barton."

"Don't *'sir'* me, kid...I'm enlisted," Chief Petty Officer Wilkins said. The honorific was likely less to do with Wilkins's rank and more to do with the fact he was a monster of a man, an imposing wall of muscle that seemed even more so due to the confined space in the detachment's security office. "Respectfully, Admiral, this is why trained law enforcement personnel are tasked with these sorts of things, not a couple jarheads who train to repel borders or secure a beachhead on the surface of a planet."

"In hindsight, I agree, Chief," Jackson said. "However, I'd

prefer not to waste much more time talking about what *should* have happened and focus more on what *did* happen."

"Yes, sir," Wilkins said. "It's pretty cut and dry. The knife was definitely his judging by the number of prints on it. Probably something he carried on him daily. The cuts are consistent with a suicide, including a few half-hearted practice slashes before he got down to business and opened an artery up. The camera in the cell appears to have failed completely. My tech team will look at it more closely. He wasn't discovered until about three hours after he bled out, when someone went to get him something to eat."

"When did you discover the camera was out?" Jackson asked Stevens.

"It went on the fritz when your aide was down here, and then after she left, it died completely, Admiral," Stevens said, standing ramrod straight at attention. "Lieutenant Trapp confirmed that Commander Trane was alive and well when she left the cell."

"That seems to match up with the timeline we've gotten from Medical," Wilkins said. "They sent someone down to determine time of death and to officially declare the XO deceased for the ship's log."

"I need Barton with me. Is he cleared to leave?" Jackson asked.

"I've taken the Gunny's statement already." Wilkins nodded. "He's free to go."

"Let's go," Jackson said to him, pulling out his comlink.

"Yes, Admiral?" Lieutenant Trapp's voice came from device's speaker.

"Tell Commanders Corsi and McVey that I want to see them in the bridge briefing room in twenty minutes," Jackson said, killing the channel before she could reply.

"Sir? Do you really believe that Trane just up and

commits suicide like that?" Barton asked. When Jackson just glared at him, he rushed on. "Sorry, Admiral. I'll keep my—"

"Speak," Jackson demanded.

"I know I'm just a dumb grunt, sir, but the odds of both Captain Hardy *and* Commander Trane deciding to commit suicide before any real evidence was presented or formal accusations made seems...convenient."

"I'm not sure what to think right now," Jackson said. "I'm not a trained criminal investigator, so I can only go off what my people tell me. I *do* know that somehow a knife made it into that cell with Trane despite four Marines searching him when he was detained."

"I can't offer an excuse or even an explanation there, Admiral." Barton didn't shrink away from his boss's glare. "I patted him down, then two others did, and we chained him to the table in such a way that he wouldn't have been able to root around in his underwear if, for some reason, he'd happened to be storing a utility knife up his own smoke stack."

"Any other theories?" Jackson asked.

"Everything I've said is assuming that the Marines I grabbed from the detachment are on the level, but I've never served with these guys before. It's entirely possible that one of them slipped him a knife after we secured him."

"That'll be Chief Wilkins's job to sort out. Now, I've got to replace the command staff of my flagship the best I can and tell the crew that their Captain and XO apparently decided to inexplicably kill themselves just before a major engagement."

"I hadn't thought about the optics of that, sir," Barton frowned. "We've already had some unusual behavior from Task Force crewmembers along with the more credible threats on your life. The risk of a mutiny is very real right now."

"Which is why I'm contacting CENTCOM and requesting permission to withdraw," Jackson sighed. "We'll perform a series of off-ecliptic, short warp flights to clear the system, and then head back to the Eternis System with our tails firmly tucked."

"At this point, sir, is there really any other option?"

"None that I'm seeing."

"I will make these remarks as brief as possible without skipping too much detail. We're still in the middle of hostile space and will be closing in on another enemy formation within the next thirty hours." Jackson was sitting in the bridge briefing room, staring into a camera that Lieutenant Trapp had set up to broadcast ship wide.

"Addressing the rumors that are doubtlessly circulating, Captain Hardy and Commander Trane are both dead from apparently unrelated suicides. In the interim, I've assigned Commander Lazaro Corsi from Flight OPS and Commander Willis McVey from CIC to fill the gaps left in the command staff by their passing. Master at Arms Wilkins is currently spearheading the investigations into both deaths.

"I only served with both these officers for a short time since coming aboard the *Jericho*, but in that time, they impressed me with their professionalism, dedication, and loyalty to their crew. If for no other reason than to honor their memory, I hope we can all continue to perform at the level they expected. This battleship has already been under enemy fire and has drawn blood, but we're now flying into a heavy concentration of Alliance ships that are intent on stopping us from reaching the outer system. Things are going to get bumpy, but I know that this ship—this crew—is up to the challenge ahead.

"The current strategy is to reunite Task Force Vega in the outer orbits, and then use our combined firepower and defensive capability to carve a path through the Alliance blockade until reinforcements arrive. I've been notified that the *Nemesis* has been repaired and is on her way here now at maximum warp. Her arrival will begin to turn the tide of this battle and allow us to adopt a more aggressive posture, seeking out retribution for the millions of deaths on Odmena rather than letting the Alliance take shots at us as they please.

"Trust your crewmates, trust your leadership, and trust that, together, we can overcome the challenges ahead of us and return home victorious. Wolfe out."

"That seems like the right tone to set, sir," Trapp said once the camera shut off.

"I want you plugged in with Chief Wilkins during the investigation," Jackson told her. "I don't have even a minute to spare on this, and I need you to be my liaison between myself and the lower decks. Understand what I'm telling you?"

"Completely, Admiral," she assured him. He stood and left her as she packed up the equipment. The bridge briefing room was a secure location so there weren't any cameras or microphones built into it like there were in the other conference rooms.

He walked back out onto the bridge to witness Corsi and McVey getting a refresher in ship's operations by Lieutenant Orr. The situation was far from optimal, but at least both commanders had completed the requisite training to be on the bridge in command of the ship when he couldn't be. It was their complete lack of experience that concerned him, but he had no plans on leaving them alone while the *Jericho* was actually engaged with the enemy. It meant he would be running on little to no sleep while they were still in-system, but he'd done it before.

"Sir, CIC said a Bluebird dispatch from CENTCOM was received, your eyes only," Orr said.

"Have them send it to the secure tile I was issued, Mr. Orr," Jackson said. When the message came through, he nearly threw the tile across the bridge.

ADM WOLFE, UNDERSTAND JERICHO IS NOT AT FULL STRENGTH WITH LOSS OF KEY PERSONNEL. MISSION GOALS HAVE CHANGED AFTER ODMENA DISASTER. YOU ARE TASKED WITH MAKING SURE ADM KOHL DOES NOT LEAVE THE SYSTEM ALIVE—KILL OR CAPTURE AUTHORIZED. DO NOT PURSUE BEYOND RECOGNIZED FEDERATION BOUNDARY AT THIS TIME.

BE ADVISED THAT FLEET R&S HAS CONFIRMED THAT NEW ESA WEAPON IS NOT NUCLEAR, SMALLER ATTACK SHIPS ARE LOADED WITH ANTIMATTER WARHEADS. UNKNOWN IF CAPITAL SHIPS ARE CARRYING SIMILAR MUNITIONS.

"Coms! Please send out a fleet-wide message over Bluebird." Jackson put the tile away and sat down. "Do not engage smaller ships at close range. They're carrying antimatter weapons that are significantly more powerful than our nukes."

"Weaponized antimatter?" Commander Corsi asked. "I thought that was theoretical."

"For the Federation, it is," Jackson said. "It seems the ESA's partnership with the Darshik wasn't a complete waste for them."

"Anything else for the fleet-wide broadcast, sir?" the com officer asked.

"One thing more. We're now tasked with apprehending or killing Admiral Kohl, the man in charge of the armada that just killed millions of Federation citizens," Jackson said. "We need to positively identify the *Heart of Xian* and begin trying to separate her from the rest of her formation. Tell Carmichael that I want him to try and identify and track the ship but not to attempt an intercept until we've rejoined the task force."

"Aye, sir"

"What's the plan once we identify the *Heart*, Admiral?" McVey asked.

"We give the coordinates to the *Nemesis* and let Captain Barrett run her down."

20

"Tell them to get clear!"

"They say they can't, sir. Their port RDS field emitters were damaged during the last exchange, and they're pushing as hard as they can just to stay in the formation."

Carmichael swore as he watched the TFS *Liberator* begin to flag as she could no longer maintain the acceleration change he'd ordered to clear a cluster of the smaller attack ships. The *Jericho* had warned them the little boats were carrying antimatter weapons, of all unbelievable things, and that they were ordered to run clear while also trying to pinpoint the location of a single Alliance cruiser. He knew that Wolfe had a lot on his plate on the flagship since most of the command staff had apparently decided to off themselves mid-mission, but the rest of Task Force Vega was in trouble.

So far, he'd managed to keep them together and all ships intact by using their superior performance to skirt around enemy ships and stay outside of effective weapons range, but once he'd tried to start pushing downhill at Wolfe's order, the game became much more difficult. He'd ordered hard sprints away from pursuing ships so many times that their accumulated relative velocity was approaching the *Blake*'s Delta-V roll off. He was carrying too much speed, and it was hampering his ability to maneuver his ships quickly enough to evade the enemy.

His trailing frigates, the *Liberator* and *Victory*, had both taken damage when a handful of missiles had gotten through the point defense shield and detonated. They weren't direct impacts, but they were close enough that, even in the vacuum of space, they had caused moderate system damage to both ships. He'd ordered the task force to decelerate a bit so they could cover, but the Alliance fleet tasted blood in the water.

"OPS, is there any way the *Liberator* can break clear and head back uphill out of the fray?"

"Negative, sir. We've been cut off from higher orbits in this quadrant," his OPS officer told him. "We won't have a clear path to transfer up until we come around to quadrant two."

"She won't last that long," his XO whispered. "Their RDS output has been fluctuating badly for the last sixteen hours. These sons of bitches took out two unarmed supply ships, and hit a planet with an antimatter bomb. What do you think they'd do to a surrendering frigate or a bunch of lifeboats?"

"That's not an option," Carmichael said, his guts tied into knots as he realized his hands were tied when it came to trying to help his stricken ship. They were being pursued by sixteen of the smaller attack boats, and behind them were five Alliance cruisers. If he slowed significantly or tried to turn and fight to save the *Liberator*, he'd almost certainly lose more ships in the process...maybe all of them.

"Okay, we're going to take a page from Celesta Wright's playbook," Carmichael said after staring at the tactical plot on the main display. "Here's how this is going to work..."

Over the next ninety minutes, CIC worked with the two ships ahead of the *Liberator* and *Victory* in the formation to put the plan into action. The captains of the two damaged frigates weren't too thrilled about the idea at first, but they realized their options were limited.

"The *Fairfax* and the *Ghost Dancer* are in position and ready, Captain."

"Deploy," Carmichael ordered.

A moment later, the two heavy cruisers began spitting Shrike missiles from their aft launch tubes, but the missiles' engines didn't ignite. Instead, the munitions drifted slowly away from the two ships but still carried most of their initial velocity to keep them tucked up behind the two cruisers but also shielded by the two trailing frigates.

The last few times Carmichael had ordered his ships to fire on the smaller attack boats harassing his formation, they would immediately begin braking and allow the Alliance capital ships to move up and shoot down his missiles with overlapping fields of point defense fire. One Shrike had gotten through out of the twelve he'd launched into the tightly packed group of ships. While he was dutifully impressed with the ESA's improvements in defensive fire capabilities, he also realizes that if he kept it up, he'd deplete his store of ship-busters without putting a dent in the enemy fleet.

Now that he knew what the smaller ships were carrying, it was clear why the bigger cruisers were mostly keeping their distance. One lucky hit and the antimatter charge could take out half the formation. It was also what he was counting on...assuming he was executing the maneuver properly. He held no delusions about himself: he was no Celesta Wright. But this strategy was fairly straightforward and the Alliance skippers hadn't shown themselves to be master tacticians either.

"All missiles are expelled and trailing along behind *Fairfax* and *Ghost Dancer*, sir."

"All right...order all ships to begin decelerating," Carmichael ordered. "Two percent reverse power." Over the Link all the ships received the command to begin braking and executed in near unison. On the main display he could see the enemy ships beginning to close the gap, their drive power output spiking as they eagerly went after the two flagging ships. Carmichael hoped the ESA commander would think he was slowing his entire force to provide cover for the damaged ships and would be overconfident as they approached.

"All ships responding, sir."

"Tell the *Liberator* it's show time," Carmichael said.

On the composite image the computer created of the frigate using optical, radar, and Link data, Carmichael watched as the ship appeared to flounder and a great gout of vapor was released from her exhaust vents. As he'd hoped, the enemy ships began to angle in to focus on what looked like easy prey. The *Liberator* let loose with a volley of six missiles aimed for the oncoming attack boats. They were all low-yield, non-nuclear Hornet missiles, but the enemy didn't seem to be able to tell the difference between them and a Shrike. As before, the Alliance cruisers accelerated hard to provide point defense cover.

"Hold fast," Carmichael muttered, willing Commander

Zin to wait until the cruisers had fully committed before veering off.

"Venting reactor coolant into space was a nice touch," his XO complimented him. "It looks like they're going to bite on it."

Over the next hour and forty-five minutes, they watched the ESA cruisers charge up to cover their smaller ships, slowly closing into range as the entire enemy force bore down on the *Liberator*. Once they'd crossed the two-hundred-kilometer threshold, Carmichael pulled the trigger.

"Coms, instruct the *Liberator* to clear the area. Tactical! You may engage your firing script as soon as our frigate is out of the way."

"Aye, sir."

On the main display, suddenly looking much sprightlier, the *Liberator* angled to port and poured on the acceleration. Even in her degraded state, the frigate's RDS had ample power to quickly move her from the firing lane where the ESA formation, bunched up anticipating an attack, was now looking at twelve Shrike missiles between them and the rest of the Federation task force.

"Executing script, Shrikes away!"

A dozen solid fuel first stage boosters lit up the sky as the missiles, still flying backwards, decelerated into the path of the oncoming ESA ships. Too late, the formation commander saw the danger and tried to disengage the cruisers away from the attack boats, but the range was too close, and their ships lacked the necessary power.

"Shrikes are prioritizing targets now second stage firing in five seconds."

As the crisscrossing point defense fire of the enemy ships intensified, the missiles lit off the powerful second stage boosters that would send them streaking into their assigned targets. The missiles were burning all their fuel to rapidly close the gap before the enemy could adjust their defenses.

The first Shrike slammed into the leading attack boat just fifty minutes after it had fired its first stage engine, practically close quarter combat for a munition that was designed to traverse half a star system if need be. The smaller ship was carrying one of the new antimatter warheads, and the shock of the impact alone destabilized containment and set the charge off before the Shrike's nuclear payload could detonate.

Carmichael watched in awe at the chain reaction he'd just set off. The antimatter explosion encompassed the ship above and the one to starboard, setting off their charges, as well. Those explosions wiped out two cruisers, their less energetic demise sending debris into the remaining ships. By the end of the skirmish, there was only one cruiser left intact...mostly. The ship tumbled uncontrolled and streaming atmosphere at a rate that Carmichael knew meant the crew didn't have long if they didn't get into the lifeboats.

"It would almost be a mercy to use one more Shrike on them, Captain," the XO said.

"We're all out of mercy today, Commander," Carmichael growled. "They can take their chances like the people on Odmena had to. Tell the task force to take no further action. Order the *Liberator* and *Victory* back into formation, and let's see what the next threat is. OPS! Make sure the flagship gets a full report of the encounter."

"Aye-aye, sir."

"Holy shit!" Commander Corsi whispered as he read through the after-action report Jackson had just handed him. "I had no idea Carmichael was such a ruthless fighter."

"He's a skilled tactician," Jackson agreed. "His maneuver worked so well that he could have pulled it off with far fewer missiles than he used."

"At least the Alliance fleet knows we're not going down without a fight now," Corsi said.

"They've also been taught a hard lesson about bunching up your formations in battle," Jackson said. "Whether they learned it or not remains to be seen."

He'd been beyond impressed with how Carmichael had been handling himself as he tried to bring the task force back down into the inner system to link back up with the *Jericho*. In most ways, his job had been more difficult than Jackson's since he had to worry about multiple ships, two of which had already taken damage. The tactics used in eliminating his immediate pursuers showed not only that he was cool under pressure and had a firm grasp of how to fight his ships, but he also wasn't going to leave the slower ships to fend for themselves despite being pursued by a larger force.

In fact, while Carmichael had managed his own forces with a deft touch and a bit of a dramatic flair, Jackson's single-ship command was in complete disarray, something he was not at all happy about. The *Jericho* was currently pursuing a target of opportunity—two ESA cruisers with an escort of nine attack boats—and he was beginning to see why Captain Hardy had never added Corsi and McVey to the bridge watch roster despite the fact they had been to command school and held the necessary rank: the pair seemed to suffer from crippling self-doubt regardless of how minor the decision was they needed to make.

The result was that Jackson was forced to spend more

and more time on the bridge without a break, and he wasn't a young man anymore. He was becoming concerned that trying to manage the battle on little sleep and too much coffee was going to degrade his decision-making ability. On the rare chance he did make it back to his quarters to try and sleep, one of the pair would inevitably call him back to the bridge with an *emergency* they should have been completely comfortable handling. Perhaps the fault was Hardy's in that he never had them on bridge watch enough to be comfortable with it.

"How many Alliance cruisers are still in the system?" Jackson asked the backup second watch OPS officer, a young ensign whose name he couldn't pronounce.

"CIC is tracking sixteen cruiser-class warships via their RDS signatures, Admiral," she said. "The smaller attack boats use a—"

"Thank you, OPS," Jackson cut her off. The smaller ships had limited RDS capability and switched back and forth between that and the now-obsolete MPD engines starships used to fly with. It was the switching back and forth coupled with their stealth characteristics that were making them difficult to track across the entire system.

Even though they were tough to spot from a distance, and they seemed to all be carrying at least one antimatter missile, the small ships had proven to be mostly ineffective against the Federation fleet. The high-power tracking radars would burn through the stealth countermeasures at a range that was plenty far to give them time to target and fire. The attack boats didn't maneuver particularly well, and their weapons didn't have the range of even the smaller Hornet's Jackson's fleet carried. They were still a danger when they tried to isolate and swarm an individual ship but, so far, they'd proven of little use to Admiral Kohl other than committing a war crime by wiping out most of the population on Odmena.

"It's odd the cruisers don't seem to be equipped with the new weapons," Corsi echoed his thoughts. "Just those smaller ships that can't even evade a Hornet strike."

"It makes me think their antimatter containment may not be as stable as Fleet Intel believes it to be, and they don't want to risk a capital ship when one cooks off," Jackson said. "OPS! How many Shrikes does the task force have left?"

"Sixty-seven, sir," she said, putting the Link data up on the main display so Jackson could see the distribution of weapons.

"Damn," he muttered. As he'd feared, the bulk of the remaining ship-busters were located on the *Jericho*. The Alliance ships had been trying to avoid a direct confrontation with the battleship while Carmichael's ships had been forced to burn up their supply of missiles to keep from being swarmed under. If he still had his two supply ships, he might have tried an in-flight transfer since each of those cargo barges had been carrying forty spare Shrike missiles each.

"Sir?" Corsi asked.

"That's just over three missiles per enemy capital ship left," Jackson said. "That's cutting it too close. Tactical! What's our range?"

"Target group is currently six hundred and seventy thousand kilometers off the bow, Admiral," Ensign Onley reported from tactical. He was another second watch backup sitting in while the A-team got some food and rest. "CIC thinks they're pushing hard to stay ahead of us. The reactor vents have been running hotter for the last few hours."

"Or they think we're foolish enough to fall for the same

ruse Captain Carmichael used on them," Jackson said. "Maintain closure speed and keep an updated firing solution for each. Make sure CIC is watching space just off our projected course carefully. They like to hide their smaller ships along the way."

"Aye, sir."

The *Juggernaut*-class was really more of an updated version of its predecessor, the Dreadnaught-class battleship that had served at the end of the Phage War. Fleet R&D had equipped her with the latest and greatest in stand-off and close-in weaponry, but the command and control systems were still antiquated compared to the streamlined bridge and computer integration he'd enjoyed while commanding the *Nemesis*. There was still too much manual input on the *Jericho* that made him have to shout out streams of orders to multiple stations to get anything done. Losing two competent command officers like Hardy and Trane—and overlooking the fact they were likely traitors—made the inefficiencies that much more apparent.

"New RDS signature on the board, sir! It's...it's really big," OPS reported.

"The *Nemesis*?" Jackson asked hopefully.

"Unlikely, sir," she said. "This one transitioned in from the New Kazan jump point. CIC is trying to match the profile now in the database."

"New player for the other team?" Corsi asked. Jackson didn't bother answering.

"CIC says it doesn't match any known ship class, but the field power of the drive suggests the ship is much larger than the cruisers currently in-system. Much faster, too."

"Tell them to coordinate over Bluebird with the rest of the task force to try and ID the newcomer. Leave that task to them and focus on what we're doing here. Tactical, what's our closure rate?"

"Rate of closure is still ninety-four kilometers per second, Admiral."

Jackson did the math in his sleep-deprived mind and realized that at less than seven hours to intercept, they were closer than he'd thought to being within firing range. He toyed with the idea of bumping his acceleration curve up to catch them faster, but he was still leery of the smaller ships that could deploy their stealth shrouds and virtually disappear. The *Jericho* didn't have the maneuverability required to skirt around one if she was barreling down on the target at full speed.

Three more hours dragged by with Jackson staring a hole through the main display. As he closed in on what should be an easy kill, the adrenaline of the coming engagement erased the fatigue and mental fog that had come from being on-duty for seventeen hours straight. He was just about to order an engine power change to sprint the last two hundred thousand kilometers so he could fire his spread, and then pull off before the smaller ships had a chance to lob an antimatter missile at him, but the Alliance fleet had other plans.

"Two more RDS signatures have popped up, Admiral. One is similar to the first newcomer, the third is another unknown. CIC is asking permission to use Bluebird to contact Fleet Intel and see if they have a match for the new ships."

"Granted," Jackson said. "They should have been doing that already."

"Sir, the first contact is moving onto an intercept course for Captain Carmichael's group," Commander Corsi said, looking over the OPS officer's shoulder.

"Bold," Jackson muttered, a knot starting to form in the pit of his stomach. So far, Kohl had shown nothing but timidity and a hesitation to try and meet his ships in the open, now a powerful RDS signature appears and starts steaming right for eight Federation warships. His gut told him there had just been another shift in the balance of the fight and that he wasn't going to like it when he figured out what that was.

"The smaller attack boats are breaking formation too, sir," Ensign Onley said. "CIC is updating the tracks. It looks like they're all breaking for the outer system near the New Berlin jump point."

"Did that first newcomer actually appear at the New Kazan jump point, or just near it?" Jackson asked, spinning on his OPS officer.

"Standby, sir," she said. "The transition flash was observed just over fifteen million kilometers spinward from the New Kazan jump point."

"Has the number of observed RDS tracks fluctuated since Carmichael took out that first cruiser?" Jackson asked. "Specifically, have ships been appearing and disappearing in that region of space?"

"CIC can't say with certainty that—"

"I'm not looking to blame anyone for missing this, Ensign, I just need the information."

"The number of RDS signatures has fluctuated the entire time we've been in-system. There have been eleven incidents that match the Alliance attack boats operating around that area. Since these ships are switching between gravimetric and thrust drives, CIC has been logging each incidence and letting the computer track them."

"Sir?" Corsi asked.

"Admiral Kohl has a staging point somewhere beyond

the boundary of this system," Jackson said, speaking to Commander Corsi but mostly thinking aloud. "It has to be fairly close, and he's able to move in reinforcements or pull back damaged ships without sending them all the way back to ESA space. There's no way of knowing what sort of flotilla he's got out there. For all we know, it could be a full-fledged expeditionary force preparing to move deeper into Federation space."

"We've had no indication that the ESA has the ability to navigate outside of established warp lanes with that degree of accuracy." Jackson turned to look at the person speaking, unaware that she had come onto the bridge.

"This doesn't require much accuracy, Lieutenant Trapp," he said. "He's simply placed his forces outside of our detection range, likely just on the other side of the heliopause, and then executes timed hops from a fixed point within the system."

He hadn't seen his new aide since the unpleasantness down in the holding cell where an officer she'd just spoken to had killed himself. Jackson assumed she was still working diligently to track down exactly what Hardy and Trane had been up to and made a mental note to check with her later. Just because they were gone didn't mean the problems ended with them.

"Sir, CIC has heard back from Fleet Intel. They'd like a word with you over a secure channel."

Jackson raised an eyebrow at that and went over to the command chair, pulling out a wired headset from a compartment near the armrest. If CIC needed to talk privately, that meant Fleet must have given them something that's still not cleared for general dissemination. While it was annoying that something pertaining to the battle at hand couldn't be discussed openly on the bridge, he did just have two high-ranking officers who were apparently communicating with the enemy.

"This is Admiral Wolfe," he said once someone in CIC accepted the secure channel request. "What do you have for me?"

"Standby, sir...linking you to Lieutenant Hoffman."

"Admiral?" a youthful male voice asked.

"Go ahead," Jackson said.

"Fleet Intel and CIS haven't been able to complete a full workup yet...but they're telling me unofficially that the RDS signatures we've provided look similar to a new class of battleship the ESA has been developing behind the communication blackout," Hoffman said. *"Since we couldn't provide the full RDS profile over Bluebird due to bandwidth restrictions, they're not willing to say one way—"*

"Stick to the pertinent details, Mr. Hoffman."

"Yes, sir. The hull design is based on the TCS Dao."

"She was a Third Fleet battleship that was lost at the Second Battle of Xi'an during the war. The last of her class, if I remember right," Jackson said, closing his eyes for a moment as the memories came back.

"Er...yes, sir," Hoffman stumbled, seeming unsure of what to say. *"The Dao was the last battleship in service until the Dreadnaught-class ships. Anyway, CIS had managed to get some long-range observational data of these new boomers, but nothing that will likely help you if they're in the system with us. Performance, armament, armor, countermeasures...all unknown."*

"Do they think there's much Darshik tech in the new ships?" Jackson asked.

"Standby." Jackson drummed his fingers while he listened to Hoffman type furiously on his Bluebird terminal.

"Possibly. The RDS profiles indicate the ship has a lot of

power, but that the design isn't a derivative of our own Class IV drives in use now."

"That's useful," Jackson said. "Anything else?"

"No, sir. I'll maintain this connection and keep picking at what they know and contact you should I learn more," Hoffman said.

"You do that," Jackson said. "Good work, Hoffman."

He pulled the headset off and ignored the questioning looks from his crew to take a half-minute to reflect on what he'd just learned. The TCS *Dao* had been destroyed early in the Phage War and had been an outdated design even then. Why would the ESA base a whole new class of battleship on a hull that had been designed over a hundred years ago?

The Asianic Union had always been the most secretive of the enclaves under the old Terran Confederation political system. It was their covert colonization program that had precipitated the war, and then they spent most of the actual fighting making excuses as to why Third Fleet ships weren't ready when they needed them. Maybe these new ships weren't new hulls, but battleships they'd already had lying around that they kept a secret to protect their own worlds while Starfleet was slaughtered at Haven and Nuovo Patria.

"Sir," Onley said, pointing at the main display. Jackson looked up and saw that the other two ships that had arrived were also now heading for an intercept of Carmichael's ships. He could see that all the smaller ships had pulled off and were regrouping in the higher orbits, and even the remaining cruisers had taken a less aggressive posture and were angling down into the system to clear the way for the newcomers.

"How long would it take the *Jericho* to reach Carmichael at full power?" Jackson asked. A moment later, the hypothetical course plots and estimated times were put up on the main display in blue. He swore when looking at how long it would take him to get back up to the rest of his task force compared to how long the new arrivals would take to intercept them.

"Helm! Pull off the target and put us on a direct intercept course for Captain Carmichael's formation," he said. "All ahead flank."

"All engines ahead flank, aye!"

"Sir, we're under three hours to the target," Corsi said.

"I am well aware of our current position, Commander," Jackson said harshly. "We will be moving the *Jericho* into position so that our cruisers and frigates aren't forced to defend themselves against two battleships, and to do that, we need to change course now. Do you have a problem with that?"

"No, sir!" Corsi said, looking stunned at the rebuke.

"I'm pleased to hear that," Jackson said. "You have the bridge for now, Commander. Keep her making way for Captain Carmichael's ships and call me if the Alliance fleet changes strategy again on us."

"Aye-aye, sir."

"You need to get some rest, Admiral," Barton said softly as he fell in behind Jackson when he strode off the bridge.

"You've been awake as long as I have."

"Yes, sir...but I'm a young man."

"You were," Jackson said.

21

"Transition in five minutes, Captain!"

Barrett just nodded to his OPS officer as she began prepping for the *Nemesis* to transition back into real-space. He'd spent the first few days of the flight out convincing CENTCOM to let him continue on and not request that he turn the ship back to New Sierra. They'd reluctantly agreed, mostly due to conversations with Wolfe that he hadn't been privy to. Accari, through his carefully cultivated intelligence network of smitten young women, had learned that things were going poorly in the Odmena System.

He'd taken his XO's reports of ESA super weapons wiping out most of Odmena with a certain skepticism until he was contacted directly by Admiral Wright. She'd told him that she would be just over a full day behind him into the system with an ultra-secret strike force that, she claimed, was a joint venture between CIS and Starfleet. If they'd moved Celesta back over to an active combat command from her duties at Prowler Fleet, things must *really* be getting out of hand in the Odmena System.

"Standby for transition!" Lieutenant Hori's announcement was picked up by the computer and broadcast throughout the ship. Spacers in all the work centers paused and grabbed onto a handhold while the destroyer's shuddered slightly as she was spit back out into real space once warp drive shut down and the fields collapsed.

"Federation transponder codes coming in now, Captain," Hori said. "The computer is populating the system from the Link data we're getting."

"All weapon systems are active and ready, sir."

"OPS, fire up our own ident beacon," Barrett said. "Fleet codes only, no ship ID. Coms! Contact the *Jericho* through Bluebird and get an update on the situation and find out where Admiral Wolfe would like us deployed."

"Aye, sir...messaging flagship now."

"Sir, Engineering reports full engine power is available at your discretion," Hori said.

"Helm, clear the jump point and begin tracking into the system," Barrett said. "All ahead full."

"All engines ahead full, aye!"

"Sir, the *Jericho* is sending through a detailed report of the encounter so far through Bluebird," the com officer said. "It's going to take five more minutes or so to get it all."

"Do we have a position for Task Force Vega?"

"The data is over four hours old, but their last beacon location and RDS signatures show that the task force is split up, sir," OPS reported. "The *Jericho* is on her own down near the fourth planet, and the rest of the group is in a higher heliocentric orbit between the sixth and seventh planet. It looks like the *Robert Blake* is the lead ship and is taking them down for a rendezvous. The two supply ships aren't showing up, but Admiral Wolfe may have left them in the upper system running dark."

"Let's wait for their status to come through before speculating," Barrett said. "Helm, put us on an intercept for—" he paused to think about where the *Nemesis* would most likely be needed, "the bulk of Task Force Vega. If Admiral Wolfe wants to redirect us, we'll wait for his orders."

"Coming onto new course, aye!" Petty Officer Kyra Healy said.

"Sir there's been...a lot." Lieutenant Hori swallowed hard as she read through the compiled report. "The planet of Odmena has suffered a devastating strike by three antimatter warheads from the ESA fleet. Both of Vega's supply ships were destroyed, and two frigates have suffered critical damage."

"How heavy were the casualties on the planet?" Barrett asked.

"Millions dead," Hori said. "Admiral Wolfe has sent word to get Starfleet rescue and recovery assets into the system, but there's not much hope they'll arrive in time."

"This is how it starts," Accari said matter-of-factly. "The ESA had been careful to not cross the line, playing games hitting military targets, but there's no way the president will let this go. We'll be in a declared state of war before the ash settles on that planet."

Barrett didn't answer. He was concentrating on the familiar, comforting thrum of his ship's engines, feeling the mild vibration through the deck as they strained to shove two hundred and fifty thousand tons of starship through space. Anything to focus on besides the unimaginable loss of life his OPS officer was reporting.

He'd fought on the front lines of two wars and had seen death before, even death on a planetary scale. But this seemed...different. In ways he couldn't articulate even in his own head, the millions lost on a comparatively sparsely populated world like Odmena offended him more than when he had learned Haven—the old Confederation's capital planet—had been completely slagged by the Phage.

The next thought that entered his head as he realized the Federation would now be forced into a fight with the ESA was how completely war-weary he was. He'd been the tactical officer on the TCS *Blue Jacket*, the first ship to fire a shot in anger during the Phage War, and was there right up until the end as the captain of the *Aludra Star* when the Darshik were finally defeated. In both conflicts, he'd always been at the pointy end of the spear and the idea of yet another brutal war, this time with an enemy that understood them far better than the alien threats, seemed to weaken his resolve.

"Captain, we have two Alliance cruisers that will cross below us," Lieutenant Commander Mikaël Brageot reported from tactical. "They're just above the orbit of the fifth planet, following it around to where the larger formation is rallying."

"Could we intercept them and still make it to our own rendezvous with Task Force Vega?" Barrett asked.

"Just," Brageot said. "Nav, want to check me on that?"

"We'll have to push her hard, but we can shallow out our intercept vector for Vega's orbit at the last minute and get within Shrike range of the cruisers with time to spare, sir," Haley said from the helm. Barrett realized she'd already been running the numbers when she heard there was a potential target ahead of them, anticipating what he'd be asking.

"Make it happen, helm," he said. "You're clear to execute any course and velocity changes needed. OPS, tell CIC that I want direct Bluebird access up here at the bridge com station and make sure the flagship knows we'll be pursuing two targets of opportunity before joining the formation."

"Aye, sir."

Barrett watched the *Nemesis's* vital statistics on the main display as Haley swung her about smoothly and pushed the drive to full power. The destroyer was roaring down the well towards the two cruisers that the tactical computer had bracketed and showed were now thirty-nine hours ahead of their maximum effective missile range. He thanked his good fortune that his ship had transitioned in far enough away from the main engagements that he could get his bearing and read all the Link data so that he wasn't hit with any nasty surprises...like an ESA super-weapon that had crippled his ship after a glancing blow in the Eternis System.

"Captain, CIC is done going through all the data the *Jericho* sent, as well as what we've received on the Link so far," Accari said. "It looks like the bulk of Alliance forces are in the middle of an orderly withdraw out of the AO while they move in three new arrivals, apparently real-deal battleships, that are coming down to intercept the admiral's task force.

"The smaller ships in this system match the profile of the Dagger-class attack boats CIS sent us intel on before leaving Eternis Pax, and we're being warned that possibly all of them are carrying at least one antimatter warheads each."

"That makes sense," Barrett said. "Nobody in their right mind would want that weapon on a capital ship. One hiccup in containment and you vaporize a cruiser. Much better to risk a smaller, cheaper ship with a minimal crew."

"Right," Accari went on. "It looks like the ESA commander in this system, Admiral Vadim Kohl, screwed up royally and three of the Daggers collided with each other in low orbit over Odmena, resulting in a disaster when the warheads detonated on the surface."

"Vadim Kohl... I know that guy," Barrett said. "He was a

Lieutenant in Eighth Fleet that had been serving on a survey frigate when I was an Ensign graduating from SWO school and getting assigned to Black Fleet. He was waiting for a class slot after he'd washed out of training for Fleet Intel."

"Do you actually know him, or just know *of* him, sir?" Accari asked.

"He would mill around in transient berthing on *Jericho* Station so we spoke a few times." Barrett shrugged. "Seemed like sort of a loner. Someone told me he made it through training as an SWO and had gone back to Eighth Fleet on a light cruiser."

SWO—Space Warfare Officer—was an all-encompassing designation that included officers who were assigned to the operation of mainline warships within the fleet. The more specialized designators like the engineering officer and flight officer also served aboard starships, but in a more focused capacity.

"Do you have anything you'd like me to give the admiral that might be useful, sir?" Accari asked.

"Nothing the CIS profile hasn't already told him. He has an underserved sense of entitlement coupled with a screaming inferiority complex…or at least that was the rap on him after he'd washed out of Intel and got recycled back through SWO school. You can include that in the log as a note, I guess."

"Yes, sir."

The *Nemesis* continued her headlong rush down the system, bearing down on the helpless Alliance cruisers that, judging by their acceleration profiles, had spotted the destroyer and were now trying to outrun her. Barrett was a bit gun shy after being baited into a trap by the Alliance fleet before, and the idea that this could be another was firmly in his mind. He kept his stoic, cool demeanor he'd tried to adopt from his mentor, Wolfe, while the crew was watching, but his anxiety was ratcheting up in proportion to his ship's increasing velocity.

Nine hours into their charge, he turned the bridge over to Commander Accari and left, rotating out first watch to get some sleep and chow while the *Nemesis* was still repositioning from the outer system. He wanted his crew fresh and ready when they entered the fray. He stopped off at his office that was just outside the bridge on the command deck and brought up the tactical situation composite that CIC updated in real-time based on all the inputs coming into the *Nemesis's* combat nerve center. It was an aggregate representation of the star system, viewed top-down, that let him see their latest intel and the computer's best guess projections for enemy movements all at once thanks to Bluebird and the Link system.

It all looked pretty straight-forward. The Daggers were all moving away from Federation ships at full speed, not bothering to try and hide by deploying their stealth shrouds. The cruisers, including the suspected command ship, *Heart of Xi'an*, were all sweeping up into a holding area while the Alliance's big battleships were on a direct intercept for Captain Carmichael's formation, while the *Jericho* was under power and steaming hard to get there first. It was exactly what he'd expect to see if two flag officers were using standard Fleet doctrine to counter each other, so why did it bother him so much?

The whole scenario was too obvious. From what he'd read so far, Kohl had shown no inclination to want a direct confrontation with Wolfe on equal footing. Instead, he'd relied on clumsy traps, the fact he'd been able to position his ships first, and his numerical advantage. He'd also shown no compunction when it came to destroying non-combatants and putting the population of a planet at risk, both things that were considered off-limits in space warfare going back to the time of Earth nations fighting each other above Mars and Titan. Accident or not, the destruction of Odmena would have vast implications going forward even if they miraculously managed to avoid a full-scale war from this incident.

"What are you up to now?" Barrett muttered.

After another forty-five minutes of staring at the diagram, he gave up and shut the terminal down. He wasn't learning anything new from watching the dots crawl around their orbits, and he was beginning to feel the fatigue of staying up for twenty-eight hours straight. A fresh look when he woke up in a few hours might tell him what he knew, deep down, that he was missing when he looked at the formations on the holographic display.

"Admiral Kohl has begun to move his reserve forces into play."

"He needs to withdraw completely," Zhang said. "We've lost the initiative here...you must see that."

"How do you figure that?"

"The entire point was to try and goad Wolfe into a rash action we could sell to the public, and the Council, as proof that the Federation intended to move against us. Kohl wiping out a planet hurts that narrative."

"We control the narrative," Councilman Chan said. "Who's to say that Wolfe's recklessness wasn't the cause of the atrocity on Odmena? A planet, mind you, that came to us in good faith asking for entrance into our mighty alliance...and now it's a smoldering cinder, destroyed while Wolfe's battleship was in low-orbit."

"The point of this operation was to use Kohl's forces loyal to him to get irrefutable proof of Fed intent by letting Wolfe take out a handful of aging cruisers," Zhang said carefully, aware he was treading on dangerous ground. "You're suggesting simply fabricating a story to sell the public, but the opposition party won't be so easily fooled. When I agreed to facilitate this plan, I made it clear—"

"You agreed because deep down you're a coward, and even the hint of a threat towards your family was enough to secure your cooperation," Chan scoffed. "You're in this to the end, Zhang, and don't forget it. You can forget any ideas you have rattling around up there about betraying us to save your own skin. You'll never make it to the Council Hall to testify, and the people involved you don't even know about are too well-connected."

"My point is that a doctored video and a planet that has obviously been hit with one of our own antimatter weapons aren't going to convince the committees to risk a direct confrontation with the Federation." Zhang ignored the implied threat for now. Chan, for all his bluster, was a junior councilmember that the others in the cabal used as a courier since he could walk freely throughout the capital without being harassed by the state police or capital security. "We've also lost our stream of live intelligence from the battle so, for all we know, Kohl's fleet has already been wiped out."

"Just...stop," Chan sighed. "We're moving forward with what we have. When we get word back from Kohl, along with all the raw sensor data, we'll adjust accordingly. Just keep up as you have been and keep trying to re-open communications with the plant in Wolfe's fleet."

Once Chan left, Zhang knew that most of the cabal would be going to a military prison. They were too fixated on the goal to realize they'd lost an opportunity and had, in the process, facilitated an atrocity that would mar their family names for generations. Sadly, the architects of the failed plan would still get their war. He had no doubt that with Joseph Marcum advising President Stark, the Federation Parliament would move quickly to first condemn the ESA's actions, then move to formally declare war.

He knew that his nation had more ships, and that they'd received upgrades in weaponry and propulsion from the Darshik, but he still didn't think they would prevail. More than that, though, was the potential for destruction a war between the human factions would unleash. Humans had fought wars with each other before, centuries ago, and had managed to mostly contain the collateral damage even in the age of the strategic nuclear weapon. He almost couldn't imagine creating such weapons to aim them at an enemy that was on the *same planet* you were. How short-sighted his ancestors must have been.

Those weapons were only used four times in all those wars, and none of the warheads detonated were more powerful than twenty kilotons. The massive gigaton warheads were dismantled shortly after the armistice agreement following the Third Great War. But now humans had access to an even more powerful weapon to turn on its enemy: starships. More specifically, mainline warships.

A ship like the *Nemesis* or the *Jericho* could depopulate a planet in short order if she turned her weapons on it, and do so quickly enough that it would be difficult to stop them. Now that Kohl had set the precedent, he feared what would happen if weapons meant for deep space combat were brought to bear on inhabited planets.

The war could be a holocaust the likes of which had never been seen. As these thoughts bounced chaotically in his head, Zhang knew he had to do something. He had no real power here in the capital, and he knew of no ally he could turn to that might stop this madness. His only option left to him would be to beg Anders to take him back to New Sierra, where he could ask for asylum and turn everything over to their CIS and hope that Starfleet could head things off before they moved beyond the point of no return.

"I can't win, no matter what I do," Zhang sighed bitterly at his lot in life. On cue, his comlink pinged once on his desk with a simple message on the screen:

Mr. Anders will be in to see you shortly.

He knew this visit was no coincidence, and that the Agent knew Councilman Chan had just been there to see him. His mind made up, he began to formulate his strategy on how he'd convince Anders to spirit him and his family away and get them back to New Sierra before his cohorts decided he posed too much of a risk.

22

"That makes twenty-six of the smaller ships that have broken off from their original course, Admiral," Lieutenant Orr reported. "The *Nemesis* has identified them as *Dagger*-class small attack boats."

"What about the remaining Daggers?" Jackson asked. "What are they doing?"

"They're off-scope, sir," Easton reported. "CIC lost track of them when they shut down their drives and deployed their stealth shrouds."

"So, they're cold coasting along towards the same area near the New Berlin jump point Kohl's new forces have rallied. Ignore them for now, they can't reverse course without lighting up their drives again. The real question is where the other twenty-six are going. This new course doesn't give them an obvious intercept vector for us or the rest of the task force."

"There's nothing along their new course of any interest,

sir," Orr confirmed. "Perhaps they've received new intel about Federation reinforcements heading this way?"

"They know the *Nemesis* has arrived by now, even with Captain Barrett not broadcasting his ship ID. They'll have radar profiles for all our mainline ships," Jackson said. "Make sure CIC is keeping track of any changes to their course or speed."

Jackson rotated his people out, left the bridge himself to try and catch a few hours of sleep where he could, and watched things unfold as Kohl began redeploying his forces for what would be the final push in what had become a one-sided battle. Despite Wolfe's superior range and firepower—something he hoped would overcome the enemy's numerical edge—he'd so far been stymied by Kohl at every turn including failing to prevent three antimatter charges from hitting a Federation planet.

The chaos aboard the flagship with double agents, traitors, and an entire command structure in upheaval after two inexplicable suicides were distracting enough for him. Adding to that was the fact that the battle itself, something he ostensibly was supposed to excel at, was not breaking his way no matter what he tried.

Kohl had put him back on his heels and chased his broken formation all over the system with a few aging cruisers and a clever gimmick with his smaller attack boats. Jackson's confidence in his ability to command a ship and to manage a battle had been shaken, and now he was second guessing every move he might make in response to the Alliance fleet. Each time a ship changed course, he felt that Kohl must be following some master strategy and that he was floundering, struggling to keep up.

"Admiral," Commander McVey nodded to Jackson as he walked back onto the bridge after choking down a late dinner and grabbing five hours of uninterrupted sleep, a rarity lately.

"Commander," Jackson said, walking over to the OPS station and scrolling through the master log. "Anything of note to report?"

"The formation of Daggers that broke off has changed course," McVey said. "CIC says it's likely they're heading back to Odmena."

"Define likely."

"Seventy-two percent chance of certainty from the analysts."

"Can we move to intercept?" Jackson asked.

"They'll reach the planet well before we could move anything back down the well to stop them, sir."

Jackson seethed at the news. While there wasn't much left on Odmena for Kohl to threaten him with, there were five massive orbital installations over the planet that, between them, had another one hundred and sixty thousand people. It was almost certain Kohl was going to move his attack boats back into orbit and threaten those facilities unless Jackson conceded to his wishes.

"Could the *Nemesis* make it down there in time?" he asked.

"The top acceleration and velocity numbers for the *Nemesis* are classified at a level that—"

"Have CIC ask them over Bluebird," Jackson interrupted.

"Captain Barrett says it would be close if he ran at full emergency power, but he still wouldn't get there until sixteen hours after the Dagger fleet," McVey said after a few moments of talking with the com officer on watch.

"Coms, let the Odmena orbital platforms know they have incoming hostiles and that we are no longer in position to offer aid," Jackson said, the words combining with stale coffee to leave a sour, alkali taste in his mouth.

"Aye, sir," the com officer said quietly. Jackson could hear it in her voice, too. Her confidence and resolve were shaken. He looked around the bridge and saw other crewmembers quickly avert their gaze and could only guess what they were thinking.

"Admiral, you have an incoming transmission from... unknown source," the OPS officer said. "Point of origin is within the Alliance cruiser formation."

"What type of transmission?"

"Unencrypted data packet addressed to you personally, sir. Likely a bundled media transmission."

"Mr. McVey, you still have the bridge. Send the message to the terminal in my office."

"Aye, sir."

Jackson made his way to what used to be Captain Hardy's office and closed the hatch. He looked around for a moment, uncomfortable at all the personal effects still there, including pictures of his wife and their four children. He'd wanted to have the office cleaned out and packed up, but the master at arms had wanted to maintain it as it had been for the investigation.

He sat in the well-worn leather chair and logged into the terminal, waiting as the message that the com shop had received was bounced to him. He wasn't surprised when the bundle unpacked itself and the prominent item was a video from Admiral Vadim Kohl.

"Greetings, Admiral Wolfe," Kohl began. "I wish we were meeting under different circumstances. I consider myself a student of yours, having studied your career and mastery of space combat, modeling my own style after yours.

"As you now must see, you cannot win here. I'm holding

the high ground with superior numbers and now, with the arrival of my battleships, have shifted the balance of firepower in my favor, as well. I have fulfilled my mission and, with the regrettable incident over the planet, we no longer are worried about vying for Odmena's favor. I am declaring this system as part of the Eastern Star Alliance. As a token of my respect for you, I will allow your ships to jettison your Shrike II missiles and exit the system back into Federation space. This is a time-limited offer that I make in good faith. You have six hours to signal your compliance, and then I will be compelled to remove you from Alliance space by force."

Kohl looked like he had more to say, then abruptly ended the recording. An odd mix of emotions washed over Jackson as he stared at the black terminal screen. He knew the offer Kohl had made was a trap he wasn't expected to accept. If Jackson were foolish enough to dump his Shrikes overboard and try to leave, the Alliance fleet would swarm his task force, and they'd be wiped out. They'd worked hard to get him here, and they weren't about to let him leave freely. It was interesting that Kohl hadn't mentioned the Daggers moving back down towards the orbital facilities. Perhaps he intended to wipe them out regardless now that he'd laid claim to the system. More likely, he meant to use them as leverage once he realized Jackson wasn't complying with his demands.

"Wolfe to bridge, status?" he asked, holding down the intercom button on the desk.

"No change, Admiral."

"Tell Commander McVey no change in his orders. Steady as she goes towards Captain Carmichael's position."

"Aye-aye, sir."

The tile in his thigh pocket chimed, letting him know

that a Bluebird communique had been received addressed specifically to him. He pulled the device out, dreading what he was about to read. It took him two full passes through the message to fully absorb what it told him. Slowly, a smile spread across his face as a cool wave of relief crashed over him. Finally, there had been a stroke of luck in this Godforsaken operation, and he quickly began adjusting his plans accordingly.

Once he had what he wanted to do firmly in his mind, he fired off a response to the message and began programming the tactical simulation software with the changes to make sure he was covering as many contingencies as possible. He couldn't let Admiral Kohl leave the system once he realized what had happened.

"This is an utter fucking disaster."

"That's one way to put it."

Everyone in the room sat silently for a moment, nobody wanting to be the first to speak.

"You think Wolfe's past his sell-by date? Should we pull him and let Wright take command of the AO?" Marcum asked. It was a small, private briefing on the surface of New Sierra that would allow the senior military leadership to get on the same page before they briefed the president later that afternoon. "I've never seen him lose control of a ship and a battle this spectacularly, not even when we were almost wiped out at Nuovo Patria."

"A ridiculous assertion," Pitt said. "He's not infallible. He put himself into a bad position by not recognizing in time that the orders we'd saddled him with were no longer achievable. When he moved the *Jericho* to make his presence felt over the planet, he put things in motion he couldn't undo. He also had no way of knowing that Vadim Kohl would be so willing to risk an entire planet's population to achieve his goals."

"I wasn't being serious about reliving him...mostly. So, what's our best-case scenario here?" Marcum asked.

"Wolfe will capture or kill Kohl, not lose his entire task force, and the Odmena System remains in Federation hands...what's left of it anyway. Without a habitable planet or a com drone platform, it's become less of a logistical asset and more of a strategic outpost given its unusually high number of jump points."

"And if we lose Task Force Vega, including the *Jericho* and the *Nemesis*?"

"We'll be in real trouble," Pitt admitted. "We'll be relying heavily on Vega to spearhead any operations into ESA space now that a war seems imminent. Losing a battleship and the Fleet's most capable destroyer wouldn't be crippling but damn, close."

"Fucking disaster," Marcum repeated.

"What has Pike found? Pitt asked CIS Director Perez.

"Quite a bit, actually," Perez said, clearing his throat. He tended to not talk much during discussions of Fleet operations since that wasn't his area of expertise. It was refreshing to Pitt to find a political appointee who didn't feel the need to interject themselves into every conversation regardless of whether they were needed or not.

"It appears this Odmena operation is not sanctioned by the ESA Council. It's a small cabal within the Council and Alliance Fleet Command that have decided to kick off what they see as an inevitable war while they still hold the advantage. They're afraid if they give Starfleet too much time to rebuild, we'll roll right over top of them."

"They're not wrong there," Marcum groused. "What about specifics? Has he been able to ferret out what the Darshik may have given the ESA in trade for selling us out?"

"He's working on it," Perez said evasively. "While not entirely germane to the conversation, the person who he's working to turn—the facilitator for this small group—is the same man who ran the Asianic Union's illegal expansion program that stumbled upon the Phage."

"*That* asshole?" Marcum groaned. "How is he even still alive after all the damage he's done? Never mind. You think Pike can bring him here, and we can really put the screws to him?"

"I have every confidence my Agent is up to the task of extracting any useful information from a bureaucrat, even if the subject is less than willing," Perez said. His precise manner of speech and urbaneness were in sharp contrast to Marcum's perceptible twang and casual profanity. "But he has been instructed to bring Zhang back to Federation space if he thinks there's an advantage to that. We currently have a more pressing problem in that area that I need handled first, however."

"That being?" Pitt asked.

"Someone from my organization has a Bluebird transceiver and has been feeding leaked information from Wolfe's task force to Zhang." Perez squirmed. "We know who it is and have taken steps to cut off the flow of information, but I want Pike to eliminate the traitor before we send the remote destruct command to the box."

"There's no way you can use this to your advantage?" Pitt asked. "All Bluebird messages get routed through one of our com ships. Perhaps a counterintelligence operation to feed your traitor inaccurate intel?"

"Too risky," Perez said. "We've gone over the messages,

and they're speaking in some type of prearranged code. We could crack it, but one slip up, and we'll have alerted the enemy we're on to them. I'm also concerned that group isn't the only one we have within Starfleet and CIS with sympathetic leanings."

"We need to dig into that further, and do it quickly before this war escalates on us," Marcum said, pushing his chair back. "Admiral Pitt and Director Perez are due to brief the president in twenty minutes, and the man despises people being late for appointed meetings. The rest of you, I better not hear a word about these off-book meetings. Understood?"

The rest of the fleet officers and government officials that Marcum had brought into the circle mumbled their agreement and began filing out of the room. He paused at the door while the others collected the comlinks and tiles they were forbidden from bringing into the secure room and put a hand on Pitt's shoulder, holding him back.

"You had something else, sir?" Pitt asked.

"Who has operational control over Wright's strike group?"

"For the duration of this mission, CENTCOM has overall control, but Admiral Wright is to remain...unencumbered... by the traditional chain of command per CIS," Pitt said.

"We both know when she arrives at the Odmena System, she'll report to Wolfe and take his orders," Marcum said. "Do we have any way to supersede that and step in if need be? My point is that those ships cannot fall into enemy hands. Preferably, I'd rather the ESA not even know they exist. If we have to withdraw her, even if it leaves Vega flapping in the breeze, will she follow orders and do the hard thing?"

"Honestly? I don't know," Pitt said. "At this point, given the things we've put in motion, we'll have little choice but to let his play out as it will and trust the people we've put in charge."

Marcum just grunted but said nothing. Pitt understood his concern, but his outlook was tempered with a bit of realism. Wolfe's legend had been built up to mythological proportions, even among those who knew him well, and to see him stumble as he had in this mission was frightening. He was viewed by those in power as the secret weapon that could be unleashed to save the day, but the truth was much more complicated. Pitt knew that the Odmena operation was going poorly for other reasons than Wolfe being outmaneuvered by Kohl.

Despite all of that, he remained confident his man would come through as he always did. Perhaps he was no more immune to the hero worship of the man who had seemingly pulled off miracles than those in the lower ranks.

"You better get going. The president will have a fit if you're late," Marcum said, moving so Pitt could leave. "I hope you're right about this."

"Me too."

23

"The two battleships have peeled away from the main formation to intercept the *Jericho*, ma'am. The third large, unknown target is still loitering near the boundary."

"I see that," Celesta said. "What about the Dagger-class ships approaching the planet?"

"The leading ships of that element will be within the assumed weapons range for that class in nine hours, ma'am," the *Broadsword*'s OPS officer said. "They've begun braking and are splitting up into three smaller groups to go after the larger platforms. Admiral Wolfe has warned the orbitals that the enemy is inbound, and they claim to have a few surprises for them."

"I can't imagine they have anything more than the outdated point-defense batteries most platforms have to vaporize the larger meteors that come their way," Celesta said. "I'd like to warn them to not provoke the Alliance ships, but we can't warn them without giving away our presence."

"Has Admiral Wolfe given any indication where he

might want us, ma'am?" Captain Parker Risher, CO of the *Broadsword* was standing behind her and to the right.

"Not yet, only that he wants to make sure wherever we're deployed, it's not a frivolous use," Celesta said. "Ideally, we'd like the ESA to still be ignorant that these ships exist."

"Of course, ma'am."

The Valkyrie-class hulls that had been finished to make up the Wolfpack strike force had been named after a cultural mishmash of ancient sword types from at least four different Earth cultures, the *Broadsword* being the lead ship of the formation. After her, there was *Saber*, *Katana*, *Cutlass*, and *Gladius*.

Celesta still wasn't sure how she felt about her new command. The ships represented a lot of power that wasn't under Starfleet's chain of command or the civilian oversight. She understood the reasoning behind keeping them a secret but, historically, that sort of power in the hands of a few unelected, unaccountable people tended to end poorly. The *Nemesis* had been a significant leap forward in starship design and potential for destruction, and the five ships she currently wielded were even more advanced.

When the strike force had arrived in Odmena without so much as a flicker of light to announce their arrival, she'd messaged Wolfe's personal Bluebird address and let him know she had arrived. She'd briefly explained the capabilities of her new command, and when she stressed that the people in charge would prefer if they remained a secret, he had her hold position until he was certain about what Kohl's move was.

From what she'd been able to pick up from Wolfe's reports and the Link broadcast they were now receiving, the Alliance ships had been aware Task Force Vega was inbound and had set their pieces on the board before the first Federation ship had transitioned in. Given the fact the flagship had lost its captain *and* executive officer in bizarre back to back suicides, it was amazing that all he'd lost so far was two supply ships.

"The remaining Alliance cruisers are moving to block Captain Carmichael's formation," OPS reported.

"They want to make sure the *Jericho* can't receive any help. Kohl wants to force Wolfe into a two on one," Risher said. "Shall we prepare the strike force for battle in case the call comes into help, Admiral?"

"Ready missile launch tubes only," she said. "We can't afford to run the powerplants any hotter to charge the MAC capacitor banks or to generate plasma."

"Aye, ma'am."

Celesta was painfully aware of how unqualified she was given her unfamiliarity with the ships so she made an effort to stay out of the way and offer direction only in the broadest strokes. The crews had been carefully screened and extensively trained. She was more or less there as a political observer at the request of Director Perez. That also meant that if something went horribly wrong, she'd be the one to take the blame.

"Admiral Wright, I have a Bluebird message that's come in addressed for your eyes only."

"Send it to the auxiliary terminal," Celesta said, walking over to the station at the rear bulkhead and logging in. It took less than a minute for the message to come up and it wasn't from who she'd expected it to be from.

ADM WRIGHT... WILL HAVE SIX ASYLUM SEEKERS ABOARD MY SHIP AND WITHIN THREE DAYS AND FLYING TO ODMENA. UNDERSTAND YOU ARE IN AREA

WITH NEW COMMAND? NEED TO OFFLOAD THEM WITH YOU OR WOLFE'S GROUP AND THEN MOVE BACK INTO ESA SPACE WITHOUT BEING REPORTED. POSSIBLE? –PIKE

The message was almost written as if Pike expected it to be intercepted. Normally, against regulations, he wrote his Bluebird dispatches to her as if he were writing a sweeping epic with multiple points of view, subplots, and enough extraneous detail that they took forever to download through the system. She thought a moment how to respond before answering him. Three days plus transit for a Broadhead wasn't a long time given how long battles in space could drag out.

CAN CONFIRM LOCATION OF STRIKE FORCE AS ODMENA SYSTEM. PROCEED WITH CAUTION. BATTLE IN PROGRESS, LIKELY STILL HOT SYSTEM IN THREE DAYS TIME. SUGGEST YOU KEEP LOW PROFILE UNTIL ENEMY FORCES ARE SUBDUED OR MOVE OUT.

She didn't expect a confirmation back from him, so she logged off the terminal and moved back to the center of the bridge. On the main display, she could see that the *Jericho* had come about to a course that would take her head to head with the two Alliance battleships and was accelerating hard. Now that Kohl had committed to splitting his forces, Wolfe no longer had to hang back and worry about covering the rest of the task force. She saw another track bearing down into the engagement that was flying fleet codes, but no ship ID.

"Who is our shy friend here?" she asked, pointing to the fast-moving blip.

"Engine profile matches the *Nemesis*, Admiral."

"Captain Barrett was reported leaving Eternis Pax about the time we departed home port," Risher said. "He made good time getting out here."

"That he did," she said. "Do we have an idea where he's going?"

"From the course changes we've seen so far, he looks to be heading for Captain Carmichael's group at flank speed," the OPS officer said. "She's shallowing out too much after crossing the orbit of the sixth planet to provide aid to the *Jericho*."

"Captain, I think we can safely assume we won't be needed in the direct engagements between the Fed and Alliance capital ships," Celesta said. "I'd like a direct-jump course plotted to put us in position to intercept the Dagger-class ships moving back to Odmena Prime."

"Nav, set up jump coordinates to put us in right behind the Alliance Dagger formations," Risher said. "OPS, send it out to the rest of the strike force via the short-range laser."

"Captain, Admiral...Captain Carmichael's formation has been engaged," the com officer said. "We're receiving Blue-bird updates."

"Damn sensor data is hours old at this range," Risher said quietly. "If Carmichael is in a fight, the *Jericho* is almost in range for the opening shots of their engagement."

"Which leaves us still not knowing what that massive RDS signature is that's been lagging behind the Alliance cruisers," Celesta said. "OPS, has anybody put eyes on that thing yet?"

"Nothing reported over the Link, Admiral. Radar returns were inconclusive. Other than being larger than even the battleships, it has an oddly dispersed thermal signature along its outer hull."

"Interesting, but not pressing," Celesta said. "Let's remain focused on the threat to the larger orbitals around Odmena and be ready to move if the Alliance decides they're going to do something else stupid when it comes to firing on civilians."

"Aye, ma'am."

"Incoming channel request, Admiral. It's marked as coming from the *Heart of Xi-an*."

"That'll be Admiral Kohl," Jackson said. "What's the com lag between us and the *Heart*?"

"Just over fourteen minutes, sir."

"Send the channel through to the station here," Jackson said, pulling the monitor around on the command chair. A moment later, the face of a middle-aged man of Eastern European lineage appeared. His trim beard flecked with gray and his blue eyes piercing under a heavy brow. Jackson pressed the 'play' indicator at the bottom of the image.

"Admiral Wolfe, this has regrettably gotten out of hand. We were here at the behest of the Odmena regional government; we did not come to cause trouble. The loss of life already has been tragic," Kohl paused for a moment before continuing.

"As you can see, you are out-gunned and out-matched here, Admiral. My honor demands that I extract some level of justice for the deaths on the planet your actions precipitated. I have no wish to wipe out your small flotilla, so I have a compromise to propose. Surrender yourself, allow me to take you back to Alliance space, and you alone can stand trial for what has happened here with no need to further hostilities. I await your reply."

"He can't be serious," Commander McVey said.

"He's not," Jackson said. "This is just stalling for time." He pulled up another window on his terminal and did a quick search for something in the archive before pressing the spot on the monitor to record his reply.

"Admiral Kohl, you are already in violation of the Xi'an Nonaggression Pact agreed to by both of our governments, specifically sections six-alpha and six-bravo: transiting sovereign space with ships of war without prior notification. I'm not even getting into the issue of three of your antimatter warheads being used in the slaughter of millions of Federation citizens and the rendering of a Federation planet uninhabitable. Your crimes have been documented and sent back to New Sierra where, I'd imagine, a suitable response will be agreed upon.

"Should *you* wish to surrender yourself and be tried for your crimes here, you might succeed in heading off a war that will cost both sides dearly. Do the right thing, Admiral...ignore whoever sent you here on orders and sacrifice yourself for the greater good. You speak of your honor. We both know there's only one course of action here that will allow you to retain any of it." He pressed the stop/send indicator on the monitor and leaned back in the seat, knowing that the enemy had no intention of surrendering or taking him prisoner.

"OPS, has the *Blake* been able to get a better look at that inbound behemoth?"

"No, sir," Orr said. "The hull is oddly irregular, and there appears to be gaps in the plating that appear and disappear.

The *Blake*'s CIC says it almost looks like it's coming apart when looked at through the high-power array. They're still — Whoa! Captain Carmichael has just taken out two Alliance cruisers, sir! Updates coming in over the Link."

"Let CIC feed you updates from the rest of the task force, I need you focused on the battleships ahead of us," Jackson said. "Where is the *Heart of Xi'an*?"

"Lagging back behind the rest of the cruisers attacking Captain Carmichael's ships, sir. It's braking at full power and pulling off to keep out of effective Shrike range," Easton spoke up from tactical.

"CIC confirms that the transmission from Kohl came from that ship, sir," Orr added.

Jackson checked his own forces, running the numbers in his head, and realized none of his ships had a chance of catching the *Heart* if she continued to angle away from the engagement like she was. The *Nemesis* was coming in as fast as Barrett could flog her, but she was still halfway across the system.

Celesta Wright's top-secret strike force could do it, but she only had five ships, and Kohl had sent twenty-six of his smaller attack boats back towards the planet. Jackson could ask her to pull one off to perform a warp hop close to the *Heart of Xi'an* and try to capture her, but who knew if the remaining four would be enough to protect the orbitals or if Kohl's flagship was carrying antimatter-equipped missiles.

The other factor was that of timing. If he ordered Celesta's ships to the planet to intercept the inbound Daggers, she'd have to jump in further away because even the cutting-edge warp drives had to respect the gravitational pull of something the size of Odmena. That meant she'd have to run down the smaller ships the conventional way, defend against their missiles, and score twenty-six kills before even one of them could fire on a heavily populated orbital.

In the end, the decision was easy. Protecting civilian lives took precedent over any strictly military goal. The Wolfpack had five ships, which was really stretching it to intercept all three groups even as capable as Celesta said her new ships were. He pulled out his secure tile and fired off a message to her while waiting for Kohl's response to his last transmission.

ADM WRIGHT, ORBITALS OVER ODMENA HEAVILY POPULATED. SUGGEST YOU USE YOUR FORCE TO ENSURE THEIR SAFETY. YOU MAY ENGAGE THE ENEMY AT YOUR DISCRETION. GOOD LUCK. –ADM WOLFE

He continued to monitor Carmichael's battle while waiting. So far, it looked like the veteran captain was really taking it to the Alliance formation. He'd destroyed three ships outright with Shrike hits, and a fourth was taking heavy hits, unable to defend itself. Jackson wanted to warn Carmichael not to outrun his own flanking ships, but he couldn't micromanage the battle from where he was sitting hundreds of thousands of kilometers away. Carmichael had proven himself more than capable thus far, so Jackson tamped down his instinct to step in and let the man run his fight.

"Incoming response on the open channel, Admiral," Orr said. A split second later, the green icon of a received message flashed. He pressed it and sat back to see what Kohl had to say in reply.

"It would appear we have nothing more to discuss,

Admiral," Kohl said. "I would have liked to have faced you in your prime, not this shade of your former self that you've shown me here in this system. Lodge any protests you wish about treaty violations like the politician you've become...by the time your com drone reaches New Sierra, this will all be over. Godspeed, Admiral."

"Tactical?" Jackson asked.

"In range, Admiral," Easton replied. Both incoming battleships on the main display had been marked in purple, now they both had pulsing red crosshairs on them to indicate the tactical computer was locked on and tracking.

"Fire first volley and reset for our second run," Jackson said, his calm voice belied the excited tension he felt now that he was about to unleash the *Jericho's* full might upon the enemy. Any doubts he'd harbored about fighting humans had been ground down to a nub as Kohl showed a shocking lack of compunction when it came to killing noncombatants. Since he'd not been removed from command, he could only assume his officers were complicit in acts that the Federation Parliament would view as war crimes.

"Firing! Spitting out tubes one through ten, stagger fire patter," Easton said. "Tubes clear! Reloading."

"Firing solution for the MACs," Jackson ordered as he watched the tracks of his ten missiles crawl away from the green icon of the *Jericho* on the display. It was a basic opening salvo with five missiles to each target a number that showed respect to the Alliance boomers, but not enough to tip his hand just yet.

"MACs charged and ready, sir," Easton said. "Firing solution locked."

"Helm, all ahead emergency."

"Safety locks disengaged, all engines ahead full emergency power, aye!"

The deck of the *Jericho* shook harshly as the engines ramped up, the massive field generators greedily sucking up every bit of power the reactors could give them as the power levels shot past rated maximum. Jackson watched as they leveled out at one-hundred and twenty-two percent and made a note to compliment Chief Engineer McKenna for keeping the drive so finely tuned it could achieve such an impressive output. As the cooling systems were taxed, the computers would keep pulling the power back to keep the field emitters from overloading unless Jackson entered the command codes to disable the secondary safety interlocks. Then the ship would run wide open until she burned herself out.

"Targets maintaining interval and increasing acceleration to mirror us, sir," Easton said. "We're reading a marked increase in thermal energy near the prow on both ships, CIC says its inconsistent with the normal leakage they'd expect from a large-bore laser."

"If my guess is correct, we're seeing the thing that's making them rush downhill at us so confidently," Jackson said. "Have CIC monitoring for high-energy EM fields that suddenly pop up around either ship and have them cross check the thermal signature with anything Darshik we have in the database."

"Aye, sir."

"Darshik?" McVey asked.

"The RDS these ships are using isn't Federation in origin," Jackson explained. "I'm guessing their partnership with the Darshik during the Expansion War included drive and weapons tech in exchange for the location of Federation military installations."

"Darshik weapons tech wasn't any more advanced than our own." McVey frowned. Jackson ignored him and concentrated on the detailed situation display in front of him. The ships had now crossed a million kilometers of gap and were bearing down on each other as hard as their drives could push them. The closing speed between them was climbing, but still under .10C, and the Alliance ships seemed to be reducing their acceleration, content to coast the rest of the way in. The weapons Jackson suspected they had weren't optimally effective at high-speed passes, so he kept his own ship at full power.

"Shrikes have burned out their first stage boosters, cold coasting and waiting for the second fire command," Easton said.

"Acknowledged," Jackson said. "Hold fast...timing will be critical here."

The three battleships were screaming at each other, the closure speed becoming more apparent as the gap shrunk. As far as Jackson knew, this was the first time this class-type of warship had ever met head-to-head in battle. Few true battleships had ever been built due to cost and lack of mission, almost none of those had ever seen combat in the centuries leading up to this moment. Even the newer Dreadnought-class hadn't been used for anything other than a command platform during the Phage War.

"High-energy EM detected!" Lieutenant Orr said. "CIC reports that both ships are producing high-power fields emitting from the prows and thermal signature is continuing to climb."

"Both ships have shut down their drives, they're angling in towards us. It looks like they're going to try and pinch us in between them on the first pass," Easton said.

"Very good, Lieutenant," Jackson said. "That's exactly what they're going to do. They'll try and take out our first salvo of missiles, and then rake both flanks as we go by at speed. Standby Shrikes for second fire command...fire!"

"Firing!"

The Shrike missiles that had been coasting out ahead of them fired their second stage booster and accelerated away from the *Jericho* again. They were close enough now that the high-power radar array could provide a detailed picture of the incoming threat, and Jackson could see both battleships adjust their attitude again to overlap fields of fire. That would have been a good, basic strategy...if Jackson had been targeting both ships.

At the point when they'd expect the missiles to break off and head for their respective targets, all ten Shrikes veered right and went after only one battleship. The missile formation split up, some flying high, low, and right relative to the engagement plane, and ignited their final stages to try and get in past the target's point defense.

"Helm! Twelve degrees to port," Jackson ordered. "Engines ahead one half. Tactical, you have control of the MAC turrets, fire at your discretion."

"Engines ahead one half, aye!" the helmsman said and pulled the power back on the drives. At half-power, the engines had just enough push to move them onto the new course and keep their closure speed the same so the MACs would have a stable platform for their volley."

"Bogey Two is activating point defense, Bogey One has... activated a plasma lance! It's trying to hit the missiles as they go by," Easton said.

Jackson watched, knowing that the Darshik plasma lance the battleships were carrying wasn't something easily directed. The first ship tried to angle over and widened its beam, but the missiles had already skirted out of the weapon's effective range. All the captain had done was expose his starboard flank to the *Jericho*, seeming to forget that the Fed boomer was roaring down their throat.

"Two missiles collected...three...impacts! Two more!" Orr shouted, taking over battle damage assessment duties while Easton concentrated on his next task. "Four missiles made it through, Admiral. CIC reports secondary explosions within the hull."

"They're out of the fight. Keep monitoring them but don't report," Jackson said. "Tactical!"

"MACs targeted and ready...waiting for optimal range."

The remaining battleship seemed to remember there was still a threat out there and swung wildly back as the *Jericho* sped across her prow and was now angling for a shot on her outside flank. The plasma lance seemed to lose cohesion during the maneuver, and then winked out entirely. Loud *bangs* could be heard and felt as the big ship bucked as if hit with a giant hammer.

"We're being hit with laser fire...outer armor not breached," Orr said. "CIC reports no significant system damage."

"Mr. Easton?" Jackson asked, not worried about laser cannons given how heavily armored the battleship was.

"Five seconds...standby. Firing MACs!"

The two double barrel turrets, one dorsal, the other ventral, spat out six shots apiece. Unlike the old magcannons, however, Fed engineers had also taken a page from the Darshik and, instead of ferrous shells, the cannons fired plasma bursts. The hyper-heated gas streaked away from the *Jericho*, leaving a fiery trail in its wake.

"Helm, hard to port! All ahead flank!"

"Coming about, all engines ahead flank!"

The *Jericho* swung out away from the engagement, leaving the doomed Alliance battleship lagging behind and out of weapons range. The MAC—Magneto-plasma Accelerator Cannon—shots were self-contained, each shot carrying its own EM field generator to keep the plasma contained and cohesive. It wasn't a long-range weapon, but it was devastating when it hit Terran starship armor.

"Two shots missed...the rest have impacted down the target's starboard side," Orr said, his voice subdued. "CIC reports dozens of large breaches, hundreds of microbreaches, and significant internal structural damage. She's adrift and burning, sir."

The plasma charges boiled away hull armor on impact, leaving a large gap in the ship for the weapon's last little nasty surprise: a small thermonuclear charge that was piggybacking the containment field generator and would detonate within the exposed areas.

"Incoming!" Easton called. "They got two missiles off before they were hit. Point defense is tracking, aft starboard quadrant cannons are standing by."

Jackson waited quietly while the missiles closed the short gap, letting his people do their jobs. He saw one missile wink out of existence as the lasers heated it to failure, but the second seemed to find a crease in the protection and was still coming.

"All hands, brace for impact!" the call went out over the ship-wide PA. Jackson didn't bother with the restraints, just grabbed the "oh, shit!" handles on either side of his seat and gritted his teeth.

At first, he thought the missile may have been stopped, but then the deck heaved, and his shoulders were wrenched in their sockets as he held fast to keep from being tossed onto the deck. The bridge lights flickered once and damage reports began scrolling across the display attached to his seat.

"Proximity detonation, hull breach in section thirty-seven, deck nineteen," Orr reported. "Damage control teams are dispatched and pressure hatches are holding. Engineering reports the RDS is offline. We're ballistic, sir."

"Damn lucky shot," Easton grumbled as Jackson stood.

"Casualties?" he asked.

"Six minor injuries reported so far, no deaths, sir."

"Status of enemy ships?"

"Bogey Two is breaking up, Bogey One is adrift and still burning, sir. Twenty-nine lifeboat launches detected from both ships."

"Mark their locations," Jackson said. "Give me a status on Captain Carmichael's group."

"The enemy is trying to disengage, sir," Orr said. "Two of our ships have taken significant damage and have dropped back, the *Ghost Dancer* is reporting *critical* damage and may need to abandon ship if they can't get it under control. Enemy has lost seven ships, and the *Blake* is still pressing them as they retreat. The *Nemesis* is still out of range and is targeting the ship we've identified as the *Heart of Xi'an*, but it's already moving off towards the New Berlin jump point."

"Understood," Jackson said. "Inform Captain Carmichael that he is clear to keep engaged as long as he can without undue risk to the rest of his group, and then tell Commander McKenna he has five minutes to give me an answer on when my ship will be under power again."

"Aye, sir."

Jackson pulled his tile out and read the two Bluebird messages that had come in while he was engaged with the two Alliance ships. Admiral Wright had taken the initiative and moved her ships down to the planet to head off the fleet of attack boats that were still bearing down on the orbitals. He frowned, trying to put himself in Kohl's mind. The

Alliance admiral had lost the initiative, and the battle was decided. The only rational move at this point would be to order a withdraw, maybe even petition Jackson for a cease-fire and leave while he could. There was nothing to gain by further provoking the Federation with yet another attack on a civilian target.

"Sir, Chief Engineer McKenna says he's coming up to brief you personally, but that the *Jericho* will be dead in space for at least another twelve to fourteen hours," Orr said. "He's stressing that's a best-case scenario. There's the possibility we'll be stuck until a recovery ship can come out and assist with repairs."

"Tell him I don't need him up here, and that if he makes me call a recovery ship to get back to Federation space, he'll be riding on the outside of the hull for the duration of the flight," Jackson said. The comment was so out of character that his OPS officer just stared at him for a moment before slipping the headset back up and relaying the message.

"Sir, the third large target is on the move again," Easton said. "It's moving on an intercept for the rest of the task force. CIC is relaying the warning to the *Blake*."

"I guess we'll get to see what the hell that thing is after all," Jackson said, feeling helpless as the battleship underneath him drifted uncontrolled through space.

24

"What...what the fuck am I looking at, OPS?"

"Sir, I-I mean, CIC is saying this matches no known class-type configuration."

Captain Carmichael paced the bridge of the Robert *Blake*, unsure what he should do. Admiral Wolfe had just taken on two Alliance battleships in a head-to-head run and kicked the shit out of both—a beautiful sight to behold—but had taken damage to the *Jericho* in the process. His ships were showing the strain of the running engagement and he'd had to send three to the rear to keep them from taking any more hits. The *Ghost Dancer* may yet have to be scuttled, and he hadn't been able to rotate his crew for the better part of two days.

The last thing he wanted to do right now was try and take on a large, unknown bogey with his beat-up task force while the *Jericho* was making emergency repairs and the *Nemesis* was still eleven hours out.

Over the next three hours, the composite image the

computer was creating from the sensor feeds began to resolve itself and what he saw defied explanation. What they'd originally identified as shifting, ill-fitting hull plates, turned out to be retractable covers that folded up and into the structure itself. Watching the behemoth struggle to reconfigure itself gave Carmichael the impression that it was a poorly designed, hastily assembled unit. Once the covers were all retraced, and they were able to get a glimpse beneath, his confusion only deepened.

"Are those...*fighters?*"

"Can't be."

"The computer is clearly making out a transparent canopy," the OPS officer said. "The scale puts the individual ships at roughly one quarter the size of the Dagger-class boats we've been fighting. External weapon hard points, with four missiles visible per ship. I can't think of anything else to classify this other than a fighter, sir."

Starfighters had been tried a few times in the previous centuries, but the concept was always quickly abandoned. The main issues were the powerplants were too bulky, they didn't carry enough propellant, the pilots couldn't survive the g-loading, and they didn't carry enough firepower to make their miniscule range worth the trouble. Conventional wisdom said that small fighter craft had no chance against a capital ship and simply wasn't worth the effort to design or build...but that philosophy was from the days of slow, ungainly starships flying on magnetoplasma thrust engines and warp drives that had to be unfurled and powered up days before actual transition.

Now, there were more powerful, compact fusion powerplants, RDS drives, and solid-state, low-power artificial gravity systems. Had the ESA thought outside the box and brought a weapon to the fight that the Federation fleet had zero tactical answer for? A cold sweat trickled down Carmichael's spine as he watched dozens of small ships detach from the skeletal framework of the carrier and form up to face his ships.

"Coms, make sure the flagship is aware of the new... developments," he said. "Tactical, have CIC working on whether or not our point defense guns are enough to take one of these...fighters...down. OPS, make sure the rest of the task force is ready."

"Given what radar and spectral analysis is showing, CIC is less than confident our current point defense systems are up to the task of destroying one of these ships, sir. They say without a flight profile to work with, it's impossible to say whether our Hornet missiles will have a chance either."

"They'll have their chance to collect some data," the tactical officer said. "Here they come."

On the main display, Carmichael watched in awe as thirty-nine miniscule attack ships surged towards his formation at accelerations that a capital ship couldn't hope to achieve. The leading elements zipped towards him at over nine hundred g's of acceleration. That was approaching what missiles did when launched, and the danger of what he was facing began to really sink in.

"OPS! Order the formation to scatter! Everyone, pick a line and get clear so we don't shoot each other when they get close," Carmichael barked. Normally, he'd try to pack his ships in tighter and take advantage of overlapping fields of fire and sensor coverage, but these fighters could get inside his formation, and they wouldn't even be able to open fire for risk of hitting one of their own.

"Helm, all ahead flank! Drive her right at the incoming wave!"

"All ahead flank, aye!"

The fighters may be fast, but they were still piloted by humans...apparently. Carmichael wanted to get the closure speeds so high that human reflexes became useless. If he could shoot through a gap in the formation, maybe he could get behind them and exploit any vulnerability in their coverage with his aft missile tubes. If not, then he will have made a grave mistake and took the *Blake* out of the fight early.

"Range is four hundred and ten thousand kilometers and closing fast," OPS reported. "The enemy formation is breaking up and going after individual targets."

"Tactical, snap fire tubes three through seven," Carmichael ordered. "See if the Hornets have any luck clearing a hole for us."

"Snap firing Hornets, spitting out tubes three through seven, aye! Missiles away...tubes reloading. CIC is tracking."

"Standby point defense...full power, auto targeting, no exclusions," Carmichael said, watching tensely as the missiles seemed to get swallowed up by the approaching fighters. There were detonation icons on the main display, but nothing confirming they'd scored a hit.

"One hit, the rest missed completely, sir. The hit fighter is tumbling uncontrolled and streaming reactor coolant," Tactical reported.

"Helm, aim for that hole...emergency power."

"Ahead emergency, aye...bearing to the gap in their—"

"Incoming! Two— No, four missiles coming dead ahead!"

"Steady as she goes! Let the DSO worry about them," Carmichael said tensely, looking over his shoulder at his Defensive Systems Operator as she managed the point defense batteries and ECM suite. The systems were entirely automated, but she could coax them as needed to pay special attention to threats she saw. He hit the ship-wide on his seat as he began to pull on his restraints. "All hands! Brace! Standby damage control teams!"

Boom—BOOM!!

Two distinct hits, one massive, rocked the heavy cruiser. Alarms blared, and the damage control computers began routing teams to where they were needed. Carmichael could smell the first hints of burning plastic wafting through the environmental ducts, and two of the terminals on the bridge winked out. The main display stayed on and, despite the heavy hits, the *Blake* shot through the dispersing group of fighters without taking another shot.

"We're through!" Tactical shouted over the alarms. "Aft launch tubes are offline, sir!"

"We took both impacts on the belly," OPS said, silencing the bridge alarms. "Structural damage in section nineteen and hull breaches near the reactor exhaust vents in section twenty-two. Power to all tactical systems in the aft of the ship has been lost including point defense and missile tubes. Engineering is warning us that we may have reduced engine power depending on how bad the damage is in nineteen."

"Tell them to get on it," Carmichael said. "I want—"

"The *Liberator* is signaling mayday! They're abandoning ship, sir!"

"Have—"

"*Victory* and *Fairfax* are also critically damaged," the OPS officer interrupted. "Both are— *Fairfax* just exploded! Holy shit!"

"Get a hold of yourself, Mister!" Carmichael barked.

"Helm, how long to bring us about and get back into the fight?"

"She's responding sluggishly under reduced engine power, Captain," the helmswoman said. "Best case is six hours to bring her about and come back into range."

"Goddamnit," Carmichael muttered, looking up from his hands to the main display again. The *Nemesis* would get there before he could get back. He studied the tactical threat display again, his eyes narrowed. "What's our range to the carrier that brought those fighters in?"

"Three hundred and sixty thousand kilometers, sir," the OPS officer said. "It's drifting to port and slowly clearing the area, but they're not making any obvious move to avoid us."

"They either can't maneuver quickly, can't be out of range of the fighters, or think that we were critically damaged in the exchange and are adrift," Carmichael mused. "Tactical!"

"Working the numbers now, sir"

"Good man."

"That's it. They're moving in, ma'am."

Strike Force Wolfpack had been sitting silent high above Odmena, the five ships separating so they could provide maximum coverage. The Dagger-class ships below them had been parked near the three largest orbitals left over the planet but, so far, had not made any other aggressive moves.

Celesta would have been happy to wipe them out on principle after looking down at the roiling atmosphere on Odmena, trying to imagine being on the surface as the sun was blotted out and the land passes were pummeled by tsunamis and high-speed winds. The problem was that one of her overarching directives was to keep the existence of her strike force a secret, so engaging with the enemy for any other reason than to defend directly threatened Federation civilians or military assets was out of the question. The risk that the gun boats below would get a clear look at one of the destroyers and transmit that data was too high for her to indulge her desire for revenge.

"How long until we have to launch?" she asked.

"Forty-six minutes, and they'll pass the point where our Hornets can get to them before they launch their missiles, ma'am."

"If they don't deviate course, fire in twenty minutes," Celesta ordered. "Let's not cut this any closer than we have to. Wait for the first volley to impact before committing to repositioning."

"Aye-aye, ma'am," Captain Risher said, turning to relay her orders.

"Admiral, we have an incoming Bluebird from the flagship... Actually, it's from Admiral Wolfe himself," the com officer said. "He says that Task Force Vega is taking heavy losses from a squadron of...*starfighters?*...that's moved into the area. The *Jericho* is disabled and adrift and Captain Carmichael has already lost two ships."

"Starfighters?" Celesta asked, worried that her mentor had fallen back into old habits and was drinking heavily again. She moved over and read the message in its entirety, shocked by what it said. Apparently, the ESA had taken their new technological advancements and resurrected a long-dead idea. Now, they were using it to take apart Wolfe's task force bit by bit.

Celesta stepped back and chewed on the inside of her lip, stuck in a rare moment of indecision. Even if she fired now on the ships below her, it would be hours before she'd be able to verify her missiles had found their marks and reposition the strike force to aid Wolfe's ships. There was also the concern that her ships might not be any more effective than his. The new upgraded Valkyrie-class ships were still designed with established Fleet doctrine in mind, and her weapons were built to take on other capital ships, not speedy little fighters.

"Ma'am?" Risher asked.

"Protecting the civilians on the orbitals takes priority," she said with some reluctance. "Maintain posture but prepare the strike force to move on my command. Nav, prepare a warp-jump to a point well outside of the main battle. Once we're certain every attack boat below us is eliminated, we'll reposition and assist Task Force Vega."

"Might I suggest a compromise, ma'am?" Risher asked, lowering his voice so that the conversation was private.

"You may."

"If we fire now, then reposition the *Katana* and *Saber* immediately, we'll have the remaining three ships for cleanup duty," he said. "The *Cutlass*, *Broadsword*, and *Gladius* would have to come around the planet before jumping anyway."

Celesta carefully considered his idea. It would put at least two of her fresh ships in place to cover the battered cruisers in Task Force Vega, but if the plan failed it would mean not only loss of life here over the planet, but possibly the loss of two ships the Federation couldn't afford to lose right now. On the other side of the argument, she'd never been known for playing things safe when backed into a corner.

"You may execute your plan, Captain," she said. "Issue the necessary move orders for the *Katana* and *Saber*, and then fire Hornets at your discretion."

Aye-aye, Admiral."

Six minutes after she gave her approval, a synchronized barrage of Hornet missiles streamed from five warships sitting above the planet. The destroyers were at an altitude of one hundred and sixty thousand kilometers, well above the orbital platforms and the attack boats moving towards them.

"*Katana* and *Saber* have jumped away," the OPS officer reported fifteen minutes later. Celesta didn't respond as she watched the medium-range missiles continue their march. Unlike the Shrikes, Hornets were smaller missiles with high-explosive warheads as opposed to nuclear. Celesta had ordered three missiles fired at each target, almost depleting her strike force's store of the missiles, but she didn't want even a single boat getting a lucky shot off.

The wait for the leading missiles to start hitting their targets seemed to stretch on forever. It still amazed Celesta that even before the missiles they'd fired detonated, two of the destroyers were already over a billion kilometers away across the system. Watching the ships below on passives, two things became apparent. First, the small attack boats weren't equipped with very good sensors. The destroyers themselves were somewhat stealthy, but they should have easily spotted the inbound missiles, and they had yet to react. The second thing she noticed was that they didn't appear to be very well built. On the long-range optics and multispectral sensors, she could see that the hull panels were roughly cut and ill-fit to the internal structure. Most ships were venting atmosphere from at least one place, and the fields from their RDS drives were fluctuating wildly.

What this told Celesta was that these ships were conceived and designed hastily, and then thrown together with limited resources. It was bothersome that such a shoddy flotilla of poorly built ships had been able to get the jump so thoroughly on one of the Federation's mainline task forces. Likely ESA scientists had successfully weaponized antimatter, and then Alliance Fleet Command ordered a delivery vehicle built quickly and cheaply after the capital ship captains refused to carry such an unstable munition.

"First missiles reaching their targets now, Captain," the tactical officer said, his baritone voice smooth and calm. "Six targets destroyed...ten...fifteen—"

"Five of the ships have fired their missiles," the OPS officer interrupted. "Two appear unguided, three tracking for the Proto-Ignis facility. That platform houses a hundred and eleven thousand people."

"Can we intercept?" Risher asked.

"We're completely out of position. The *Cutlass* is moving in at full burn," OPS said. "Captain Gefter thinks he can hit them with a Hornet if he can get in closer."

The ESA's antimatter missiles were very large, probably why the gunboats only carried one each, and also comparatively slow. Theoretically, a Hornet missile should have no trouble knocking one down...but three? Celesta held her tongue and let her people work.

"CIC reports all ships destroyed, Admiral," the tactical officer said. "The only outbound transmission detected was a truncated mayday over a clear channel. Nothing else, though, encrypted or otherwise. Once the antimatter warheads began detonating, it was pretty chaotic in their formation. I'm not sure they realized they were even under attack."

"Come on," Celesta urged, willing the blue dot on her main display that represented the *Cutlass*. "Get there!"

The *Cutlass* roared down towards the planet at full power while trying to get in a position to give the Hornets a fighting chance of intercepting the ungainly missiles chugging towards the defenseless orbital. The destroyer was accelerating so hard, and had to cut so close to the planet, that the thermal imagers on the *Broadsword* could see the hull heating as she rubbed against the lower layers of the thermosphere. Celesta held her breath as she realized how close Gefter was coming to the planet. At that speed, there was no room for mistakes or the ship would slam into the mesosphere and possibly be pulled down to the surface from the violent deceleration.

"*Cutlass* is firing. Damn they're close," the OPS officer said. "Two missiles intercepted...the third is a miss! Third intercept failed!"

"Can they try again?" Celesta demanded.

"Negative, they're already past the orbital plane the missiles were traveling on. They're reporting they were already out of range and position to try a shot with the aft tubes."

"Coms, contact the platform and tell them they have incoming...recommend they get into lifeboats and abandon ship," Risher said grimly.

25

"It's moving away, sir, but slowly."

"Maybe it really has no defenses of its own," Carmichael said. "Just like the aircraft carriers of ancient Earth blue water navies. The only offensive system it carried was the fighters themselves."

"And they're all busy shredding our— What the hell?"

"Report!" Carmichael demanded of his OPS officer.

"Two more Federation ships just appeared near the fray...and I do mean *appeared*. Both ships claim to be Valkyrie-class destroyers."

"That's...not possible," the XO said. "The *Nemesis* is the only ship of that class, and she's hours away still."

"I'm just reporting what our ships are seeing, sir." the OPS officer threw his hands up. "Apparently, two ships appeared out of nowhere and have taken out a handful of fighters with laser cannon fire."

"Leave it for the flagship to figure out," Carmichael said. "Tactical, do we have a targeting package?"

"It just came up now, sir. CIC has picked out what they suspect are critical components and places they think might be point defense emplacements. Firing solution is locked and ready."

"I feel like this is an all or nothing moment, people," Carmichael said to all of his bridge crew. "Tactical, load firing solution into *all* remaining Shrikes in the forward launchers. Fire at your discretion."

"Aye, sir! Firing tubes one through six...reloading."

The *Blake* cycled through the entire load of Shrikes in her forward launchers, three complete volleys. While his munition crews began moving missiles from the aft magazine up to the forward launchers, Carmichael watched his eighteen precious Shrikes streak away on their chemical rocket first stages. That many ship busters would be viewed by most as complete overkill, but the fighters' mothership was massive, and he had no idea what sort of defenses the ESA had packed into her. All he knew was that he had a chance to take out a major piece of strategic hardware right now, and he was taking it.

"Eighteen missiles burning hot and clean, sir," tactical reported.

"OPS, sitrep on the rest of the fleet," Carmichael said.

"The *Jericho* is underway again, sir...limited engine power, but she's on her way. The two newcomers have turned the tide a bit, and we've taken out two thirds of the enemy fighters, the others are moving out of range and keeping their distance. *Ghost Dancer* reports they've stabilized their powerplant and are upgrading their status to partially mission capable."

"Tell *Ghost Dancer* to keep her distance and continue with repairs," Carmichael said. "Helm, begin turn to port to bring us about. It's time to rejoin the formation."

"Coming about, aye."

The Robert *Blake* groaned as she pushed against her own inertia, the compromised RDS unable to completely nullify the effect. Carmichael saw that there was only one Alliance cruiser remaining in the system now, and it was steaming hard for the New Berlin jump point. He assumed it was the *Heart of Xi'an*, staying behind to see if the fighters could carry the day as the rest of the fleet limped away. Once Wolfe had taken out the two battleships, the battle had been decided. He just hoped his missiles found their mark, and he would have contributed something to the battle other than the gross incompetence that had cost the Federation a cruiser and a frigate.

SINGLE ANTIMATTER MISSILE MADE IT THROUGH... MIRACULOUSLY MINIMAL DAMAGE TO THE ORBITAL. THE CREW HIT IT WITH INDUSTRIAL PARTICLE BEAM USED TO SECTION DERILICT SHIPS AND IT DETONATED ELEVEN HUNDRED KLICKS OUT. FOURTEEN KILLED IN BREACHED SECTION, OVER ONE HUNDRED THOUSAND ALIVE.

Jackson breathed a huge sigh of relief as he read Celesta's message. The *Jericho* had limited engine power available and was pushing back uphill to meet up with what was left of Task Force Vega. Celesta's two destroyers had retreated back to their own formation now that the immediate threat of the fighters seemed to have passed. His forces had managed to down three-quarters of them, but at a heavy cost. The remaining fighters had moved out of range and were either out of things to shoot at them or the tiny ships had already burned through their fuel load.

He also saw that Kohl had been sneaking his remaining cruisers out of the system while the Federation fleet dealt with the fighters and battleships. One remaining ship was pushing hard for the New Berlin jump point, and it looked unlikely that the *Nemesis* would reach it in time. He flicked his tile open and began composing a message, asking Celesta if she could use her warp-jump capable ships to intercept it when he heard a chorus of gasps and hisses.

"Admiral! That...carrier...just blew up!" Lieutenant Orr said. "The *Robert Blake* said they'd fired a full salvo of Shrikes at it before turning back to the main engagement. I guess some got through."

"Sir, the *Heart of Xi'an* has transitioned out of the system," Easton said. "They went to warp well short of the jump point."

"They saw the carrier go down, too," Jackson said. "Kohl knew it was over at that point."

"Did...did we win?" Orr asked.

"Nobody won today, Lieutenant," Jackson said wearily. "Coms! Begin negotiating with the remaining fighters for their unconditional surrender of themselves and their ships. OPS, coordinate with the *Blake* and begin reassembling the task force. Have CIC contact CENTCOM and get an update on what they're sending out to help survivors on the planet and support ships to get us back to a shipyard."

"I'll take care of it, Admiral," Orr said.

"Mister McVey, you have the bridge. Alert me to any changes in status."

"I have the bridge, aye."

Jackson trudged through the hatchway, nodding to Barton as he walked into the corridor. He was exhausted, heartsick, and angry with himself. He'd failed spectacularly in this fight, missing key hints along the way that this wasn't going to be just a simple force projection mission. Not only had he been taken by surprise when Vadim Kohl had laid not one, but two traps for him, he had also let his flagship descend into chaos as traitors worked with the enemy and the entire command crew killed themselves.

Had he begun to believe his own hype? Too impressed with the legend of the "Implacable Jackson Wolfe" that he forgot how to keep his head on a swivel and trust nothing? It would be a long, uncomfortable debrief when he finally dragged the *Jericho* back into port at New Sierra. He fully expected to be yanked from operational status and stored somewhere on the Platform, likely analyzing wargame scenarios, until his contract was up or he decided he'd had enough and quit.

He went back to his quarters and, as much as he wanted to sleep, began typing up his report while it was all still fresh in his mind. It was three hours later when he felt like he'd managed to get all the pertinent details out of his head and into the personal report he'd submit to CENTCOM, along with the ship's log and CIC's mission report. As he read it, something was tickling the back of his mind, something he was missing. He tried to focus on it, but his sleep deprived mind just couldn't get a hold of the thread and pull it out no matter how he looked at it.

Giving up, he set an alarm to wake him in four hours and collapsed on his rack without bothering to take his uniform off.

26

"This could have been a lot worse," Pitt noted as he finished the brief preliminary report on the Battle of Odmena, as it was being called.

"Agreed," Marcum said. The pair had met alone before the others got there to discuss the issue. They had an initial planning meeting later in that day, where they'd begin to craft a recommendation for the Parliament to present to President Stark regarding any retaliatory action against the ESA.

"CIS and Fleet Intel both really stepped on their dicks this time. Not even a whisper that this asshole, Kohl, was moving so much firepower into the system with the express purpose of going after Wolfe. How the fuck do you miss something like that? Hell, they didn't even know the Alliance fleet had battleships at all, much less two fully operational hulls sitting in Fed space."

"I might word that a bit more diplomatically when Perez gets here," Pitt said blandly. "But when you're right, you're right. Between that, the antimatter weapons, *and* a fully functional starfighter squadron complete with rapid deployment carrier. This is a *lot* to overlook as just some sort of mistake."

"What're you saying?"

"I'm saying that the same intelligence apparatus that failed to know about high level operatives within Starfleet—specifically on the TFS *Jericho*—are the same people giving us this 'we don't know what happened' act when it comes to the ESA having so many new weapons advancements," Pitt said. "How do we not have better information on Vadim Kohl? Some Eighth Fleet lackey just happens to get his hands on a full battlefleet and flies it to Odmena and nobody knows shit?"

"Either we have epic levels of incompetence, or we haven't rooted out all the traitors." Marcum nodded. "Neither is a particularly pleasant prospect." He leaned back in his chair, staring at the ceiling, and then let out a chuckle that startled Pitt.

"Sir?"

"I was just thinking...how much would you have loved to see the look on Kohl's face when Wolfe took the *Jericho* and blasted both his shiny new battleships out of the sky?"

"Or when Carmichael turned their fighter carrier to slag with enough Shrikes to take out a small moon," Pitt said, smiling briefly. "The loss of life on the planet isn't something Parliament is going to be willing to ignore. They're going to demand blood."

"I know," Marcum sighed. "I know. From what Pike is telling us, this wasn't officially sanctioned by the Alliance Council, but the Parliament won't make any distinction now that the death toll is in the millions."

"How do you suggest I handle Wolfe, sir?"

"Are you asking for advice from me as a friend or as someone who used to have to ride herd on the man?"

"Maybe both."

"I read his full report, *and* I've known him long enough to read between the lines," Marcum said. "He blames himself for the losses his task force suffered and for the atrocity on Odmena. We view this operation as a strategic victory in the face of overwhelming odds. He'll look at it as an utter failure on his part to not recognize the true threat sooner. My advice? Don't let him sit around here and think about it. Put him in command of a strike package, ask for Parliamentary approval for a mission to find and apprehend Vadim Kohl, and turn him loose. Give him a tangible mission to focus on."

"That'll be tricky," Pitt said. "The decision we've come to is to completely disband Task Force Vega in the face of what happened on the *Jericho*. The crews need further screening and, honestly, it looks like we'll be digging into the backgrounds of our entire force. I don't even want to think about where all this is going to lead, but for now, it'll be a scramble to get something together until the first squadron of Mickeys is ready for deployment."

"You'll figure it out...you always do," Marcum said, looking down at his watch. It was built to look like an antique mechanical watch, but it had everything a full-featured comlink had. "I've got to run. My committee is meeting prior to the full session this week. Tell the others I'll be in touch."

"Will do," Pitt said, pulling out a tile and making some preliminary notes before the rest of their secret group started showing up.

He thought Marcum was right. Wolfe would not take the loss of life that happened on this mission well. Pitt thought it was because he'd been too successful, for too long. He also tended to take direct action himself, putting his own ass on the line rather than delegating when he should. It was a symptom of his inability to accept that decisions he made could, and did, result in the deaths of people under his command or, in this case, innocent civilians.

Pitt felt, knowing Wolfe as he did, that it could go one of two ways. He might internalize the entire affair and some of his less savory self-destructive tendencies could come out. Or, he would take those feelings of regret and helplessness and use them to stoke a fire within himself and want to be at the tip of the spear when Starfleet punched back. If that happened, and the Jackson Wolfe that took on the Darshik *Specter* came out, Pitt almost felt sorry for Vadim Kohl. Almost.

Celesta watched from the bridge of the *Broadsword* as a flotilla of Federation support vessels and warships flooded into the Odmena System. Her destroyer was flying along the edge of the system, just outside the orbit of the ninth planet, waiting for an inbound Broadhead to transfer over a group of political refugees. She'd sent the rest of the Wolfpack back to home base and requested one of her own Prowlers meet her in the Eternis System so she could turn the asylum seekers over to them for transport back to New Sierra. After that, she'd return the destroyer to the ultra-secret organization that had let her borrow it and get back to her normal routine of managing her own office.

During the after-action brief with the other ship captains, she could tell how badly Wolfe had missed being in the thick of the action after he'd taken command of the *Jericho*. She also realized, with surprise, that she didn't.

It wasn't that she was scared or felt she'd lost a step from her days commanding Ninth Squadron in the wars; it was more that she no longer felt she had anything to prove on that front. She derived immense satisfaction from her work as the head of Prowler Fleet, proud of the job she and her office had done in turning it around, and no longer heard the horns like Wolfe did when there was a battle to be met.

And now there was a new enemy to defeat, a new threat that had singled Wolfe out and threatened the things he held dear. Celesta vaguely remembered Vadim Kohl, recalled meeting him in passing on Haven once, but didn't know enough about him to guess at his motivations. She'd read the report Wolfe's new aide/intel analyst had provided her, but Trapp's summary only left more questions than it answered. All she knew at this point was that if Alliance Fleet Command was anything like CENTCOM, Kohl would have a lot of explaining to do.

"Admiral, we've received a Bluebird message," Captain Risher said. "The Broadhead is in the system and flying around to these coordinates. The pilot says he needs no beacon or navigational aids to find us so we're maintaining strict EMSEC protocols."

"Thank you, Captain," she said. "Please tell me when they've made dock."

"Of course, Admiral."

"Quite the fancy ride you have here, Admiral," Pike said, sauntering into Celesta's office, and flouncing into one of the seats. "Pretty amazing I haven't even caught a whiff of rumor about this secret strike force of Perez's."

"And you need to forget you saw it this time," Celesta said. "I'm serious about this, Pike. The existence of these ships breaks about a dozen Federation maritime laws."

"You forget who you're talking to?" Pike laughed. "My entire career has been doing illegal shit for the people in charge. This is a little bigger than poisoning the occasional diplomat or blackmailing a regional governor, but at least they can't try to pin it completely on you if it's discovered."

"So, who are the people I'm ferrying back to Federation space?"

"Mr. Zhang was the program manager for the Asianic Union's ill-fated—and illegal—colonization efforts that preceded the Phage War. He'd cultivated a lot of contacts within a lot of offices in the old Terran Confederation, contacts that still exist today under the new government. Currently, he's being used by a cabal of ESA politicians and military officers to try and draw the Federation into a war while they think they have the upper hand. The other people with him are his family."

"Good God, Pike. I'm sure that information was highly classified!" Celesta said.

"It will be." Pike shrugged. "But as I'm currently the only one who knows it, I get to decide its classification level until CIS overrides me. I trust you not to get drunk and blab when you get back to your cushy existence in the Prowler Fleet program office."

"Piss off," Celesta said. "So, Vadim Kohl is—"

"Working with a secret group within the ESA government that's trying to kick off what they see to be an inevitable war while Starfleet is still trying to rebuild," Pike confirmed.

"I guess it's a good thing he failed," Celesta said.

"That's what you think?" Pike asked, raising an eyebrow. "Sure, their original plan was to try and bait your old boss into firing first since Wolfe's name is pretty well trashed in the ESA already. They use his actions as proof of Fed aggression, convince the Council to take a retaliatory action, and let it snowball from there. Kohl may have shit the bed in that regard, but the cabal will still get their war."

"There's no way Parliament will believe he wasn't acting on official orders." Realization dawned on Celesta. "*Our* side will have little choice but to respond given the loss of life here in the Odmena System."

"Exactly. I don't think the schemers wanted their admiral to lose two battleships and a carrier, as well as leaving behind a handful of antimatter warheads for us to analyze, but they'll get what they want in the end."

"Maybe cooler heads could yet prevail," Celesta said. "The Alliance Council will have to investigate *why* Kohl had a full battlegroup in a Federation system in the first place."

"He was invited." Pike shrugged. "Someone within the Odmenan regional government had been flipped and had sent an official invite to an ESA delegation. Kohl's fleet was here responding to that invite."

"Nobody is so stupid to believe that Kohl's force was here on a diplomatic mission."

"Won't matter. The Council is mostly seated with former AU political hacks, and while they may deal with Kohl internally, they'll never admit to New Sierra that they'd had a rogue faction operating without their knowledge. It'd weaken their hold over the entire Alliance."

"That's a cynical way to look at it, but also fits with what we know about current ESA politics," Celesta sighed. "What a fucking mess."

"Yep," Pike said, rolling forward in his chair and rising smoothly to his feet. "I leave the Zhang family in your capable hands until you dump them off in the Eternis System. I need to head back out."

"Where are they sending you?"

"I'm cauterizing the leaks we have in Starfleet...at least the leaks on one end," Pike said cryptically. "I need to get back to ESA space before the cabal realizes Zhang has bolted and my lead dries up."

"Be careful," Celesta said, also standing. "You...you're not going to be running ops during the coming conflict, are you?"

Pike knew what she was really asking. Their relationship had been simmering for years, constantly interrupted by the demands of lifelong careers and one inconvenient war against the Darshik, but had never been given the opportunity to grow. Both of them having Bluebird access had helped tremendously, but there was simply no substitute for proximity. Being thousands of lightyears away at any given time had strained things between them and, sometimes, Pike thought it would have been less painful if they'd never admitted they had feelings for each other.

As a program office administrator, Celesta would be sitting back on New Sierra, rarely venturing out on deployments. Pike was still technically an Agent and had not been approached about moving into operational control or supervision. He knew Perez was frustrated by the fact he couldn't be used in covert actions anymore thanks to his overzealous use of the 'Aston Lynch' persona, but the CIS didn't have so many full Agents that they could afford to retire one just because of his notoriety. Unfortunately, that meant Pike would be on tap for the more dangerous direct interdiction-type missions rather than the covert intelligence gathering he preferred.

While all of this was bouncing around inside his head, Celesta had never taken her eyes off him.

"I'll put in for retirement once I take care of this last thing," he said, the words surprising him as much as they did her.

"You're serious? Pike, there's a major war coming that could determine who controls all of human space, not to mention the lives at risk, and you're going to just sit it out?"

"Yes," he said firmly, the idea solidifying in his head. "I've done more than enough dirty little deeds for two different governments. I think it's someone else's turn. I'm becoming of less and less use to the Federation. I've lost a step from my youth, I'm too easily recognized, and I've ruffled too many feathers. Maybe they ask me to come on as an advisor, maybe they happily process my retirement and throw my ass into the street. Speaking of, I don't actually have a place to stay so—"

"So, you'll already be freeloading off me?" Celesta asked, arching an eyebrow.

"Freeloading is a strong word," Pike said. "I'll be your live-in house keeper...who won't actually do any housework."

"I think we can find something you're qualified for," she laughed before turning serious again. "You're sure about this? I don't want you doing this on a whim because you're afraid I'll get bored and end up resenting the fact you're on the sidelines in the coming months."

"You know, this is actually one of the few things I've been sure about in a long time."

"You sound surprised by that."

"You have no idea."

27

"We finally received word from the Odmena System," Chan said. He, Councilman Makov, and three others from their shadowy cabal were sitting in a secure room deep within one of the generic administrative buildings that dotted the capital. "The news is...not good."

"How *not good* are we talking about? And where is Zhang?" Makov demanded.

"Zhang left word that he was going to meet with his source of information directly, try to get him to relinquish control of the alien device he'd been using to communicate with our assets in the Federation fleet," Chan said, waving a tile at Makov. "This report came in via courier ship, directly from Admiral Kohl.

"In addition to the...*mishap*...with the antimatter bombs that hit the planet, Kohl is reporting that Wolfe destroyed both battleships and the carrier in his armada. Most of the fighters were destroyed, the rest abandoned. Over half of his cruisers are gone, and he thinks some of the antimatter missiles may be dormant and recoverable within the system." The groups sat in stunned silence as they processed the sheer scope of the debacle they were facing.

"We diverted all of those ships and personnel to Kohl on your request," an aging fleet admiral finally spoke up. "There's no way we can hide the fact they were lost nor lie about how. The battleships alone represent a significant part of our fleet's total firepower, and you're telling me that bumbling fool lost them both?! And the starfighters, another secret weapons program now exposed along with the antimatter warheads. How do you propose to hide all of this from the Council? Everyone in this room will be executed if the truth comes out about what—"

"Calm yourself, Admiral," Makov said. "You seem to forget, we're the only ones who really know what happened so far. We control the narrative because we control the means of communication. Kohl returns from his diplomatic trip, reports that Wolfe showed up with his task force and attacked them, and the media runs with that. The citizenry won't question it, the Council will be compelled to act, and in the end, we get what we wanted."

"Maybe. If it works out as simply as you say, I assume we'll be *retiring* Vadim Kohl upon his return?"

"Tempting, but impractical," Chan said. "We needed someone like him as a focal point for within the Alliance military structure. He's seen as our answer to Jackson Wolfe, and if he was replaced or...*retired*...we'd not likely find a replacement. As helpful as you are, Admiral, you're not a mainline officer anymore, and we need someone the rank and file look to."

"Moving on," Makov said smoothly, rushing ahead so the old logistics officer didn't have time to realize he'd just been insulted. "We'll begin putting together the press releases immediately. I want it done in stages, a little more information given each time, until we culminate with the news that Wolfe attacked and shot down two of our ships over the planet Odmena, causing them to crash into the surface, killing the crews and millions of innocent civilians."

"It should work," Chan said. "We've been using Wolfe as a convenient scapegoat for years, and the people always seem eager to believe any story about a stupid, aggressive Earther. The old AU worlds especially still hate him."

"Then it's settled," Makov said. "We won't meet in person again until Kohl has moved his fleet—or what's left of it—back to port and we can begin assessing the damage there." The others correctly interpreted the comment as a dismissal and began filing out of the room. Chan moved out with them, made some show of forgetting something, and went back in after everyone but Makov had left.

"So, we still have no idea what really happened to Zhang?" he asked.

"No, and that worries me more than a little bit." Makov frowned. "His family is gone, too. The home looks as if they left in a hurry. We checked discreetly with immigration. He didn't leave the planet."

"Or he didn't leave through the commercial system," Chan interjected.

"Please, travel to and from this planet is tightly controlled. If Zhang had a private shuttle, we'd have known about it. Besides, he'd still need to go somewhere once in orbit, and we've checked every outbound starship. No, he's still here. He's just hiding in a hole somewhere."

"He's a timid man, but what do you think spooked him?"

"His contact likely gave him advance warning of Kohl's failure via their alien device," Makov said. "He likely thought the whole thing was coming apart and wanted to get out of the city before Kohl returned and the official investigations started."

"He knows enough to bring this whole thing down on our heads," Chan warned. "We need to find him. Quickly."

"We will."

Task Force Vega limped back into the DeLonges System to little fanfare as the battered formation skirted around the system before flying a direct course for the New Sierra Platform. Just called 'the Platform' by most, it was a sprawling complex that had started life as the New Sierra Shipyards and had been hastily repurposed and expanded after the Phage had destroyed the Confederation's former capital world, Haven. The flagship Jackson was standing upon was named in honor of *Jericho* Station, the orbital facility that had flown over Haven for over a hundred years as Starfleet's headquarters, also lost when the Phage attacked Haven.

Now, CENTCOM used the Platform as a combination headquarters and refit yard, taking advantage of the extensive docking system that had come with their new place. Jackson was exhausted and wanted nothing more than to take the captain's launch and ride ahead to the Platform, but neither Corsi nor McVey were qualified to bring her into dock. Instead, Jackson was stuck on the bridge as the harbor pilots came aboard and the tugs were hooked up to haul them out of their holding orbit and into the berthing cradle, where tech teams would begin pulling damaged hull armor off and repairing the *Jericho's* RDS field emitters.

The worst part of the whole damn thing, the part that made Jackson's gut churn and jaw clench, was the parade of dignitaries that had flown out to the lumbering warship as she wallowed down the well at less than half power. PMs, flag officers, each of them with media crews in tow, had flown out to the *Jericho* to congratulate him on the mission.

To fucking *congratulate* him.

On a mission that lost four ships and *millions* of innocent civilians, it sickened him to receive accolades. They were even talking about giving him a fucking medal because his guns took out the two Alliance boomers before they could shred the *Jericho* with the plasma lances Fleet Intel didn't even know they had.

He had been on the bridge in his dress blacks when the battleship transitioned in, fully expecting to be met at the heliopause boundary and relieved of command, possibly arrested, for gross negligence resulting in the loss of life. Instead, he was being lauded as a hero again. The parallels between this and his failure to stop the first Phage combat unit that ventured into human space before it wiped out two entire planets were obvious.

He wasn't foolish enough to think that maybe he was just being too hard on himself. The people flying out to get their photo ops with him were politicians, or aspiring politicians, and weren't sincere in their praise. They were simply opportunists trying to be first in line when the news began to propagate out from New Sierra on the com drone network.

"That'll do it. Welcome home, Admiral," the docking supervisor said, waving his pilots from the bridge. One final *clang*, and the *Jericho* was secure in her berth.

"OPS, instruct Engineering to begin final power-down

procedure once they've verified we're on dock power and the gangways are all secure."

"Aye, sir," Lieutenant Orr said.

"Admiral Wolfe, there's a message coming in from the Platform," the com officer said. "Chief of Staff Pitt would like to see you in his office as soon as you disembark, sir."

"Understood. Tell them I'm on my way now." He nodded to Barton on the way off the bridge and waved to Lieutenant Trapp. "You're still assigned to me. We'll do the paperwork later, but consider yourself my new aide."

"Sir, I'm an intel analyst. I'm not sure that I—"

"Stow it, Lieutenant. I need people I can trust around me, and right now, that's you and Gunny Barton. If that changes anytime soon, I'll personally cut order for you to go back into CIC on any ship you want."

"Aye-aye, sir."

Barton gave her a sideways look Jackson caught, but the Marine said nothing. Jackson's mind was on his upcoming meeting. He assumed that Pitt would also have CENTCOM's Chief of Operations there and that the discussion would be quick and to the point. They'd likely want him to transition over to a strategic advisory position and relinquish control of Black Fleet Combat Ops to someone else. At least that's what he would ask if he was in charge and one of his subordinates had managed to screw up this badly.

"Sit down, Wolfe. I believe you know Director Perez?"

"I do. It's nice to see you again, sir," Wolfe said, extending his hand to Perez.

"Likewise, Admiral," the CIS Director said, giving a firm handshake.

"Drink?" Pitt asked.

"No thank you, sir."

"Bullshit," Pitt said and filled three glasses from a decanter. Jackson accepted his, could smell the expensive scotch, and tried to figure out the meeting dynamic. Director Perez was not the person he'd assumed would be in attendance with Pitt.

"I think I'll go ahead and start us off, if nobody objects," Perez said, taking a long sip from his drink before continuing. "Admiral Wolfe, I'd just like to say I admire your ability to adapt quickly in a situation like you had on the *Jericho*. We're still trying to figure out how Captain Hardy and Commander Trane were compromised, and if they were working together the whole time or individually.

"What's not widely known right now is just how effective the ESA has been in corrupting high-level officers and officials within the Federation military. We're now beginning to see a complex network of sleeper agents, people who've always had questionable loyalty, and some who were turned through old-fashioned blackmail. While the *Jericho* is in berth, my people will tear into her and try to begin piecing together what was happening. We do know for a fact that one of your Bluebird transceivers was used to send updates on your position and posture to a double agent who was working for the ESA. That person would relay orders back, and then someone on your ship would transmit that to Vadim Kohl by piggybacking onto the Link broadcast."

"That's disconcerting," Jackson said. "A single person couldn't do that, not even the captain."

"Agreed," Perez said. "That's why we have no choice but to quarantine the crew here on the Platform for a while and begin a more thorough background check of them all coupled with an investigation of the ship herself. Needless to say, the *Jericho* is going to be on the sidelines for some months."

"And that brings us to the next thing," Pitt said. "The orders will come officially through Fleet Admiral Lazonic's office, but we're going to go ahead and dissolve Task Force Vega."

"I understand, sir," Wolfe said, unable to hide his disappointment despite agreeing with the decision.

"I doubt that," Pitt said. "We're not abandoning the task force idea or the Wolfe Doctrine altogether, but we'd like to divide Vega assets among the rest of the fleet. Upon your recommendation, Captain Carmichael is going to get his own group of ships to command, and so is Captain Barrett. The *Nemesis* is ready to go right now, but the *Robert Blake* needs a few weeks in the yard. After that, two new task forces will make way for the border. You, however, will have an entirely different job. Director?"

"The ships that Admiral Wright brought to your aid were highly classified, though she admitted to me she divulged their origins to you after the battle," Perez said. "That strike force will be rolled into Seventh Fleet Special Operations Group."

"There's no such thing as a—"

"We're making it up as we go," Pitt growled. "Shut up and listen."

"This new Black Fleet covert group will be responsible for the deployment and operation of the five ships that comprise Strike Force Wolfpack. The reason we need to roll them in under your command structure is that right now, technically, they don't exist."

"You can't possibly mean that I'm going to be commanding this strike force, sir," Jackson said. "Not after that clusterfuck in Odmena."

"It wasn't your finest moment, for certain," Pitt said. "But you still managed to dig yourself out of a hole and come out swinging. You'll be put in charge of the Wolfpack and given a specific mission: we want Vadim Kohl brought back to Federation space where he can stand trial for the massacre of millions at Odmena. You'll be given a full complement of Marines as well for the inevitable boarding actions you'll be seeing."

"We're ready to take you to the secret facility where we've built and housed these ships so that you can begin training on their operation, Admiral," Perez said. "Is there anything you require?"

"So, I'm being given a strike force with the express order of violating the ESA border and dragging Kohl back out?" Jackson asked.

"Yes," Pitt said.

"When does my ride leave?" Jackson asked. "I'll be bringing my personal security and new aide with me."

"Have they been cleared?" Perez asked.

"Gunny Barton has for sure, Lieutenant Trapp was an intel analyst on the *Jericho*. She's the one who warned me about the com irregularities when I came aboard."

"We'll get her cleared before you depart," Perez said.

"Try to get some rest and be ready to hit the ground running," Pitt said. "We have frighteningly little intel as to where Kohl might have gone to ground, but we'll try to get you what we have so you'll at least have a place to start."

"I'll get the job done, sir." Jackson stood and placed his glass on the table beside him. "I fully intended to walk in here and announce my retirement, but I'll make sure this one last thing is finished."

"Damn right you will," Pitt said. "Now, get out of here."

Once Jackson had left, Pitt looked at Perez, finishing off his drink and reaching to pour another.

"You didn't tell him about the other attempts on his life when he was on the *Blake*. Why?"

"Sometimes, it's not helpful," Perez said. "The attempt on the *Blake* was clumsy and was thwarted when the would-be assassin saw Barton standing in the corridor with his weapon drawn. There will be no one lurking in the shadows to kill him aboard the *Broadsword*, so we'll simply deal with the traitor Pike named for us once the *Blake* docks and nobody needs to know just how bad our little problem has gotten."

"Sometimes I wish— What?" Pitt had been interrupted by Perez's comlink chiming in his pocket. The director pulled it from his coat pocket and had a brief, tense conversation with whoever was on the other end.

"We've received word that the ESA news agencies are issuing a preliminary report claiming that Alliance ships were attacked unprovoked by Wolfe. They're promising follow up reports and hinting that Starfleet is responsible for the catastrophic disaster on a planet," Perez said. "It looks like the propaganda war has kicked off fully."

"What does that mean for us?" Pitt asked. He was a lifelong military man. The murky marriage between politics and intelligence was something he'd never fully understood.

"It's the first step they'll take to begin getting their own people ready for a war," Perez sighed. "I guess part of me still clung to the hope this could be avoided. The citizens on ESA held worlds will begin to pressure their councilmembers for some sort of military response. The Council may try to do some half-asses strike against a couple border systems, or they might try something insane like moving antimatter weapons into this system."

"It's hard to win a PR war in a place where you have no voice," Pitt said.

"Well...maybe," Perez said cryptically. "What I'm about to tell you is so secret that even President Stark only knows the broad strokes of it." He paused, seeming to waffle about whether to trust Pitt this far or not.

"What Pike and that NOVA team were doing on the Odmena com drone platform was installing a self-replicating, self-propagating software package that will give us access to the entire ESA public broadcast system. It was developed by Project Prometheus and is an adaptive semi-AI program that's damn near impossible to dig out once it's in...and that's if you can even find and isolate it. We'll be able to push our own message directly to the people in the ESA, and the government will be helpless to stop us."

"Holy shit," Pitt whispered as the enormity of what he was being told sunk in. "Is...is this even legal?"

"It sits firmly on that wide gray line between legal and not," Perez said. "We'll frame the broadcasts as if they're coming from within the ESA, sent out by a guerrilla hacking group that's only interested in spreading the *truth*. Yes, I understand the ethical dilemma here, and I can see the objections written all over your face, but this is our best chance of swinging public opinion on a group of planets that have been fed nothing but anti-Federation propaganda for years. The ultimate goal is to bring the ESA back into the fold, ideally via a diplomatic solution. Nobody has ever willingly submitted because you brought in a fleet of starships and wrecked their worlds."

"I almost wish you hadn't told me what you were up to," Pitt grumbled. "But don't worry, I'll pretend I never did as soon as you leave this room."

"I appreciate that," Perez said. He stood and nodded to

the veteran flag officer, pausing by the hatchway. "I'm trusting your assertion that Wolfe is the man for the job when I agreed to give him my strike force. You're certain about this?"

"Just sit back and watch." Pitt smirked. "He got a long-overdue bloody nose this time. The next time Wolfe and Kohl go head-to-head, he won't be taken by surprise, and he won't be interested in showing mercy."

"As I said, I trust your judgment," Perez said. "Good day, Admiral."

As Perez walked the corridors of the Platform, he could see the recognition on the faces of those he passed and smiled grimly to himself as they dove into whichever open hatchway they could find to avoid him. He had put a lot of faith in Pitt by revealing the details of their latest psyops operation, the crowning jewel of a years-long campaign to try and collapse the ESA from within so the member worlds would begin coming back to the United Terran Federation. It could have been a mistake.

The old warhorse had a reputation for being uptight and a by-the-book Starfleet officer, the kind they used to make movies about, but Perez thought he could see past that. He saw the officer who knew when playing it straight wasn't necessarily doing the right thing. Perez was one of the few people who knew Pitt had gone completely off the reservation and ordered Jackson Wolfe to take the *Nemesis* without orders and hunt down the Darshik *Specter*. That had been the right call, and it had almost cost him his career. That was the type of ally Perez needed if he was going to have the resources to fight a covert war while the ESA and Federation postured and threatened each other with their fleets.

Perez had only one goal right now: try to end the war before it moved past the initial stages. Humanity could not afford to be fractured, and the potential loss of innocent lives kept him up at night. That idiot, Kohl, had already set the bar too high by letting three of his super-weapons hit a populated planet. Accident or not, the precedent was now set, and it wasn't a stretch to think some desperate Federation captain, when backed into a corner, would turn his mag-cannons on a planet and begin erasing cities.

He felt he had Pitt on board. Now, he just needed to convince Marcum. The ex-Fleet officer was calculating and cunning, so Perez would need to be careful not to overexpose himself. But Marcum was on a trajectory to keep moving higher in the Federation government, and he tended to be sympathetic to what it *really* took to win a war. There were others who could help grease the wheels within Parliament, but Marcum was still his best option.

28

Glyn Burson knew when it was time to leave, and it was time to leave.

Zhang had completely disappeared and his discreet poking around hadn't turned up anything. He's stayed as long as he dared on the planet now that his benefactor was missing. The most likely scenario was that Zhang and his cabal were discovered and collected by the secret police and were now rotting in cells deep underneath Midi Tower. Now, Burson had to send word back to his coconspirators, shut down his operation in the capital, and exfil out of the city to where his ride off the planet was hidden.

The stealthy ascension pod would get him past orbital security and out to the pickup point where his ship waited for him. The Dagger-class attack boat that Zhang's people had refit and provided him would then take him back to where he'd left a retired Tsuyo Broadhead—the original class from before the Phage War—that would take him back to Federation space.

He wasn't sure what the final outcome had been in the Odmena System, but the state media had been running wall-to-wall coverage claiming that Jackson Wolfe had attacked an ESA armada and then, inexplicably, the planet itself. Unbelievably, the people he encountered that were seeing the same thing he was were swallowing the story without question, becoming visibly angry at what the news was calling an "inexplicably savage, unprovoked attack."

"Maybe Zhang's plan is actually going to work," Burson mumbled, almost tripping over his own feet as one of the public information screens that dotted the walkways changed from the usual, mindless pro-Council garbage to a computer-generated image of someone standing in a dark room with a single light source above. The person was also wearing a highly stylized version of an ancient shamanic mask. Burson looked around and saw that *all* the screens on this walkway were showing the same image. Creepy.

"We...are the Jian Huren," the mask said in a mildly modulated, generic sounding male voice. "We are...everywhere. We are inside the Council's secret rooms, we are sitting inside Midi Tower, we are watching Alliance Fleet Command prepare to go to war...all based on a lie. We. Are. Everywhere.

"You have been told the Federation savagely attacked our ships at a place called Odmena. This is a lie. A lie meant to make you angry and to accept the coming war as necessary. Here are the images—the *real* images—from that battle."

The screens changed and began showing what everyone would recognize as composite sensor feeds from a ship in space. The first few showed an Alliance cruiser firing on a Federation formation, then there were some images of what Burson knew to be a Valkyrie-class destroyer being hit by a Dagger-class attack ship. Lastly, and most horrifically, a full forty-five second elapsed video showed three Daggers in close formation colliding, and then falling to the surface while a Federation battleship flew underneath.

"As you can see, the Federation was not the aggressor here," the mask said, its snarling visage back on the screen. "This attack was perpetrated by an Alliance officer, in your names, in order to allow the Council to declare war without public outcry. The atrocity on the planet Odmena was the fault of this same Alliance officer who foolishly lost control of a new, secret weapon and allowed it to detonate on the surface.

"Make no mistake, fellow citizens...the fight they want us to believe in so much is a fight we cannot win. Even now, the mighty Alliance armada is limping home from this place, having been decimated by the Federation forces after the attack on their planet. Do not be a pawn. Do not allow them to perpetrate war crimes in our names! DO NOT LET—" the video winked out, all of the screens going dark at once. A moment later, a rattled looking media personality was sitting at a desk and began trying to explain that they'd been victim of some elaborate hoax.

Burson moved on, now rattled. He heard the buzzing conversations around him but ignored what they were saying. The fingerprints of the CIS were unmistakable on the video. The melodrama and urgings to rise up were counter to the culture here in the old Asianic Union, so in his mind the video had obviously been done by New Sierra to look like there were a group of all-seeing, all-knowing computer hackers loose in the ESA government.

The imagery was obviously real, but Burson had not heard the CIS possessed the technological capability to infiltrate an entire public broadcast system like that. Given that this section of ESA space was his responsibility it should have been something he was made aware of. Had this been across the entire Alliance, or just the capital world?

He managed to make it back to the small, first level domicile that Zhang had procured him in the swanky Government District. His building was home to mid-level aides and bureaucratic underlings that, while not major players themselves, were tangentially attached to power. He rushed inside, locking the door behind him, and flicked on the lights. It wasn't a full panic yet, but he was starting to feel trapped in the crowded city.

The secret police weren't stupid, they'd know the video had come from the Federation. If they'd captured Zhang and made him talk, they'd also know there was a CIS Agent living in their city. He had to make arrangements quickly and get the hell out of town.

After checking his comlink one more time, he went to the tiny kitchen and grabbed a glass off the counter, filling it twice, and chugging down the cool water. It wasn't until he set the glass back down that he heard a rustling sound behind him. He spun about and reached into a cabinet where there would usually be a small, untraceable sidearm.

"Sit down, Glyn," a voice said from the living room. "I've already collected all your weapons."

"Pike," Burson said, recognizing the voice before the light in the other room flicked on. "So, how did you want to do this?"

"I already did it," Pike said, not bothering to get up or even aim a weapon at him. Burson could feel his heart beginning to race and had a sudden metallic taste in his mouth.

"You put it in the glass, didn't you?"

"You know me...I love the classics." Pike shrugged and

smiled. "Before you die, you should know that you helped that psychopath Kohl kill over four million innocent Odmenans and will likely have helped cause the death of millions more when this war really gets going. Was it worth it?"

"Now that I'm going to die after being poisoned by some sarcastic prick? No," Burson's words were beginning to slur and his vision was double. "So, you're not even going to question me first?"

"I already have Zhang. I found your ascension pod with the coordinates of both your ships, as well as the Bluebird transceiver you had stashed in a hole you dug in into the cement under your bed," Pike said. "I really have little use for you other than to enjoy the final act, which should be starting right about now."

As if on cue, Burson felt his airway constrict, and all his muscles began to cramp and spasm. He fell to the floor and as he suffocated. He could feel the muscles in his back tear from the force of the spasms and electric lances of pain shot through his entire body. The last thing he saw was Pike standing over him, a bored expression on his face, as he mercifully lost consciousness from lack of oxygen.

Pike stared down at the body of his fellow Agent with the same clinical, bored expression he'd had the entire encounter. He'd been ordered to kill many times in his career, rarely was he able to do so with such satisfaction.

"You know, Burson, I could have picked a far less painful poison to use...but the truth is, I've never really liked you." He moved to the door to make sure it was locked before he began the unpleasant task of cleanup and disposal.

"Now the gross part," he said as he dragged the body into

the surprisingly large bathroom. He stripped Burson of his clothing and flopped him into the bathtub. Once he'd tucked in the arms and legs, having to break the left leg to get it to stay down, he went to his kit and pulled out three, half-liter bottles and set them carefully on the floor. After pulling on a rebreather mask and elbow-length gloves, he opened and poured all three bottles into the tub. The contents combined and immediately began hissing and foaming. Pike quickly pulled out a large plastic sheet and stretched it over the tub, yanking on a yellow cord to activate the barrier.

The plastic adhered to the edges of the tub and formed an airtight seal. He reached over and adjusted the stubby cylinder in the middle that was actually a one-way air valve to prevent a vacuum from forming and to provide oxygen to the catalyst. The concoction he'd dumped on the body was something CIS developed for just such an occasion. Within three hours, the body of Agent Burson would be completely liquefied and able to slip down the drain with the barrier keeping the fumes and horrific smells out of the domicile. The enzymatic agent was so thorough it broke down the tissue to the point that DNA analysis would be impossible.

Once he was certain Agent Burson was moving along in his well-earned journey to a sewage treatment center, he began sanitizing the rest of the place. When he was done, the secret police would have a very hard time getting any useful evidence from it. The first thing he destroyed was the Bluebird transceiver, activating the self-destruct to destroy the quantum-paired molecules inside, and then opening the case to break the rest down into unusable scrap he'd carry out with him.

Six hours after he'd slipped into Burson's residence, he

casually walked out with a courier bag slung over his shoulder, a happy bounce in his step.

"This ship is impressive," Lieutenant Trapp said as she walked alongside Jackson. "I've been in intel most of my career and had never even heard a whisper about a group of Super Valkyrie-class destroyers."

"I'd be surprised if you had," Jackson commented. "They were built by crews who had gone through the most stringent of security background checks, and then moved to this location and cut off from access to com drones."

"And these are going to be rolled in under the Black Fleet umbrella for operational control?" she asked.

"That's the plan."

"Interesting." Trapp had been fast-tracked through the required auxiliary background check so she was cleared to even travel to the secret base. Jackson felt like he knew her well enough to trust her, so he'd pushed to have her approved as his personal aide rather than pick up yet another ambitious young officer when he got here. His experience trying to command Task Force Vega in a combat operation made him realize that he had to begin delegating some of the tasks down to his subordinates. It was either that, or find a way to operate without any sleep.

Once he'd arrived and had sat down with the five captains of his new command, he'd decided he would fly his flag aboard the *Saber*, not the *Broadsword* as Celesta had. Captain Risher seemed to take the news in stride and, if anything, looked relieved that he wouldn't be the ship carrying the flag officer of the strike group. After that had all been settled, he began the task of familiarizing himself with the new class of ship, annotating differences between the *Saber* and the *Nemesis* as a sort of reference point that would allow him to better understand the capabilities of the new ships.

They were impressive. More than impressive. The word *terrifying* came to mind when he began to see the tactical possibilities of a group of destroyers that could hop around a system undetected like ghosts. The deeper he went, the more Perez's departing comment made sense to him. The CIS Director told him it would be better to lose all five ships completely than to allow even one to fall into enemy hands.

Jackson could plainly see that Perez was less than thrilled about turning the ships over to Starfleet but understood the politics of the situation better than most. After seeing that the ESA hadn't been just sitting idle and had developed a host of new, advanced weapons of their own, Perez had little choice but to turn over the strike force so that whoever they sent after Kohl would at least have a fighting chance.

There wasn't a day that went by where Jackson wasn't consumed with a seething rage by what had happened in the Odmena System. He vowed he would never again underestimate his opponent, and he would never stop until Vadim Kohl was hunted down like the rabid animal he was and brought to justice.

EPILOGUE

Vadim Kohl was a proud man. He also considered himself a warrior, a man of honor. His Dagger crews' screw up over Odmena had people accusing him of things and calling him names that enraged him. The "Butcher of Odmena" wasn't the sort of legacy he'd planned to leave behind to his son when he found out he was going to confront Jackson Wolfe.

His crew looked at him different, too. There was a tinge of fear and caution now where once there had only been trust and adoration. The incredible losses his armada had suffered had them whispering in the corridors about him, and he could plainly see they didn't believe in him as they once did.

He'd show them. He'd show everybody. He was not a man to take an insult like that lying down. Now that he'd seen how clumsy and unprepared the vaunted Admiral Wolfe had been when he came bumbling into the Odmena System, he knew that he would be victorious the next time...*if* there was a next time.

The word coming from their spies in New Sierra was that Wolfe had disappeared, Task Force Vega had been disbanded, and the mighty *Jericho* was still sitting in port being disassembled by technicians. Perhaps there would be no next time, and Starfleet would quietly retire Wolfe and bring up another of their big guns. Maybe Celesta Wright would come after him this time, or maybe they'd foolishly send Barrett and the *Nemesis*.

It didn't matter who they sent. He would meet them in battle and prove to everyone he was not a coward and a butcher of innocent civilians. He gave the cabal the war they wanted, and now he had his chance to prove himself again. Vadim had initially worried they would take his fleet from him given the losses he'd sustained, but Councilman Makov had waved it off as inconsequential and assured him that his losses would be replenished soon enough, and then he would deploy for his next mission.

That was good enough for him. He knew that Chan and Makov were ambitious, and that their goals didn't necessarily align perfectly with that of the rest of the Alliance Council, but they'd shown themselves loyal to the ESA and to remaining independent from the Federation. As long as that remained, he'd be willing to fight for them.

"The next time we meet, Jackson Wolfe, I will erase your legend from the stars."

Thank you for reading *Battleground.*

If you enjoyed the story, Lieutenant Brown and the guys will be back in:

No Quarter

Book 8 of the Black Fleet Saga

Subscribe to my newsletter for the latest updates on new releases, exclusive content, and special offers:

Connect with me on Facebook and Twitter:

www.facebook.com/Joshua.Dalzelle

@JoshuaDalzelle

Check out my Amazon page to see my other works including the #1 bestselling military science fiction series: *Terran Scout Fleet* along with the international bestselling *Omega Force* series:

AFTERWORD

It was interesting climbing back into Jackson Wolfe's head after such a lengthy break between *Destroyer* and this book. I'd spent nearly two years exclusively with the insane, kinetic world of Omega Force along with the more abstract story of Blueshift. This series has always been a more precise, detail-driven story and it was a joy to get back into the groove of the tech-oriented space battles.

    This is the beginning of the third and final trilogy within this overarching saga. By the time we get to the third book, *Empire*, we'll have reached the end of Jackson Wolfe's character arc and his growth from a stigmatized screw-up to a hero of the people. He's been an interesting character to write because of the drastic changes he's been forced to go through. For those that read Omega Force, you'll see that while Jason Burke gets kicked in the teeth from time to time, he's very firmly established in who he is and sees no real need to evolve past his "hit it with a rock until it works" mentality. While Burke lacks much introspection, Wolfe tends to live a lot of his life in his own head dealing with his crippling self-doubt as it does battle with his sense of duty.

To be honest when I first outlined this story Wolfe's character wasn't so prominently featured and the first versions even had him dying within the first trilogy. I had an idea that there shouldn't be a single character that overshadows the others and consumes so much of the story. In hindsight, I'm glad I decided against that.

Thanks for the patience given how long ago this book was promised versus how long it took to write and publish. It's bittersweet rolling into the final stretch of this series and I appreciate all of you who've taken the ride with me.

Cheers!

Josh

Printed in Great Britain
by Amazon